DATE DUE

AUG 3 1993			
AUG 25 1993			
OCT 27 1993			
MAY 2 1994			
JUL 22 1994			
DEC 20 1996			
SEP 24 2012			

NATURAL
ENEMIES

NATURAL ENEMIES

A NOVEL BY SARA CAMERON

Turner Publishing, Inc.

ATLANTA

Published by Turner Publishing, Inc.
A Subsidiary of Turner Broadcasting System, Inc.
One CNN Center, Box 105366, Atlanta, Georgia 30348-5366

Printed in the United States of America.

LC #   FIC CAM   Inграмs #19.95

First Edition 10 9 8 7 6 5 4 3 2 1
Cameron, Sara
Natural Enemies
ISBN 1-878685-37-6
Distributed by Andrews and McMeel
4900 Main Street
Kansas City, Missouri 64112

Alan Schwartz, Editor-in-Chief
Katherine Buttler, Associate Editor
Robert Benard, Copy Editor
Crawford Barnett, Editorial Assistant

Michael Walsh, Design Director
Elaine Streithof, Book Design
Karen Smith, Design/Production
Nancy Robins, Production Director
Anne Murdoch, Production

Turner Publishing, Inc.

ATLANTA

Printed on recycled paper

TO GEORGE

ACKNOWLEDGMENTS

Thanks to Joyce Poole; Cynthia Moss, and Iain and Oria Douglas-Hamilton for their inspiration; my father, Don Cameron; my husband, George McBean; and our children, Fergus, Ainslie, and Ramsay.

I N 1979, AN ESTIMATED 1.3 MILLION ELEPHANTS survived in Africa. By 1989, when the ivory trade was banned, only half that number survived. Most of this drastic loss is attributed to ivory poaching. Not all countries agreed with the ban. Several southern African states, including Zimbabwe, Botswana, and South Africa, had experienced little poaching and today claim to possess too many elephants. They control elephant numbers by culling and have demanded the right to start trading ivory again.

PROLOGUE

EADLAMPS BOUNCED over the rutted dirt road, and engines sliced across the gossip of tree frogs, crickets, and other night-gatherers. The trail led along the Tana River, which the tracker knew to be a red river, stained by the rust-colored earth. He sat up front, feeling heat in his heart because the night should bring more money than he earned in a year. He grinned nervously at the driver and the other men, out of fear, worried that the elephants might have moved on or been taken by a rival band of Shifta tribesmen. The tracker wasn't a Shifta, didn't understand their Somali talk. They laughed with each other but were suspicious of him. He was afraid also of their weapons, cradled like children in their arms, and wished many times that he did not need the money so badly.

They found the place, parked upwind, and traveled on foot to the elephants, who were dozing among the acacias. The family had settled in a tight group, bodies close enough to touch, the younger animals lying with their trunks draped carelessly across each other. The adult females stood, trunks hanging down, almost brushing the ground, but the largest of them, the matriarch, had curled hers into a snake which lay across her two long, upcurved tusks.

The Shifta carried heavy flashlights, as well as their weapons and ammunition. Two of them moved east: the rest spread out towards the north.

1

The movement disturbed the animals. The matriarch looked up and shook her great head. Another large female paced towards the north, her trunk raised into the wind. The matriarch issued a sharp rumble that woke most of the other animals. The babies, three of them, had to be nudged to their feet, tusks tucked under their slumbering bodies.

Lights flashed on from the east and with them came the first deluge: men relishing the power of the weapons jumping in their hands, bullets smashing into trees, leaves, earth, and making contact with flesh.

The family was thrown into screaming, squealing chaos; bodies clashed together as gunfire tore into their hides; babies screamed, trunks whipped through the air, mouths gaped wide open trumpeting fear and rage. The matriarch, incensed, aggressive, mounted a charge: trunk rolled up, ears pressed back flat against her head, she ran straight at the lights. A magazine-load smashed into the ground. The next caught her right flank, the steel core of the bullets ensuring the deepest penetration. She spun around, bellowing with pain, legs collapsing, head thrashing, blood gushing from the wound. Screeching with effort, she struggled to her feet, but fell again before she'd gone five paces. A fresh clip of ammunition slammed into the weapon. Gunfire cut into her underbelly and up across her head.

The other large female led the survivors north, where they ran into fresh fire. Lights poured out of the trees, carrying bullets like rain. As the front runners fell, those behind stumbled and wheeled around, roaring because there was no place that seemed safe. Their leader launched her own last impressive charge, straight into the relentless hail, the momentum of her body somehow carrying her forward until she fell onto her knees, head twisting in an agonizing arc, trunk flying up to the stars, her great body falling through space and thumping heavily onto the ground.

When all was still, the weapons ceased and the silence that descended was full of death.

They drove the truck down. Four of the Shifta operated chainsaws that sliced through the flesh around the base of the tusks, turning it into a bloody pulp. The machines whined and sparked but they were careless of noise. The park boundary was miles away. The ivories were pulled free of the skulls and tossed into the back of the vehicle. The night stank of blood and gore, which also covered their clothes and faces. They labored hard over the peg-like stumps of the child-animals, swearing at each other and laughing in their throats. The tracker stood apart from all this, uneasy about the chainsaws, which they wielded with such confidence, and unable to decide if this was easy money or not. Yet a couple of hours later, he stood smiling on the bank of the blood-red Tana River, a wad of shillings in his pants, watching the vehicle drive away into the yawning mouth of the morning.

Cash flowed at every stage of the journey, first to the Shifta when the tusks were transferred from their truck to the vehicle belonging to Wong, who ran a juice factory down in Mombasa. The consignment was taken to the factory where the tusks were cleaned and transferred to crates marked "Pineapple Juice. Product of Kenya." Wong's Swiss bank account swelled as the tusks moved into the port. He paid off the customs officials on duty himself. Money also pumped into the Gulf account of the captain of *The Pearl of Sidon* as he accepted the consignment, and trickled into the hands of customs officials in the Gulf as the shipment entered their country. There, the tusks were lightly carved and, by the time they were shipped out of the Gulf, the payoffs were complete. The ivories, fully certified, official and legal, headed for their final destination, Chinese Hong Kong.

The tusks were recarved into ornaments, chessmen, signature stamps, piano keys, bangles, bracelets, beads, and even the shavings were swept into minute bottles to be sold as souvenirs. These artifacts, carrying labels proclaiming their origin as Zimbabwe or Botswana, or one of the other southern African countries which had recently legitimized ivory trading, were re-exported to other Asian countries or fed the burgeoning market on the Chinese mainland.

In Kenya, where the vulture-pecked flesh of that elephant family decayed into the dust, the ivory trade was still banned.

CHAPTER ONE

A JEEP RATTLED ALONG the highway, heading towards Nairobi. Inside was Sam Hawthorne, a mess of gear, and a CD player lying on the front seat playing old Southern blues. The road ahead stretched in a dead, black line to the horizon, slicing the desolate, mesmerizing plains in two. For thousands of square miles the terrain was the same; scrub, thornbush, and the red dirt of the earth. Over a hundred miles away, on his left, the first rays of the sun were stroking the iced cap of Mount Kilimanjaro. He was on the stretch of the Mombasa Road that cut across Tsavo National Park, and the roadsigns indicated the presence of wild animals. In the ten years that he'd been traveling it, Hawthorne had not seen anything much bigger than a baboon on the road, but the creatures were there, somewhere.

Hawthorne was forty-three and the color of sand: straw hair, bleached eyebrows, beige skin, a chameleon in that semi-desert. He drove with sandaled feet, leaning forward over the shuddering wheel. His face had a hard-edged look, handsome and full of angles. He was trying to shake off a cold and get his mind ready for Lumbumbashi. The separatist movement there was gaining momentum, and rioting had broken out in half a dozen towns. The Front for New Africa's goal was to reunite the communities with a shared language and culture which lived on both sides of the Zaire/Zambia

5

border. Land claimed by the FNA also happened to coincide with one of the richest mining zones in the world. It was the biggest African story of the new millennium, which was just eight months old.

Hawthorne sneezed, and swore. He hated flying with a cold. The Kinshasa flight was leaving at six that evening. Supposedly, the connecting flight to Lumbumbashi took off early the next morning. Even if everything flew on time, which never happened, he would not get much sleep that night. Yet, if he pushed it, he might get to Nairobi by lunchtime and catch some rest.

Dawn was a good time of day to be on the road. There was hardly any traffic. No vehicle going in either direction had passed him for twenty or thirty minutes. The air rushing through the open window still possessed an edge of coolness. A couple of weaver birds darted in front of the jeep, making for their nest hanging in the branches of a thorn tree. His eyes tracked them and also took in the ethereal image of Kilimanjaro, the ice cap glowing and tinged with pink. Seeing Kili he thought of Maya again. She'd lived most of the last decade in the shadow of that mountain.

It was three months since they'd seen each other. He'd been traveling most of that time, to Chad, the Ivory Coast, and Uganda. In between trips, he'd been back in Nairobi for less than forty-eight hours. It was a ridiculous schedule, but he'd given it to himself. Five days ago he'd at last taken some time off and had gone down to the coast with two other hacks, Gene Simmons and Fred Askew. Gene was into scuba diving and Fred was looking for some female recreation, so they'd had a little of both, taken a boat over to Shimoni with three bikinis on board. Fred was ruthless over women, and tried to keep them all to himself by telling tall stories about the life of a foreign correspondent. The females had definitely been impressed.

Hawthorne enjoyed a little scuba, but he wasn't a fanatic like Gene. On the boat he couldn't figure out why the hell he was listening to Fred, or pretending to join in the fun with the women, when he would much rather be with Maya. In the end, it had got to him so badly that he'd left them, taken himself up the coast, and rented a *banda* for a couple of nights, just to try and work out how he was going to get her back.

Lately, her face had been cropping up in newspapers and glossy magazines. She'd even appeared on a couple of the satellite news channels, supporting the attempt to ban the ivory trade again. Ever since it had reopened in southern Africa, poaching elsewhere had been on the rise. Maya had also been interviewed about her Amboseli project, which studied the way elephants communicate with each other, over distances as great as five or six miles, using infrasonic sound too low for humans to hear.

What Hawthorne liked most about Maya was her strength, independence, intelligence, and the fact that there were things she cared about more than her own life. She was also beautiful. Her face had the sculpted look of many Maasai, and her eyes were wide ovals with languorous lids. When he looked into them, they seemed full of challenge and laughter; perhaps mystery too.

She sometimes said, "You cannot understand me, Sam, because you are not an African."

Color had not mattered. He hardly saw it and she didn't care, though she sometimes laughed at it. It was culture she held up between them like a shield.

"You do not understand, Sam, how African women are supposed to behave."

Maybe that was true, but Maya was no average African woman anyway.

He remembered the time he took her to Zanzibar, recalled the baking lanes, shimmering white houses, women clothed in black *bui buis*, minarets soaring over the mosques, and the call to prayer covering the town like a blanket of peace. He remembered lying with Maya on a bed in a tiny room high on a Zanzibar rooftop, the fan-whipped air bathing their hot bodies. Moving slowly with her, looking at each other, daring the other to be the first to give in. A slight smile touched her lips as he pushed towards the mouth of her womb, glaze covered her eyes, but she pulled away from the crest, delaying it, murmuring "not yet, not yet," pushing against him and making him sweat over the effort to retrieve control. They moved like music, rhythmically, lyrically, like creatures performing an ancient dance. It was close to sunset and the room was bathed in orange light.

They'd been driven apart because they just hadn't made enough time for each other. Either there would be a crisis that required his presence on the other side of Africa, or else an elephant would be giving birth or copulating or dying or doing some other elephant-thing, and Maya would have to be there. Hawthorne never understood why she had to witness these things over and over. Wasn't one elephant copulation much like any other?

The rows had started to dominate the little time they shared, so they'd finally agreed to loosen the relationship, to become friends who might occasionally sleep together, rather than monogamous lovers. Then she'd turned up at his house unexpectedly and found him with a barely-clothed traveler. What had her name been? Julie or Jilly or something. It didn't matter. Maya Saito had walked away and had refused to answer his calls. Hiding himself in work since then had done nothing to ease the emptiness Hawthorne felt inside.

Driving the highway, he thought about going down to Amboseli to see her. He'd have to be careful, maybe put in some time elephant watching with her. Perhaps he could persuade his boss to send him down to do a story, but he probably did not have to be so devious. They'd shared too much for her not to care. Maybe he should just come right out and tell her what he felt. He decided to do it, as soon as he got back from Lumbumbashi.

A massive, dust-colored, double-bellied truck came hurtling along the road towards Hawthorne, sending clouds of black exhaust into the pure morning air. The driver could probably smell the end of his journey and was powering down the center of the road as if he owned the whole strip. Hawthorne pulled over and got his window up in time. The truck thundered past, leaving a trail of purple smoke in its wake that slowly disintegrated into the yellow light of the morning.

About thirty feet ahead of the spot where Hawthorne pulled over, a Peugeot was parked by the side of the road. He thought it must have broken down and been abandoned by its driver. Releasing the clutch of the jeep, Hawthorne moved back onto the road and was still in second gear when he passed the Peugeot slowly enough to take a good look. He swung back hard onto the shoulder, slammed on the brakes, got out of the jeep, and walked back towards the other car.

He glanced through the driver's window; the stench was sickening. Turning away, adrenaline shivering through his body, he scanned the land, searching, partly out of suspicion and partly to collect and store the details. Nothing stirred. He knelt down on the red soil and looked under the car. Between Zaire, the Ogaden, Uganda, and the Sudan, Hawthorne had seen half a thousand dead bodies. The sight of new violence brought back the memory of those atrocities, but as quickly as the ghosts rose up, he'd learned to shut them away. Finding nothing of interest on the ground, he stood up, slowly brushing the dirt off his hands, and walked all the way around the vehicle. Taking out a pen, he wrote the car's license number on the back of his hand and then took a closer look at its occupants.

The driver was stone dead, shot in the temple and slumped so that the top half of his body lay on the passenger seat. A man in the back was lying face down on the floor, his legs awkwardly crumpled. The woman was sitting up, her clothes so bloodied that Hawthorne could not see how she'd been killed. All three were African. The woman was the only one he could see clearly. She looked about forty, not rich but respectable. Her light blue handbag lay on the back window ledge. A file was on the back seat.

The rear door closest to him was slightly ajar. Untying his bandana, Hawthorne used it to cover his hand while easing the door open. The bile rose in his throat. The man on the floor had lost one of his feet, chewed off by some beast, and the tattered stump was covered with flies.

"Jesus," Hawthorne whispered, turning his head away. He coughed and went back to the file, using the same protected hand to lift the top cover. It was some kind of government report. He was about to turn the next page when the woman moaned. Hawthorne swore under his breath and let go of the file. The blood on the woman's flowery blouse had soaked into the fabric and dried. She must have been like that for hours. He spoke to her but got no response, then leaned over to feel her pulse. It was weak and slow, but she was alive. Again she groaned.

Hawthorne stood up and looked around. There was nothing but the road and the wilderness: no telephone or hospital, no police station or even gas station for sixty miles or so in both directions. A vulture circled in a

9

downward spiral against the pale blue sky, emphasizing the isolation. Then a chorus of crickets started shrieking louder than an electrical substation, making Hawthorne jump inside his skin.

The nearest place he knew was a research base known as the Sutcliffe Institute, perhaps fifteen miles away, where he thought there might be a medical unit, or at least an airstrip. Going over to the jeep, he opened the rear door and started arranging a space for the woman to lie in. There was not much to make her comfortable, and it was not particularly clean. He tossed everything onto the front passenger seat, swept the dust out of the back with a T-shirt, and laid out a sleeping bag with a towel on top. He went back to the Peugeot, to the door nearest the woman, and opened it. The woman fell towards him and he caught her. Her eyes opened briefly, and her pupils floated deliriously across their sockets. Cradling that fragile life, he realized the futility of his efforts. The road to the institute was bad for at least five miles, and the suspension of his jeep was practically nonexistent. The sleeping bag would give the woman little protection from the metal floor. A jeep was no vehicle for transporting a seriously injured person. Gently easing her back onto the seat, he leaned across and saw the keys, still in the ignition of the Peugeot. He stood up, expelling air through his teeth.

He could take her in the Peugeot, but it would mean taking all of them.

He rejected the thought as soon as it entered his head. It was tampering with the scene of the crime. The woman moaned again, and a wave of frustration swamped him. He had to do something. Something had to happen.

He searched the road again, more desperately this time, stamping up and down beside the car, kicking up small drifts of red dust. If only another car would come along.

"Right now!" he demanded. But there was not even a wisp of smoke on the horizon.

He stopped. He could chase down the truck that had forced him off the road. That idea was rejected too. The driver would never turn back, and he could go faster for help by himself. He looked inside the car and the truth hit him square between the eyes. The woman would just die right there while he made up his mind. If anything was going to save her, it had to happen now. In one decisive movement, he walked back to his jeep, lifted his camera bag, slammed the door—and froze.

Something was out there. Something had moved. His eyes swam across the scene. There was a vast baobab, its light grey branches curling skyward in agony. The landscape beyond was scattered with flat-topped acacias and giant red termite pillars. His skin crawled and his senses screamed. With fear flooding his gut, he ran to the Peugeot, pushed the driver over to the passenger seat, and got in behind the wheel. The car roared away up the road.

Hawthorne had the air-conditioner going full blast and all the windows wide open. He took short, shallow breaths until he was gasping for a deep one, then pushed his head out of the window and sucked in a lungfull of warm, rushing Tsavo air. The windshield was spattered with dried blood. The woman had not made a sound since they'd started driving. Hawthorne considered that she might be dead already and his effort to save her quite pointless. He swore at himself. It was too late to turn back anyway.

He pulled up close to the place where a degraded *murum* track turned off for the Sutcliffe Institute. Fifty miles further along the main road at Makindu there was a police station and hospital, but the Sutcliffe Institute with its airstrip was only about five miles away. Hawthorne turned round in his seat. The woman's mouth had fallen open and her lips seemed to move. He was overwhelmed. She was trying to speak. He leaned over, trying to catch her words, but the sounds that came out were too faint.

"It's okay," he said, filled with new hope, "I'm getting you to a doctor. Hang on."

He swung onto the dirt track that led to the research station. The Peugeot rode a lot smoother over the rough road than the jeep would have done, but even so it bounced around. Hawthorne drove as fast and as gently as he could, but a pothole surprised him and sent the vehicle flying. The woman slipped off her seat, landing on top of the dead man on the floor. He stopped, gently lifted her back, and drove more slowly afterwards. The car became hotter and sweat poured down his neck. Wiping a hand across 11 his forehead, he left traces of the woman's blood. His shirt and pants were also smeared with blood.

Two miles from the institute the track entered a gully. Traveling between densely packed thorn trees that had smothered the road with debris, Hawthorne slowed down. He knew the risks. He'd almost cleared the worst stretch when he heard and felt the sigh of a punctured tire. He tried to ignore it, but, with a gut-wrenching grind of metal, the vehicle sank onto the stony track. Hawthorne threw himself out of the car and found the culprit, a pristine six-inch thorn. His fury knew no bounds. He held off from physically abusing the Peugeot with its precious cargo, but he cursed it loudly, and the gully, and that wilderness. Glancing briefly at the woman, he took off on foot.

Hawthorne did not look it, but he was in poor shape and an uneasy runner; the ground hit his feet hard, sending shock waves through his knees. His senses were strung out. It was that time of day when big cats went hunting. There was a good possibility of running into a pack of baboons or a stray buffalo. Then he remembered that all the windows of the Peugeot were left wide open, and thought of vultures and hyenas, but he'd gone too far to turn back.

The track entered a wide, dry plain where there was no shade, and the temperature was beginning to soar. His neck stung with sweat. He focused on the ground, jerking by under his stumbling feet, and imagined he was traveling faster, even though he was slowing down all the time. His heart raced, and his vision grew blurred.

Then, looking up, he saw a vehicle approaching. Too desperate to feel relief, he carried on running until the car, displaying the Sutcliffe Institute logo, was pulling up beside him, and he started speaking before it had even stopped. He told the African couple inside about the Peugeot and the woman close to death, and climbed into the back before they'd said a word. The couple looked at each other and then back at him.

Hawthorne snapped in Kiswahili, "A woman is dying in a car down there. Now go!" He breathed out hard, thinking he should apologize for the tone of his last remark, but he was too wound up. As the vehicle started moving, he sank back in the seat with his eyes closed, trying to regain control. He heard the driver speaking into the radio, summoning assistance.

When they pulled up close to the Peugeot, Hawthorne sat up, leaned forward, and pushed his head between the couple, noticing the way they shrank from him. A scent of rosewater came from the woman and Hawthorne, feeling his shirt sticking to his body, knew how bad he must look.

He grunted. "I know this is hard. The woman is in a mess but we've got to get her into your car." Then he swung out of the door and strode away towards the Peugeot. Because he had no real desire to go anywhere near it, he felt every step of the way, the motion of his body, the sensation of hot air hugging his sweat-drenched head. He pulled the bandana up over his mouth and nose, purposely averting his eyes and practically holding his breath until he had the back door open and was ready to deal with the woman. He looked at her and saw the open, glazed-over, dead eyes.

There was an eruption inside: anger, disappointment; he felt absurdly cheated. He figured that he'd always known she would die. If he'd left Mombasa half an hour later, she would have been dead already, and none of the morning's "heroics" would have been necessary. It had all been for nothing.

The driver told him that Owen Sutcliffe was coming down with a couple of security guards. Hawthorne sat on a large sun-bleached rock, watching a land-cruiser streak towards him, a trail of red dust flying up in its wake. He stood as the vehicle pulled up next to him and grinned half-heartedly as Sutcliffe stepped out of the car.

The two men had met a couple of years earlier in the States. Hawthorne had been back home recuperating from a bad bout of malaria contracted while covering a famine in southern Sudan. Sutcliffe's stateside fund-raising operation had been in full swing, and Hawthorne had caught one too many of the "Adopt an Animal" commercials. These showed middle-class parents "giving" hippos to their children for Christmas; photos, adoption certificates, and twice-yearly letters giving news of wild "pets" were exchanged for tax-deductible contributions. After the horrors he'd been witnessing in Sudan, Hawthorne wanted to puke, but the media was in love

13

with Owen Sutcliffe. Even in a tuxedo, he looked as if something wild and alive was trying to break out. Hawthorne got himself invited to one of the "Adopt an Animal" gala evenings. There, he'd witnessed hundreds of diamond-chested matrons with itchy purses, drooling over Sutcliffe as he presented himself as the sole voice of reason in the African wilderness. Hawthorne had interviewed the philanthropist and then produced a scathing criticism of the whole business. It just boiled right out of him.

That morning Sutcliffe was wearing his Tsavo uniform: an upmarket version of a safari suit and scuffed Nikes. As he recognized Hawthorne, his rich-lipped mouth smiled, but his eyes recoiled as they took in the journalist's appearance. Hawthorne looked down at himself.

"It's been a hell of a morning."

Sutcliffe asked him about what had happened. Hawthorne answered. They even chuckled a couple of times out of nervousness.

The security guards who had come down from the institute were over looking at the bodies. One of them gave a shout, which took Sutcliffe jogging off towards the Peugeot. Hawthorne lagged behind. He heard Sutcliffe gag over the stench, saw him take a white, freshly-laundered handkerchief from his pocket, and shake out its folds. For Hawthorne, it was a symbol of the man's phoniness. No one who really lived in the bush had ironed handkerchiefs in their shorts.

Sutcliffe took a close look at the dead woman, jerked upright, and rushed around to the other side of the car. On the way he snagged his shirt on a thorn branch, tearing the fabric as he pulled his arm free. Hawthorne realized something was going on and started running himself, reaching the hood of the Peugeot just as Sutcliffe yanked open the rear door and knelt down to look at the dead man on the floor.

"What is it?" Hawthorne demanded.

"Unbelievable," Sutcliffe murmured.

Hawthorne moved down the side of the car but the open door barred his way. Leaning over, he couldn't see much except for the dead man's awkwardly twisted head.

14 Sutcliffe stood up, pushing a hand through his hair. He jerked his head in

the direction of the dead woman. "That's Helen Kariuki."

The name meant nothing to Hawthorne.

"She was my neighbor for six years. This was her husband, David."

"David Kariuki?" Hawthorne gasped. The dead man was practically a national hero. He'd come up through the ranks of the original Game Department, battling poachers in the old days with pitiful weapons. He had a reputation for outspokenness and for applying a Draconian management style to the Kenya Wildlife Service, which he'd directed for the last four years. The KWS was charged with managing the country's protected reserves. Since tourism brought in over forty percent of the national revenue, it was an important job. Kariuki had been appointed to it by his "close personal friend," the president.

CHAPTER TWO

HAWTHORNE GOT ON THE phone to Nairobi, and the story was on the wire within the half hour. There was not much going on in the world that day, so an unconfirmed report of the killings caught both the BBC and Voice of America broadcasts at the top of the hour. A flock of foreign correspondents and local journalists turned up at police headquarters in Nairobi twenty minutes later, demanding to know more. There was hardly one who did not harbor some unspoken thoughts about the possible political motivations behind Kariuki's death.

James Wangai, the senior detective assigned to the case only ten minutes before it made the world news, was at Wilson Airport waiting for the police Cessna to be made air-worthy. Wangai was a round, shabbily suited man in his late forties with a dusty-black complexion. He was already regretting the decision to fly down to Tsavo rather than drive. He silently cursed the police pilot for not having the aircraft ready to go, but could not afford to show how he felt. If he demonstrated the slightest annoyance the Cessna would not get fixed at all, at least not this week. The pilot had promised that the aircraft would be ready within the hour. The only way Wangai could hurry the job along to meet this probably optimistic deadline was by standing over the mechanics and the pilot while they dissected and tuned the beast.

The police Cessna was being worked on in one of the

17

large Wilson hangars. It did not take the press long to find it. They surrounded the detective, separating him from the aircraft, so that Wangai did not see his pilot and the mechanics slip off for their morning *chai*. Wangai refused to answer any of the journalists' questions. He demanded instead to know who had leaked the story. Specific orders had come to keep it quiet until more information was available. Kariuki's name had been on a priority list, along with another thirty or so prominent citizens. If one of these worthies stepped on a *siafu* trail and got nipped by a single soldier ant, the president's office had to be informed. The police were in double-deep over Kariuki's death because he was supposed to have been under police protection. He'd received several threats over the years, but apparently Kariuki had got tired of being followed around. He'd made a deal with the officers assigned to him to keep out of his way, and they'd been working holiday shifts ever since.

The journalists laughed when Wangai got upset over their information source. That was when he discovered that the bodies had been found by an American journalist, and that Helen Kariuki had been alive at the time. The detective was forced into quizzing the journalists about what they'd heard on the radio. It was very demoralizing.

Wangai eventually flew out of Wilson Airport in a twin-engine aircraft hired by a news team from CNN. He was annoyed by the insult this posed to his professionalism as a police officer. He should have been at the scene of the crime before the press, but when Vanna Deacon offered him the ride he had to accept because the alternative was frightening to contemplate. The journalists had already banded together to hire the necessary air transport. If they got down to Tsavo before him, they could do untold damage to the evidence. He called headquarters before leaving Wilson, just to make sure that the forensic team had already departed for Tsavo by road. No more delays could be tolerated, he'd told them. If everything about this case was going to become public knowledge, they'd better get it right.

The small plane bumped through the air over Nairobi, crossing the rich district of Muthaiga with its five-acre estates and brilliant blue swimming pools. Muthaiga's cruel juxtaposition with the crush of polyethylene and tin-can housing in Mathare Valley was obvious from the air. On the ground, the eyesore of Mathare was so well camouflaged that the ambassadors and company directors driving to their Muthaiga mansions would hardly notice it. Wangai knew Mathare too well, but it was still interesting to see that sprawling mass of poverty, vice, and violent death from the seclusion of the aircraft: a silent, scentless sea of glinting rooftops, divided by sandy trails that were scattered with the sharp shadows of tiny ant-like beings.

The city soon petered out into tidy *shambas* of deep green maize and the shining corrugated roofs of rectangular mud-walled houses. Still further out, the corrugated rooftops became more scarce, giving way to brown, thatched, round huts and thinner soils pathetically supporting a few sickly maize plants. The terrain grew rougher and drier, and settlements more scattered, until they were flying over scrub that went on for thousands of square miles. Far below Wangai saw a herd of Thommies, their black gazelle shadows stark against the rough redness of the earth.

Wangai looked at the dry earth, thinking that Tsavo, where Kariuki had died, was very different from the place where he'd been born. The detective knew it well since his wife also came from the reserve beyond Karatina. It was a green, fertile place on the edge of the forest surrounding Mount Kenya, where farmers produced three harvests a year of bananas, yams, sweet potatoes, maize, beans, and millet. Kariuki had grown up in the atmosphere of secrecy and rebellion surrounding Mau Mau, and had said publicly that this had been his inspiration. The man had possessed a legendary reputation for breaking the law just to get his job done. Years ago, as warden of Samburu, he'd pursued Shifta poaching gangs into the heart of the Northern Frontier District, far beyond his legal jurisdiction. He'd bartered grain from the famine relief centers for information, and traded confiscated ivory for AK-47s to replace the old carbines used by his men. Many poachers had been killed, and it had even been rumored that Kariuki had worn the shriveled balls of his victims around his neck, like a talisman. The image did not match the suited, overweight Kariuki of later years, but Wangai had seen earlier photographs, including one of the young Kariuki in ragged bush clothes, a necklace of boars' teeth around his neck and a machine gun cradled casually in his arms. His mouth had been grinning, but his eyes had been as hard as bullets.

Vanna Deacon turned round from her seat next to the pilot and shouted at Wangai over the racket of the engines. She had thick red hair not so different in color from the land they flew over, and wore a slim-fitting khaki shirt dress with a large belt; more glamorous than practical. It took the detective a while to understand that she was asking a question about Kariuki and his wife. He tried shouting back but eventually gave up and zipped open his attaché case, taking out Kariuki's file. Among the papers inside was the man's personal history. It was a dry, bloodless piece of officialese, containing no mention of shriveled balls or illegal killings; the Kariuki of this report was as spotless as a boy scout. Wangai handed it to Vanna, shouting that she would have to give it back once they got on the ground. The newswoman gave him an appreciative look. Wangai smiled to himself. He wasn't going to let Vanna Deacon leave Tsavo with the impression that he was just a dumb detective who had to hitch a ride to the scene of the crime.

Wangai had been with the police department for twenty years, and had done well in the beginning, with his career nurtured by a police inspector uncle. But the uncle had died, followed by Wangai's mother, and he had been left an orphan. Possessing few connections to the great web of support and obligation that binds African society together, Wangai's career had faltered. Matters had worsened after he uncovered a racket involving drugs, prostitutes, and several members of the Mombasa police force. Publicly, he'd been commended for his contribution to the war on corruption, but within the department he'd become regarded as someone who could not be trusted.

Remaining a senior detective hadn't been hard for Wangai. He enjoyed the challenge of his work. Years ago, he'd told his wife that detection was like paleontology. She'd been impressed by that. He'd read in a newspaper about the work going on around Lake Turkana, how these paleontologists tried to build up pictures of prehistoric beings, when they had no real idea what the creatures looked like, or even whether they possessed all of the pieces. Detection was the same. It was easy to be misled by preconceived ideas or just your imagination, but Wangai had experienced no greater boost to his stolid ego than the realization that a solution to a crime lay within his grasp.

Despite the detective's years of experience, the Kariuki slayings took him by surprise. The gut-wrenching stench made observation of the bodies a ghastly experience, though the photographers and journalists did not seem to object. Wangai could not believe that so many press people had got down there so fast. There were even a couple of local journalists from Mombasa, yet his police team was still nowhere in sight. Reporters swarmed all around the Peugeot until Wangai finally prevailed on them to go away and let him get on with his job.

He spent maybe half an hour looking at the bodies and the Peugeot, with a handkerchief tied over his mouth and nose, though that hardly helped. Looking at the dead was the least tolerable, but sometimes the most important, aspect of his work. He could tell, for instance, from the pattern of blood stains, that each of the bodies had been shifted in some way after the fatal wounds had been delivered. He also noticed Mrs. Kariuki's handbag on the back ledge. Carefully checking its contents, he was able to rule out robbery as the prime motive for the murders. In any case, he already favored the lingering assumption that Kariuki himself had been the primary target. The wife and the driver had probably just got in the way. Wangai imagined what it must have been like for Kariuki, to have lived a life like his and have death come to him like that. In this state he was not much different from the corpses they found in Mathare. He thought also about Helen Kariuki, and how her last hours alive must have been a nightmare.

Turning away and heading up to the institute to interview his first witness, Wangai ran through the possible motives for getting rid of Kariuki. Over the years the man must have created hundreds of enemies, among his colleagues as well as poachers and their families. He was on record as having fired more rangers than anyone else in the whole history of Kenyan conservation. The detective soon realized the impossibility of sifting through such a phenomenal list of potential suspects. His only hope was that the evidence would point him in the right direction.

Owen Sutcliffe's house overlooked the broad Galana River. Tsavo dirt had turned the river red, and the current ran sluggishly between banks stacked with bush and trees that were a profligate green in comparison to the parched ground in the rest of the park. The vegetation in front of the house had been cleared to preserve the view without spoiling the impression of wilderness. On the opposite bank a couple of giraffes were splay-legged, stretching their necks down to the water to drink.

Wangai knew something about the institute and its flamboyant benefactor, Owen Sutcliffe. For a foreigner, Sutcliffe had a fair amount of influence with the Kenya government because of the generous contributions he made to wildlife projects around the country. The institute provided a field base for scientists conducting research in Tsavo, and Owen Sutcliffe lived there six months of every year. Wangai had read somewhere about the institute's lavish accommodations but, glancing along the bank of the Galana, he saw only a few white painted *rondavels* with thatched roofs.

Owen Sutcliffe's house was made from four connecting *rondavels*, with a veranda stretching all the way along the front, where the press swarmed around a middle-aged white male lounging in a green cane chair. Wangai took this man to be Sam Hawthorne. Vanna Deacon was beside him; others were scattered around, sitting, squatting, or leaning up against the railings of the veranda. The atmosphere was playful, with a lively banter going on among the journalists. Wangai stiffened. There was laughter where there should have been respect. They had no sense of decency. It was an insult to a good man like Kariuki. He caught Vanna Deacon's eye, and perhaps she read his face and understood, because as she stepped forward to introduce the detective to Hawthorne the merriment subsided.

Sutcliffe let Wangai use his personal office to interview Sam Hawthorne. Wangai invited the journalist to sit while he closed the office window. Outside, on the veranda, a couple of Hawthorne's colleagues had been hovering.

"There have been enough leaks this morning," Wangai remarked. He sat down in Sutcliffe's chair, saying, "Kariuki was an important man in this country. Did you know him?"

Hawthorne shrugged. "I interviewed him a couple of times. I'm familiar with his . . . er . . . anti-poaching activities in Samburu and Tsavo and some of his recent work. I didn't know him."

Wangai nodded. "What happened this morning? I'm going to record our conversation." He took a Sony recorder out of his pocket and set it on the desk with the tiny microphone pointing at Hawthorne. He tested it, asking the journalist's name and address. "Right, you can begin."

Hawthorne eyed Wangai warily. There wasn't anything intrinsically wrong with recording his statement, but he automatically distrusted any member of the police or armed forces anywhere in Africa. None of them were known for their love of the foreign press. Also, the journalist had some difficult ground to cover. There was no doubt that Wangai would be annoyed about his moving the Peugeot. Any irregularity, let alone something as stupendously against the rules as removing all the murder victims from the scene of the crime, was sure to be seized upon by the police. If the crime were never solved, Hawthorne would be blamed for having interfered with police procedure by destroying vital evidence. The fact that someone as famous as Kariuki was involved made things much worse. The need to apprehend the killers would be much greater, and therefore the blame for interfering in that process would come down much harder.

Earlier in the day, while showering off blood and sweat in Sutcliffe's bathroom, Hawthorne had cynically asked himself whether he would have risked trying to save Mrs. Kariuki in such a reckless manner if he'd known that her famous husband was lying dead at her feet. In any case, he'd been dumb to move the Peugeot. He should have just taken the woman in his jeep. The result would have been the same.

Hawthorne found Wangai's face unreadable, but at least it did not have the slippery, shifting, ingratiating look that he'd come to associate with most corrupt bureaucrats. He took a deep breath and began.

Wangai listened in silence, making no comment even when Hawthorne talked about driving the Peugeot. When it was over, the journalist found the detective studying him carefully. The silence between them had a tangible quality, and Hawthorne felt uncomfortable. If the detective had shouted at him it might have been easier, but this silence was ominous.

"Look, I am real sorry about shifting the car but I just did not think I had any choice." He laughed half-heartedly. "I thought I could save her, you know."

Wangai stood up, his face expressionless. "I understand, Mr. Hawthorne. Now, shall we go and find your jeep?"

Sutcliffe gave Wangai and Hawthorne a vehicle and driver. Unfortunately for the detective, he also made the same provision for the other journalists. The two vehicles set off down the *murum* track, passing the Peugeot on the way. After reaching the highway, they swung left in the direction of Voi and had traveled perhaps twenty miles when Hawthorne realized something was wrong. They should have reached the jeep long ago.

"This is crazy," he murmured.

Wangai shifted his whole body around so that he was square to the journalist. "What is it, Mr. Hawthorne?"

"My jeep isn't where I left it."

"I see," said Wangai, thoughtfully. His voice was controlled. The news was disturbing, but the detective knew there was a time for anger and a time for calm. "Have you any idea where it is?" he inquired easily. "Or where it should be?"

Hawthorne shook his head. For a moment, he'd forgotten that Wangai was there at all. He was shocked by the loss of the jeep, not only because of the inconvenience of trying to explain its absence, but also because of all the things he'd lost with it. All his gear, his notes on Lumbumbashi, his music, CD player, laptop. Frustrated, he swung back and forth in his seat, trying to recognize the terrain.

"We have to go back," he said at last. "I'm sure we have to go back."

"All right," said Wangai, and instructed the driver accordingly. The other vehicle carrying the press swung around after them, bumping onto the shoulder and back onto the road, like a pursuit of the Keystone Cops.

Finally, Hawthorne recognized the baobab tree where he'd last seen the jeep. "Here," he said.

Wangai told the driver to stop. Hawthorne jumped down and started

walking up the road away from the vehicle, hands on his hips, shaking his head. Wangai climbed down and walked towards him more casually. Hawthorne spun around, holding his arms outstretched. "This is it! This is goddam it. My jeep was right . . . right there!" He paused and looked up at the sky. "Shit!"

The press vehicle veered past Hawthorne. One of the journalists leaned out of the window, shouting something, but Hawthorne gave no reaction. He looked at Wangai and Wangai looked back. The other vehicle screeched to a halt beyond the baobab and the "gentlemen" of the press, with Vanna Deacon, came streaming out towards them.

"Stop!" Wangai yelled, but everyone ignored him.

The Reuters man crept up right behind Hawthorne and murmured in his ear, "Sam, you and this guy have been cooped up together for too long. The boys are getting worried."

Wangai shouted at them again.

The Reuters man jumped back, holding up his hands. A couple of the pressmen sniggered.

"Lay off, Larry," Vanna Deacon said to him.

Wangai said, "Please, I want you to be very careful. Move out of this area now. Go and stand over there." He pointed to the other side of the road. "There could be evidence here and I don't want it disturbed." At last this had some effect. The journalists moved back towards their vehicle.

He walked over to Hawthorne. "Exactly where do you think you left your jeep?"

"Someone must have stolen it," said Hawthorne.

"I see," said Wangai. "Now where was it? There should be some tracks, shouldn't there? Or did you park on the road?"

"Ah, no. No," said Hawthorne, running his eyes over the ground.

Wangai did the same.

The ground was hard, but Hawthorne pointed out what he thought were the tracks of the jeep and those of the Peugeot. There were a lot of footprints; by the look of them most could have been Hawthorne's. Finally, Wangai found a third set of car tracks, though he said nothing of this to the journalist. He was not sure what to make of Hawthorne. His account of what had happened was confusing right from the beginning. But there was nothing Wangai could do until the forensic team arrived and made a thorough search of the area. Before leaving, he cordoned it off with day-glo tape, using several large rocks to hold it in place.

They arrived back at the institute to find the place crawling with policemen, far more than Wangai had requested. He did not like to have too many people around. It became too easy for the evidence to get disturbed or go missing. He found that the forensic team had already finished work at the Peugeot, and a couple of men from the mortuary were putting the bodies into bags. The mortuary men were not part of the police detail. They wore rubber gloves, ragged khaki shirts with frayed shorts, and had old bits of cloth tied over their mouths. Wangai asked a sergeant standing guard just who had given the order for the bodies to be taken away. The sergeant directed him to Sutcliffe's house and Superintendent Kamau.

Wangai sighed. He should have known that headquarters would put someone like Kamau onto the case when they realized the extent of foreign interest in it.

Superintendent Kamau was a man of style with a predilection for holidays abroad, preferably in London, and for a quality of life that required a mansion in Nairobi's Spring Valley, where diplomats and government ministers were among his neighbors. Such luxuries went far beyond the capacity of a Kenya policeman's salary, but Kamau's uncles were wealthy and influential. They supported their relation because it paid to have a friend in the police department.

The superintendent was head of Special Operations. In Wangai's eyes, this division might have been created for the sole purpose of nurturing Kamau's unlikely career, but the superintendent had delivered a few well-placed favors (due to the influence of his relatives) and his fiefdom had expanded accordingly. In particular, Special Ops. had become the main repository for high profile cases, the kind that required regular press conferences and television appearances. Kamau had sucked some good detectives into his section, but the selection of Special Ops. for newsworthy crimes had more to do with the superintendent himself. Listening to

Kamau's voice, it was easy to believe that he was a very English, very white aristocrat. The police department had been persuaded that Kamau's accent gave them extra credibility.

Wangai might have forgiven all of this if Kamau had not also been incompetent. He knew nothing about the job of detection, he had people cover for him and took their successes as his own. If anyone complained, he destroyed their careers the way he'd wrecked that of Wangai's ex-colleague, Simon Njoka. Three years earlier, Njoka had uncovered a crooked business syndicate that was falsifying coffee deals, buying beans locally that should have been sold for a fixed price to the government coffee board, and exporting them under phony certificates of origin. Since the case involved several prominent business people, Kamau had seized it, gone public, and revealed the months of painstaking investigative work as his own. Njoka had been furious and took his story to one of the independent local news weeklies. Six months later, when Njoka had been due for promotion, he'd been transferred instead to a dead-end job in Records. It had been as good as a firing notice and Njoka had been left a broken man. He started to drink heavily, and within a year was dead in a car crash.

When Wangai entered Sutcliffe's office, he found Kamau helping himself to a large scotch. He was impeccably dressed in a London suit that was almost as dark as his complexion. In comparison, the whiteness of his shirt stood out like an advertisement for bleach. Flashing a set of perfectly capped white teeth, Kamau said in a low voice, "Wangai, come in, come in. You know we don't have much time to spare. The president is very upset."

Men like Kamau bandied the president's name around, but Wangai suspected that the superintendent had probably done no more than shake the head of state's hand at a garden party.

"Where is Hawthorne?" Kamau snapped abruptly.

"Outside," Wangai replied.

The superintendent nodded his massive head. "I think we should be able to wrap this one up. The president wants to see an early resolution. I don't have to tell you the high esteem accorded to David Kariuki and the necessity of making an early arrest. The file, please?" He held out a fat hand to receive it.   27

Wangai handed over the file, an action which symbolically separated him from the case. He was deeply disappointed. The crime had engrossed him. It posed some difficult questions, but forensics might turn up some leads. He started to speak, but Kamau held up one large finger, forcing him into silence.

The superintendent gulped the scotch while flipping through the pages of Kariuki's file. Adjusting his glasses, he rubbed the side of his head with the same fat finger, then slapped his hand on the desk. "There seems to be something missing here."

Wangai remembered that he'd forgotten to take back Kariuki's personal history from Vanna Deacon. He excused himself and went outside. Hawthorne was sitting on the veranda with Deacon, who was interviewing him. Her soundman was crouched on the floor, wearing a pair of head-phones and holding up a microphone. The cameraman stood off the edge of the veranda, his camera rolling, and the rest of the pressmen were down by the river, where they appeared to be engaged in a stone-throwing competition.

Wangai hovered outside camera range and when he caught Deacon's attention, he coughed. She nodded at the cameraman, who pulled his eye away from the viewer and smiled over at Wangai.

Wangai asked for the papers. As Vanna handed them over, Kamau appeared behind him and took them out of his hand. "I don't believe it is usual practice to share police files with the press?" he said.

Wangai held up his hands and backed away. Kamau moved in and placed a proprietary hand on Hawthorne's shoulder.

"If you don't mind, Mr. Hawthorne, I would be most grateful if you would accompany me to Nairobi. There are still one or two details of the case that I would like to have clarified."

Hawthorne did not move. His eyes closed briefly. A while ago the journalist had published an anonymous story in a U.S. newspaper satirizing law enforcement techniques in Africa. He'd referred to a certain Kenya policeman as "a pin-striped egotist with a penchant for expensive wines and flashy cars." One of Kenya's leading cartoonists had quoted this description as the caption of an illustration published by one of the local newspapers. It

portrayed an over-fed man dubbed "Superintendent Smooth," his arms draped around a couple of "spring chicken" schoolgirls, while a ridiculously huge Spring Valley mansion adorned the background. The reference to Kamau had been unmistakable. Hawthorne prayed that his own anonymity had remained intact.

Kamau barked at two police officers who came across and stood expectantly behind him.

"If you don't mind, Mr. Hawthorne?" Kamau repeated, his hand tightening its grip on the journalist's shoulder. The scent of the superintendent's after-shave wafted around Hawthorne like the poisonous fumes of a spider drugging its victim.

"Are you placing him under arrest?" Vanna Deacon asked with some surprise.

Hawthorne gasped a laugh when he heard those words.

"I think that would be slightly premature," oozed the superintendent, turning a charming smile on Vanna Deacon.

"Only slightly?" she repeated.

Hawthorne caught Vanna's eye, then swung his head around and found Wangai. His expression was one of total disbelief.

The detective gave the slightest shrug. Kamau clearly suspected the journalist, but Wangai could not imagine what Kamau could have have discovered about Hawthorne so fast, or what he could have missed himself. He thought about the interview. He'd been suspicious, naturally, because witnesses sometimes twisted information, through fear or shock or, in Hawthorne's case, professional self-interest. Perhaps he was keeping something back so that he could explode it over the pages of the foreign press. But Wangai's doubts had been a matter of professional skepticism. He'd never seriously suspected the journalist of having killed the Kariukis himself, if only because Hawthorne's account of the morning's events had an untidy ring of truth, all the way down to the missing jeep. If forensics did show that the place beside the baobab was the location of the crime, why on earth would Hawthorne lead them to it if he was the killer?

Wangai's attention was drawn to the river and the gang of journalists and photographers. They'd noticed the disturbance on the veranda and were heading up from the river in a pack. Kamau held up his free hand, like a traffic cop signaling them to stop, but it was a half-hearted gesture. He stepped back, rasping an order to the police officers behind him, and they moved to the front. One of them tried to help Vanna Deacon off her chair but she stumbled and fell over her soundman. Kamau barked at the officer in Kikuyu, instructing him to be more careful, but the presspack, seeing Vanna fall, started shouting and running towards the house.

The officers pulled Hawthorne to his feet. One of them, perceiving a threat from the advancing horde of journalists, blew a whistle that brought reinforcements running from both sides of the house.

Hawthorne shouted at the journalists to stay back, but the officers holding him thought he was calling his colleagues for assistance. One of the policemen struck the journalist but his stick landed badly. Hawthorne yelled as his eyebrow split open and blood spurted out, blinding him in one eye. He rolled forward, grasping for the wound, and the policemen, momentarily shocked by the effect of the blow, let him fall.

"You bastards!" yelled Vanna, scrambling to her feet. "You can't do this! You can't . . ."

Her voice was drowned as everything went into full flood. The presspack surged forward and the police charged to meet them, their *rungus* unleashed.

Wangai waded into the fight, trying to haul newsmen aside, but an elbow winded him in the stomach and a fist struck him in the eye. He staggered out of the fray, clutching the damaged eye, straight into the line of sight of a photographer, whose motor drive hummed along, hardly pausing between shots. Wangai also noticed Vanna Deacon's cameraman, his face pressed against the viewer, catching everything. The event was televised later in over one hundred countries around the world.

CHAPTER THREE

HAWTHORNE WAS TAKEN to police headquarters in Nairobi. Iodine and a large sticking plaster were administered to his bashed eyebrow and then he was taken to a small, airless cell in the basement of the building, furnished with one wooden bench fixed to the wall. The guard told him that this was the deluxe accommodation. A stink of disinfectant drifted in from the corridor.

It felt as if someone had taken a cycle pump to his temple and blown his forehead into a lopsided balloon. The pain was only slightly relieved when he cradled the swelling in his palm. He paced the cell's twelve-by-eight floor space, struggling to figure out how trying to save a dying woman's life, putting himself through all that shit to get her to a doctor, could have resulted in this. If it wasn't so painful and serious, it would be hysterical. He guessed that one day he would be laughing about it, telling the story over dinner or something, and people would say "how amazing." Well, it *was* fucking amazing, but he wanted this part of the story to be over right now.

He went over to the door, pressed his face against the grill and shouted into the corridor. "Hey, I gotta speak to someone. I want a lawyer. I have to speak to the United States Embassy. You can't do this. I want to speak to someone. I am a citizen of the United States of America!"

A whistle came from a cell further down and someone laughed.

"I wanna talk to . . ." Hawthorne began again, but he was interrupted.

A strong, African-accented voice yelled, "I am a citizen of the United States of America!"

"Me too!" shouted another. There were shouts of laughter and several fists banged against the metal doors. "I demand to speak to de Ambassador."

Then they all joined in, shouting for lawyers, ambassadors, and even presidents.

The grinning face of an old warden eventually appeared in Hawthorne's door grill.

The journalist said, "What the hell is going on? I want a lawyer."

The old warden, still smiling, shook his head and shambled off down the corridor.

Hawthorne slept fitfully on the bench, and woke up the next morning when someone ran along dragging a *rungu* across all the doors. He was taken to piss in a stinking bathroom and returned to his cell, feeling groggy from adrenalin-exhaustion, lack of sleep, and his throbbing head. They brought him a bowl of cold *posho*, which was a stiff, maizemeal porridge, and a tin mug of weak tea. Hawthorne was starving but he could hardly eat.

Later, a couple of officers escorted him up to an interrogation room. The furniture was old and worn and the walls were smeared in places. He didn't care to think with what. At least there was a small open window high up on one wall, which made the air slightly less stale.

He was sitting on a narrow wooden stool next to a table in the middle of the room when Kamau strode in, resplendent in his uniform, blazing with medals, ribbons, and startling white cords. Hawthorne's elbows rested on the table, hands supporting his stubbled chin. He glanced up at the superintendent.

Kamau dropped a large file on the table, hitched up his trousers, and sat down on the chair opposite the journalist. He had the advantage of height, since Hawthorne's stool was at least three inches shorter than the superintendent's seat.

"I have heard the tape of your conversation with Detective Wangai, and I must say I have rarely come across a less convincing cover story."

Hawthorne raised his chin out of his palms and formed the hands into fists, replacing the chin on his knuckles. "Cover story?"

"One might think," continued Kamau, "that a journalist of your caliber," he paused over the word, "that a journalist of your caliber would be able to come up with something a little more convincing."

Hawthorne sat back. "I told what happened. The truth doesn't always make a great story."

"Is that why you are tempted to lie so often?" Kamau snapped.

Hawthorne looked Kamau straight in the eye. "I'm not lying."

Kamau's eyebrows rose into sculpted arches. "Do you deny, Mr. Hawthorne, that, when you encountered Miss Ongubo and Mr. Okech, you were actually running away from the scene of the crime?"

"That was not the scene of . . ."

"I will rephrase. When you were first sighted by members of staff from the Sutcliffe Institute, you were, in fact, running away from the car which held the bodies of David Kariuki, his wife Helen, and their driver?"

A shiver passed right up Hawthorne's backbone into his neck and face. "I wasn't running away from anything. I was running towards . . ."

Kamau flipped open the file. "Your hands and clothes were covered with blood."

"So would those of anyone trying to save a . . ."

"You were very careful to shower away the evidence while a servant washed your clothes. Washed your clothes! Are you such a meticulous man, Hawthorne?"

"This is unbelievable. I didn't ask anyone to wash my clothes. Where the hell are you digging up this garbage?"

"According to Owen Sutcliffe's houseman, you insisted."

"He's lying."

"Then there is this absurd question of your missing jeep." Kamau was contemptuous.

Hawthorne slammed his fist down on the table. He said nothing for a moment, trying to get himself under control. This was going very badly.   33

"I remember thinking that there was someone there, watching me. Maybe it was the killer. Maybe they took my jeep." He looked up.

Kamau patted the file on the table. "You've never mentioned this before."

"Well . . . I . . ." Hawthorne shook his head. What could he say? He couldn't remember everything.

"Tell me, who was the last person you spoke to before you encountered the people from the Sutcliffe Institute?"

"Helen Kariuki," said Hawthorne. "I was trying to save her life, remember?"

Kamau had a cold expression. "Before that."

Hawthorne didn't reply. His stomach sank into his boots. There'd been a fisherman who, at about four in the afternoon the day before, had come into the kitchen of the tiny *banda* he'd rented at the coast and gutted a red snapper for him. He'd dined alone, on the veranda overlooking the Indian Ocean. He'd seen no one afterwards, not before encountering the Peugeot. He hadn't even stopped for gas. He had no alibi.

Kamau clasped his hands, resting them on the file. "People have testified to your disturbed state of mind on that morning. Tell me, Mr. Hawthorne, would you not rather tell us the truth?"

Hawthorne started to protest again, then caught himself. He said flatly, "I want a lawyer. I want to see someone from the U.S. Embassy right now. I want a lawyer."

Kamau stood up so that his girth stared Hawthorne right in the face. "I am going to detain you pending further investigation into this murder."

Hawthorne turned his head from side to side in disbelief. He tried to grin but actually he grimaced. He wanted to dig a laugh out of his gut, but all that came out was a coughing sound.

It wasn't the first time Hawthorne had been in a cell. Riding with a jeep-load of journalists into the Ogaden, they'd been ambushed by guerrillas, incarcerated in the only cement building for miles around, with temperatures over a hundred, and force-fed "freedom" ideology for a week before being released. He'd done a couple of nights in Malawi for photographing the president's house. Zaire had been the worst: roach infested, mosquito-breeding pools of water on the floor; he'd slept standing up for four nights and came out with the worst dysentery of his life. In comparison, the accommodation in Nairobi was five-star, but he was more worried than he'd been any of the other times. Before, he'd been arrested because he was a journalist. This time he was just a regular guy suspected of murder.

Logically, he only had to wait for time to take its course and everything would be fine. Sit in his cell, wait, people were out there working for him, his colleagues would be stirring up the world, the embassy would come down on the Kenya government, he'd get his lawyer, and everything would be cleared up. It was impossible to keep calm, though. His mind raced away with "what ifs," and he knew he was having paranoid delusions when he thought that maybe Kamau and Sutcliffe had plotted the whole thing.

Hawthorne went back over that morning. He and Owen had been out on the veranda, waiting for the police to arrive, and Owen had asked if he wanted a shower and a change of clothes. So he'd showered and dressed in Sutcliffe's clothes. He was still wearing them now. Anyway, the shirt that he'd taken off had been in a bad way, its Dar es Salaam slogan worn out and covered with stains. He would never want to wear it again. Leaving Sutcliffe's bedroom, he'd found a door half open, leading to a rear yard where a vehicle was parked and a couple of lines of washing hung in the windless air. A trash can was open, huge fat flies were buzzing around, and he'd tossed the shirt in there. Perhaps the houseman had found it, washed it for himself, and then got scared or something.

It was a fucking stupid thing to have done, throwing away his shirt like that, but then he'd never thought that they would suspect him. He bit his lip, thinking about the man and woman in the Sutcliffe Institute vehicle. What had Kamau called them? Ongubo? Okech? He remembered them shrinking away from him; their suspiciousness. Maybe it was those two who had put the idea that he was the murderer into Kamau's head?

Hawthorne felt calmer inside as he went over what had happened, explaining it to himself. It was soothing, like writing a story, in which he   35 took the chaos of event and imposed order upon it; the when, where, how, and why. Even when he had to deal with horrific events like wars, famines, or terrible massacres, the actual process of turning them into a story, of explaining and analyzing them, allowed him to distance himself. Ultimately, he no longer felt overwhelmed; he grasped an illusion of control.

Maya had understood. He remembered something she'd said during an argument they'd had in her tent at the Amboseli elephant camp. It had seemed ridiculous, even at the time, to argue with someone in such a tiny confined space, but rain had been pissing down and Maya's coworkers had been occupying the common room. There'd been nowhere else private enough to go. He'd been complaining because he didn't want to spend all his time off in Amboseli. He liked being in his own place. He wanted her to make the effort to come up to Nairobi to see him. She'd said that she couldn't drop everything she was doing to be with him just because it suited his schedule. Actually, the argument had been about something else entirely. Hawthorne had known it. He'd been trying to loosen the bond with her because . . . because that was what he did. He hadn't had a relationship with any woman in years that lasted more than a couple of months, but he and Maya had already been together more than eighteen. He was used to being in control of his life, but she was beginning to dominate it somehow. She'd seen right through him, though. She'd said, "You know what you do, Sam? You let yourself get just a little bit involved, but when you start thinking that you are becoming dependent upon some-one, you stand back as if you are saying, 'Hold on a minute, what have we here?' And when you do that, you take yourself right out of the picture. You do just the same thing with your work. I am not one of your stories, Sam."

Hawthorne had met the lawyer, Jakob Hellman, a couple of times before and had read a lot about him in the local press. He had swarthy skin, thick black hair, a strong beard, weighed in at more than two-hundred pounds, and was over six feet tall. Despite his size, Hellman was an easy mover: He swung into the interview room, shouted in Kiswahili at the wardens outside, making them laugh, and slammed his briefcase down on the table so that it shook with the impact.

Hawthorne was leaning against the wall.

Hellman stretched out his arms as if embracing the room. "Very nice, very nice. I told the superintendent that we needed a change of decor in here. The prisoners would spill their guts much more easily, and look over there! He's arranged the nicest touch of puce."

Hawthorne held out his hand. "Glad someone sees the humor in this."

Hellman shook the hand, smoothing a subdued tie against his chest with the other. "We're going to get you out of here."

"Good. I asked for you because you always win."

"Ha, yes, well, that's because I only accept cases I can win," he said breezily. "Now, let's sit down and go from the beginning, and then we'll go through it all over again."

Hawthorne went through the story, meticulously combing his memory for details. He told Hellman why Kamau might have a personal grudge against him, about Sutcliffe, and about the missing jeep as well, and his feeling of being watched.

"Have you filed a report about the jeep yet?"

"Hell no."

"Right, well, we should. It would certainly make things easier for us if the jeep were found. Is there anyone else you think I should speak to?"

"Sutcliffe, for sure, and the other people at the institute. The first detective as well. I don't know about him, but it might be worth a try."

Hawthorne was buoyed after the meeting with Hellman, but the United States Embassy brought him right back to earth. They sent round a second officer to hold Hawthorne's hand. At least, Hawthorne thought, the guy would have held his hand if he could. He seemed perilously incapable of doing anything else. His name was Deakins; tall and thin, with stooped shoulders and a perpetual expression of concern and helplessness.

"We just want to assure you that we are doing all we can to assist the situation."

"Tell you what, Mr. Deakins," Hawthorne said, "why don't you and I just switch clothes so that I can walk out of here? I'll tie you up in the corner and make it look real professional."

Deakins blushed and stammered, "I don't think . . ."

"Just joking," said Hawthorne, without humor. "Have you guys made an official complaint?"

"We are doing everything possible."

"No official complaint, huh? An American citizen who has done his utmost to save a woman's life, and gets thrown into prison and charged with murder, and all you are doing is assessing the situation? Shall I assess it for you? It sucks. See this?" He pointed to his bandaged eyebrow. "What d'you call that?"

"Mr. Hawthorne, you have all our sympathy. The situation is highly regrettable."

"Highly."

"We are pursuing all the regular channels. If these fail then we shall . . ."

"Tell me, do they put something it in your food to make you speak like that?"

"I understand that you are very upset, Mr. Hawthorne." His voice fell to a whisper. "Please understand that we do make extra special efforts to help people like you. It is very embarrassing when our journalists are treated so badly, but frankly, the evidence against you is rather serious."

"You don't fool me, Deakins," whispered Hawthorne. "If this was human rights week, I guess that right now I would be relaxing in the Ambassador's personal jacuzzi. Unfortunately, both you and I know that the U.S. government is building up its bases on the East African coast as a backup to its operations around the Gulf, and it is not expedient right now for it to criticize the Kenya government. I know all about fucking expediency, Mr. Deakins, I've seen it up and down and all over this continent."

Deakins looked shocked. "Mr. Hawthorne, there is nothing more sacred to the heart of our country than the protection of its citizens."

Hawthorne grimaced. "Then why do I find that so hard to believe?"

By the time he got back to his cell, Hawthorne was completely depressed. He hated being dependent on others, especially when they turned out to be called "Deakins." He was so angry his insides hurt, and if

Superintendent Kamau had walked into the cell at that moment Hawthorne would have swung a punch at him.

CHAPTER FOUR

THE ROOM SAT AROUND her like a shell too large for its occupant. Since her return from Mombasa, Silvia Chi had hardly left it. She did not feel safe within its anonymous walls so much as marooned. The quietness wore her down, like a blanket of thick, suffocating air that held time in its grasp, making it stand still. She clicked on the television. It was a relief to see that KTN was not paying tribute to Kariuki. Ever since the discovery of the bodies the day before, the local media had been full of little else. Photographs showed Kariuki as a boy, as a young man, on his wedding day, at the beach, as a ranger, as the respected spokesman for wildlife conservation. The police had announced that they had detained a suspect. Silvia should have been overjoyed, but last night she'd dreamed that she'd killed the wrong man, and today she couldn't get the woman's face out of her head.

On television was a live broadcast of the opening ceremony of the Olympic Games. Like everything in the new millennium, it was bigger and more lavish than ever: the stadium crowd rippling with color; a sky glutted with doves, balloons, and parachutists; thousands of children swamping the centerfield; and massed bands marching to a martial beat. While the teams paraded round the track, the Kenyan commentators boasted of the expected success of their athletes. She switched it off.

Reclining on the rumpled bed, she was aware of the 41

muffled noise of the hotel at work: vacuum cleaners droning; crockery clashing; trolleys laden with linen rumbling along the corridors. Her hair, coarse and dark, lay across the pillows like a shawl. She lacked proportion; mouth too thick for her diminutive pale face, breasts much larger than her narrow hips. Her eyes were pale brown ovals with arched brows that gazed sullenly at the ceiling and were shocked into pinpricks of fear when someone knocked at the door. It was a deadened, sullen knock. Every muscle tensed; hands clenched in tight fists; her voice was trapped in her throat. She felt plastered to the bed. The door handle clicked, twisted, and opened. It was the maid, a large black woman with gaping earlobes hanging down to her round shoulders. She glared at Silvia, sniffed the air, jangled a set of keys in her fat hand to show she'd used a master key, and as a way of inquiring why the guest had failed to open the door. Silvia raised herself, smiled helplessly, watched the big woman clean the room, banging into furniture, clattering lamps and ashtrays. Silvia stepped from space to space, trying to keep out of the way. Once the maid had gone, solitude seemed like a friend.

She'd trailed Kariuki for days, searching for the right opportunity. Security had been too tight at his office. In the car park there were security guards and dogs. At his house, kids played in the yard, and people came and went all evening. Then on the Friday morning, Kariuki had left home with his wife, driven to the office, picked up a driver, and set off down the Mombasa road towards the airport. She'd followed, thinking that the job would be a washout if Kariuki got on a plane. She wasn't going to do it in front of the ticket counter with a couple of hundred spectators looking on. She wasn't a sniper. She didn't have the equipment or the skills. She worked close up. She'd told Zhu that she wasn't the right person for this job. In Hong Kong, it was different. She knew the territory, knew the layout, but this job had been crazy from that point of view. Everything was unknown.

But Kariuki had gone straight past the airport, beyond the signboard listing the destinations of Athi River, Mtito Andei, Voi, and Mombasa. The journey had been long and monotonous, taking her through an endless, dry, barren land. She'd never driven so far. Then the hire car had started playing up. It had looked good enough, Korean, last year's model, but the thing had coughed and spluttered, and the steering was so loose. She'd scared herself about the car breaking down altogether. What would she do in the middle of that empty, alien territory? She'd have to get someone to stop, even if there weren't many vehicles on the road.

She admired herself for the way the plan developed, the realization that she might, in fact, make Kariuki stop, right there, miles from anywhere. The steering wheel grew slippery as this plan grew in her head, making her sweat. But there were three people in the car. She would have to kill all of them. She didn't want to do that.

They'd gone all the way to Mombasa and down to Diani Beach on the south coast where the Kariukis had checked into the Trade Winds Hotel. Silvia had taken an expensive suite herself, overlooking the pool and the beach. Even there she could get no closer to Kariuki, who was attending a wildlife convention at the hotel. He was always surrounded by people. Then, after lunch on the Sunday, Kariuki and his wife had checked out and headed back to Nairobi. She'd followed, having switched cars for a more reliable, fast, Mercedes convertible. By then, she'd known what had to be done. Time had made the decision for her.

In heavy traffic at the start of the journey, she'd slipped past the Kariukis' Peugeot and driven ahead to Voi. She'd pulled in at a gas station, fueled the car, then driven into shade on the edge of the lot and pressed the button that folded back the car roof. With the roof down, Kariuki would know she was completely alone. It would make her seem more vulnerable, make them more willing to stop. She'd fixed her hair into a bun, tied a headscarf tightly over the top, adjusted her sunglasses, and waited.

The Peugeot passed the gas station; she set off in pursuit, trailing them until they were well inside the park boundary, then she roared past without giving them a glance. She drove alone, then, under the great dome of the sky that was sliding through shades of blue and pink towards the deeper colors of dusk, through that ugly wasteland of naked earth and rock, with dried out grasses and trees that clung hopelessly to life. She kept one eye on the rearview mirror, watching the godforsaken, deserted highway speeding away behind her. At last, she'd stopped on a dead straight stretch

43

of road next to a massive baobab tree, pulled a lever under the dashboard, climbed out, and raised the hood.

She was leaning against the car, arms folded, long fingers with blood-red nails tapping softly against the whiteness of her dress, studying the distant horizon of the road. Heart thumping heavily, flesh tingling, she sensed a strange elation and lightness as if she were about to throw herself off the edge of a cliff or out of an aircraft, and for that brief moment did not care what happened afterwards. All life was emptiness, nothing, like the landscape around her.

The Peugeot was crossing the horizon, shimmering through the rising heat of the tar. She was lifting the white clutch bag out of the glove compartment, slipping it under her arm, taking off the headscarf, and moving into the road, waving the scarf in the air. The Peugeot was pulling up and she was running, tottering on her heels, to the driver's window, wanting to reach the car before anyone got out. As she ran, she checked the road. If a vehicle was approaching, it still wasn't too late to stop. But the road had been empty. The job could be done.

Time seemed to slow down, becoming jerky and disordered. She saw the driver's eyes, then Kariuki's. Their faces loomed towards her, seeming to grow larger, more threatening. She was fumbling with the clutch bag. Kariuki was reaching for his door.

She had to stop him getting out.

The driver was saying something. She didn't hear what. Her hand was inside the bag, holding the gun with a finger on the trigger. She was pulling it out and shooting the driver through the open window, straight through the head. There was a strange, cracking noise and his blood spat back at her, splattering her dress.

Kariuki was yelling, leaning towards her, reaching for the gun. She was going to be sick, was overwhelmed with hate for everything, remembered firing the gun again and again, yelling at the same time, aware finally that Kariuki was lying motionless on top of his wife, though the woman had gone crazy; howling, yelling, begging, scrambling for the door handle, but at the same time trying to bury herself for protection under her husband's corpse. Silvia had had enough, wanted to get away, felt her head dragged around so that she was looking at the Mercedes, longingly, willing herself to go, get in, drive away. The woman screamed, sobbed, brought Silvia back. No one must remember, she thought.

Pulling open the rear door, she was reaching out to Kariuki, trying to pull him off the squirming woman. As she tugged at the dead man's shirt, Kariuki's wife had lunged forward, grabbing her hand. The gun saw the opportunity, guided her hand it seemed, and shot the woman, who reeled back into the corner while Kariuki's body slipped onto the floor of the car.

Silence echoed, wrapping itself around her.

Silvia had given the door a shove but it had bounced off Kariuki's feet. She remembered breathing heavily, her neck damp with sweat, chest heaving as if the air were locked inside and, glancing down at her ruined dress, the disgust she'd felt; then dragging her eyes back to the road, vision swimming unsteadily and lips moving without sounds coming out. There had been nothing in sight. Running back to the Mercedes, she slammed the hood down, got into the car, switched on the engine, and raised the roof.

She drove for a full hour before feeling safe enough to stop. After passing the Sikh temple at Makindu, she'd pulled off the road down a narrow dirt track, switched off the engine, and got out of the car. Night had fallen and the sky was loaded with stars. Bellowing toads and shrill crickets had mingled with the drone of chanting from the temple. As she began stripping off the dress, something soft and flapping had brushed against her shoulder and she'd almost screamed. So she'd struggled out of her clothes inside the narrow space of the Mercedes, wrapped the pistol in her dress, and had tied them and her shoes together using a belt, tossing the bundle into the back of the car. Dressing, then, in clean unbloodied clothes and new sandals, she'd also slipped the pins out of her hair, brushed it and sprayed herself and the car with perfume.

The Kiboko River was another ten miles up the highway. She'd stopped on the bridge and looked down on the water, running black and slow, hearing the music coming from Hunter's Lodge on the north bank of the river. The grounds of the hotel had been draped with fairy lights. She'd   45 dropped the bundle of clothes into the Kiboko; the splash was much quieter than she'd expected.

Silvia got up off the bed, poured herself a large scotch, then stood at the window sipping the drink, watching people stroll through the hotel gardens. It had been raining earlier. Glistening drops decorated the poinsettia and bougainvillea.

It was the woman. The woman screaming, trying to escape by hiding herself under her dead husband. That was the image that had stayed with her all day.

Zhu's call came in around midnight. "I heard," he said. "You did good, babe."

"They delayed the ivory vote, Zhu, like you expected. It's not taking place for three weeks."

"Good, that gives us time."

She said nothing.

"What is it?" he asked.

She hesitated. "I don't like it. I got to get out of here, you know? You bring Sen with you, let him handle the rest."

"What happened, babe? Don't do this to me. Not now."

She insisted, "I tell you it isn't good for me here." Her face flushed right up to the roots of her hair. She needed him to give way, only he never did do that. "Zhu, you gotta let me come home."

"But, babe, I ain't gonna be here. I'm coming to you. I need you, you know that."

There was a silence. She bit her lip. There were words she wanted to say but she couldn't speak them over the phone. She didn't know if she could say them ever. She wanted to tell him that she knew he'd double-crossed her, only really she didn't know, not for sure.

"Look, babe," he said softly, "you did a great thing. I'm proud of you, you know. You're feeling stressed out. I understand that. I'm with you. I'm going to be with you real soon. Listen. I'll bring Sen, okay? But you stay right there. Is the house ready?"

"Tomorrow."

"Okay, we're coming in the day after. Don't quit on me, babe. Don't do that." He hung up.

CHAPTER FIVE

WANGAI DROVE OVER to the house of Jakob Hellman on the outskirts of the capital. It was a sprawling, single-story dwelling situated in the middle of a coffee estate. A maid escorted Wangai to the lawyer, who was taking breakfast beside the pool.

Hellman looked up from the file on his knee. "Help yourself, Mr. Wangai. I won't be long."

The table was laid with a white linen tablecloth, thick napkins, heavy silverware, and fine china. In the center was a platter of mangoes, papaya slices, and watermelon, and next to this a large silver jug of coffee. Wangai ignored the fruit, poured coffee into a cup, adding cream and four spoons of sugar.

He looked around. A rich lawn, its pile as smooth as velvet, spread out beyond the pool in three loops, like a clover leaf, each loop edged with flowers, banking up into multi-colored shrubbery and surrounded by a wall of trees. It was too perfect and silent; apart from the birds and rustling leaves, there wasn't a sound, not even a distant radio or car. The pool was so still it looked like jello, and Wangai found himself staring at it, willing it to move, wishing he could chuck a pebble into it to watch the ripples spread out.

Hellman slurped his coffee, clattered the cup onto the saucer, and wiped his bearded mouth. "Well, Mr. Wangai, thanks for coming. I thought it would be more

49

discreet for us to meet here." Hellman raised his eyebrows to demonstrate just how discreet.

Wangai nodded.

"Tell me, did you feel that Superintendent Kamau was justified in detaining Sam Hawthorne?"

Wangai sipped his coffee. "Would I ask you whether a judge was right to send a man to prison?"

"I might comment on it, give my opinion, I'm only asking you to do the same."

Wangai shrugged and did not answer.

Hellman said, "You know that Superintendent Kamau has a grudge against my client."

"No," said Wangai, but it explained a lot, he thought. "Why is that?"

"Oh that doesn't matter. I looked you up, Mr. Wangai. You've had an interesting career. That corruption case you broke in Mombasa. Four or five detectives brought down. It's good to know we have men like you on the force."

Wangai looked away. He didn't want to hear this from Jakob Hellman. He wished the lawyer would just get on with the business they'd discussed on the phone. Hawthorne was innocent. Wangai had no doubt. The evidence was sitting there in forensics.

Wangai said, "Mr. Hellman, we can forget about all this foreplay. I will tell you what I know and then you can take it from there."

Hellman's eyebrows raised a fraction. "Why don't you tell me how much you want first?"

Wangai smiled. He wasn't incorruptible. If he hadn't occasionally liberated stolen goods from the police store, he could not have paid for his mother's hospital bills or have made the financial contributions demanded of a man in his position. (The latest donation came to mind, to a school attended by children of one of his Mathare Valley informants.)

Wangai viewed corruption as an unavoidable fact of life for the middle classes. It was the natural consequence of a system in which the expectations of traditional and modern life existed side-by-side on the plate of civil servants who were inadequately compensated to discharge either role. The powerful few legislated to protect their interests. The mass of humanity, confined by poverty, were always victims. The rest went out to do battle every day. Could they fix this? Could they make that happen? What could they offer? What would they provide? Most people were just trying to make ends meet.

No criminal had ever bought Wangai's silence, but he forgave this in others as long as they were otherwise doing a basically good job, and that meant putting away the habitual violent criminals. As for the rest, the white collar criminals, the accountants and politicians who bent the rules and came unstuck, Wangai understood if some of his fellow officers merely threatened exposure and extracted a hefty donation. Blackmail could be a very effective deterrent of crime. Some were too greedy, took it too far, like the Mombasa detectives. Payment for their silence had depended on a continuation of the crime. That was where Wangai drew the line.

The detective sipped his coffee, wondering how much the forensic file could be worth to Hawthorne, knowing at the same time that he would not ask for a cent. That wasn't why he was there. He shook his head.

Hellman grinned. His white teeth, ringed with the red lips and black beard, looked like a bull's-eye. "Why are you doing this?"

Wangai shrugged. There was a saying, "A wise man does not harvest his neighbor's yams." Really, he should not interfere. Even if he did nothing, Hawthorne would probably go free. Hellman was a clever lawyer. The U.S. government would step in. Foreign journalists did not get framed for murder. On the other hand, Wangai had a stubborn regard for his job. It deserved to be done properly.

In Tsavo, after the superintendent had scuttled off to Nairobi with Hawthorne, Wangai had been left to deal with that seething mob of foreign journalists, who naturally blamed him for what had happened as much as Kamau. He'd been insulted by everyone. He would have liked nothing better than to separate himself from the entire affair, but he couldn't walk away. There was still work to be done. He'd taken one of the forensic team, Michael Odile, back to the place on the Mombasa Road indicated by

Hawthorne, and they'd spent a couple of hours combing the area.

A couple of days later, Odile had called him with the results. Fragments of skin tissue, most likely from Kariuki's foot, were scattered around a large area at the highway site. The tire prints of the Peugeot matched molds and photographs of prints taken from the site. The second set of tracks was consistent with a jeep, which Hawthorne had said he'd been driving. Moreover, the pathologist's report showed that Helen Kariuki had died perhaps ten or twelve hours later than her husband and the driver of the vehicle. All of this evidence suggested that Hawthorne had been telling the truth.

There was more. A third set of tracks had been made by another vehicle on which the tires were wider, an expensive brand, in excellent condition, perhaps new. Several fingerprints had been obtained from the rear door of the Peugeot that did not match Hawthorne or any of the car's occupants, and a shred of red nail polish had been retrieved from the shirt of David Kariuki, though Mrs. Kariuki had not been wearing any. A partial footprint, from a woman's shoe that did not match Mrs. Kariuki's footwear, had also been found. It seemed possible that a woman had been involved in the murders.

Lastly, although the weapon used in the attack had not been recovered, the nine-millimeter cartridges taken from the victims revealed it as a Makarov pistol, originally a Soviet-manufactured weapon also made in China. Computer files revealed the Makarov as a favorite weapon of Middle East terrorist groups, but it had also been popular among guerrillas in southern Africa.

Wangai had told Odile to send a report over to Kamau but, for whatever reason, Kamau had failed to act on it. Two days later, Hawthorne was still detained. Kamau had to know that sooner or later the forensic evidence would have to be acknowledged, and of course it would be embarrassing for the superintendent because he'd been so quick to detain the journalist. It had struck Wangai that it might be just a little more embarrassing for Kamau if the contents of the forensic exam were revealed by Hawthorne's lawyer. It was small retribution, but Wangai liked the feel of it.

"It does not matter why I am doing this. Just do not tell anyone where you heard this information."

Hellman said nothing and gazed at Wangai. The detective could see him trying to figure out what was really going on.

"We should begin now. I have to get to work," urged Wangai.

"Sure, fine. Begin then." Hellman slipped his notebook onto the table and took a pen from his jacket pocket.

Wangai spoke, outlining the contents of the forensic exam. It didn't feel exactly like a betrayal but there was a taste of it in the still air of that perfect garden. Wangai sensed it and pushed it aside.

That evening Wangai sat at the table while his wife served up a meal of meatballs and *posho*. He watched her move back and forth to the kitchen. She was a big woman with a backside that shook to its own rhythm. Wangai liked her body. He liked *her*. Sixteen years they'd been married.

She was a traditional woman. They'd met when he was staying at his uncle's old place in Karatina. In those days the reserve had been steeped in Kikuyu custom. Wangai had chosen her for *ngweko* and they'd laid together all night, her skirt pulled in a knot between her legs for protection. Afterwards, he'd made the first formal visit to her home, taking two of his age-mates along. Her mother had given them glasses of sweet milk tea and left her daughter to entertain the visitors. He'd asked then if her family would consider his adoption and she'd assented.

The following weeks had been full of beer-drinking visits with her relatives. Once the negotiations were complete, he'd driven thirty goats to her father's farmstead as a *roracio*, which was a kind of dowry. At his uncle's place, he'd built his own hut, and the date for the marriage had been set. Everyone but his future wife had known it.

On the day of the wedding she'd gone to work in the *shamba*, and women from his uncle's place had set upon her, captured her and, since she was lighter then, had carried her shoulder high to their compound. She'd cried all the way, lamenting the loss of her family home, until they brought her to his hut and softened her with gifts and food. Then she'd been joined by her age-mates to sing the songs of lost childhood. After several days of ritual and song, they'd become man and wife, and since then he had not spoken her name aloud or even in his mind for fear of the malevolent spirits this might attract. These spirits were usually disgruntled ancestors, who lingered in death, unacknowledged, their souls untended by the old Kikuyu rituals. There was at least half a belief in Wangai's mind that the troubles of the modern world were caused by the mischief of the dead.

Wangai and his wife were cursed anyway. The table was set with only two places. Where there should have been children, there were none. Wangai felt bad about not having a son, but coming from a small family himself, he understood that children did not always happen on demand. For his wife it was a tragedy. Over the years they'd learned not to speak of it.

The phone rang. She stood up. "I will get it." He watched her listening to the receiver, two lines in the center of her forehead deepening into a frown.

"He is eating his food," she said.

Wangai smiled. It could be the attorney general on the line, but his wife would say the same thing.

She nodded at the phone and then covered the mouthpiece. "You had better come. This man is very rude."

It was Kamau, though he did not bother to introduce himself. "Did you see the news this evening, Wangai?"

"Ah . . . no, sir."

"What did you think you were doing?"

"I do not know what you mean, sir."

"Don't try to . . . Be in my office, nine tomorrow morning." He hung up.

Kamau's secretary's room was furnished in the usual post-colonial utilitarian style: plywood desk, hardback chairs, a window caked with dust, a presidential portrait (the color photographic version with a black plastic frame), and a couple of innocuous hand-written mottos stuck crookedly on the wall with sticky tape. One of them read, "If You've Got Nothing To Do, Don't Do It Here."

The secretary was a sullen, sulky man with a bad complexion, dressed in an overworn suit. The room was little wider than his desk. To get to his seat, the man had to press his back against the wall and squeeze through the narrow gap. He performed this maneuver four or five times in front of Wangai, and each time he scowled at the detective as if the positioning of the furniture were somehow Wangai's fault.

There was a third occupant of the tiny room, an overweight Maasai snoring in a threadbare armchair next to the door. His heavily jowled face fell in fat terraces, disguising his neckline; the enlarged lobes of his ears had been looped into knots that stuck out on each side of his head. His bloodshot eyes flickered open, darting towards Wangai, catching his gaze. Wangai turned away. Kamau probably had a hundred men like this one, dependent upon him for some kind of favor, charity, or nepotistic promotion. In return Kamau would earn the undying loyalty of the man, his extended family, and perhaps an entire village. It was the substance from which the deadwood of the nation constructed their great political careers. The president had made election promises that he would clear out these oxpeckers of the civil service, but even though there had been some encouraging signs, men like Kamau always survived.

Wangai had seen Hawthorne on the late evening news, which showed film of the journalist's release. Kamau had been also been interviewed, looking relaxed and happy as he praised the work of the police forensics department. Wangai had hoped for more, at least some sign of Kamau's embarrassment, some criticism, but there had been none. The previous night the detective's sleep had been disturbed by thoughts of Simon Njoka. Wangai wondered how bad life in the Records Department could really be. At least he would work more regular hours. His wife would probably like it.

He'd lain there in the dark next to her slumbering body, wondering what it would take to unravel the web of kinship and money that left the real power of the country in the hands of a few families. He thought that, even with all the changes that had been happening, it would probably take years, maybe generations. Yet power like that could be so easily abused. For instance, and this was his strongest fear, what if Kariuki's murder had been instigated at a high level, and what if this explained the rush to implicate Hawthorne? Wangai prayed that the country wasn't plunging into a dark age of assassination. If it was, then maybe he would be better off in

Records. The streets might become too dangerous.

The door to the superintendent's office opened. An official Wangai recognized, but could not name, departed, giving the detective a glimpse of the big man inside, seated behind his elaborate desk. The door closed, and a buzz came from the intercom on the secretary's desk. The sulky man stood up slowly, eased his way through the gap and, with an air of infinite boredom, sauntered into the next room. He left the door open and Wangai watched him approach Kamau's desk. As the superintendent spoke to his secretary he glanced once or twice in Wangai's direction. The secretary returned, shutting the door behind him, squeezed back behind the desk and sat down. The eyes of the Maasai slid open to assess whether it would be his turn next, but no other movement of the old man's body betrayed that hope. The slits closed again when the secretary looked moodily at Wangai.

"You," he said, with a toss of his head.

Wangai knocked on the door and entered. Kamau's office was on the sixth floor and the superintendent was standing next to the window looking out over the city. Without turning, he told Wangai to sit. Wangai found another hard-backed chair on the other side of the desk. The office was bigger than the one next door, and Kamau had added a few embellishments. There was a turquoise rug, and a small settee next to the wall, with a coffee table holding a large green malachite ashtray. The portrait of the president overlooking his desk was a print of an oil painting and had a gold-painted frame.

Kamau turned around. His eyes had a hooded look. "I have been trying to decide what to do about you."

Wangai said nothing. His hands sweated on his lap.

"You must have been aware that you had been relieved of the Kariuki case. You had no business conducting your own investigation."

"I can explain what happened, sir," Wangai stated bluntly.

"Good, you do that." Kamau slipped into his chair, leaned back, picked up the gold-tipped stick lying on the desk and used it skillfully to massage the back of his plump neck. "Why, for example, did you remain behind in Tsavo with," Kamau flipped open the forensic file on his desk and checked the name. "Odile."

"With respect, I thought there was more work to do at the scene of the crime. As it happens, I was right."

A nasty smile played behind Kamau's lips. "You were dissatisfied with my investigation?"

"I thought I was carrying out orders that you would have issued had you not been distracted by the incident with the foreign journalists."

Kamau leaned forward drumming his thumbs on the desk. "Ah yes, the journalists. Tell me, Wangai, what better disguise for a hired assassin than a press pass? Hawthorne is not off the hook as far as I'm concerned. I would say that he killed the Kariukis on the Mombasa Road and was looking for a place to hide the bodies and make his getaway when the car broke down. Perhaps he had a partner who drove away in this jeep of his. A woman, perhaps?" The superintendent barely disguised his contempt as he uttered the last phrase. "That would still fit with your Mombasa Road theory."

Wangai breathed out audibly.

"You have a problem with that?" asked Kamau sharply.

"Yes sir," said Wangai. Kamau was stumbling, Wangai could see it. Beads of sweat had formed on the superintendent's brow. Something must have happened. This attempt to still blame Hawthorne for the murders was absurd. Wangai's heart gave the smallest leap. He was not going to be banished to Records.

Kamau stood up and walked over to the window, linking his thumbs behind his back, rocking on the balls of his feet. "I don't know what you thought you would achieve with all this. Why didn't you bring the forensic evidence to me yourself? You know that is what should have happened."

"The results were sent to you."

He spun around. "We don't give police files to journalists or to defense lawyers."

"I did not give . . ."

"I know exactly what happened, Wangai. Don't you think for one moment that I don't." Kamau placed one of his large fingers inside his collar and ran it along the base of his neck.

Wangai was trying to imagine what could have happened. Perhaps 57

Hellman had gone to the top of the police department or even the Department of Public Prosecution. Someone must have come down on Kamau for not acting on the evidence.

"Your loyalty to the police department has been questioned before, Wangai. I've looked at your record. A steady arrest pattern, but it is not something of which you can be proud, is it?"

That was a little deflating, but Wangai did not answer.

"You have not courted many favors, have you Wangai? Well, I have a surprise for you. We have been discussing you and have decided that you should be transferred to this department."

Wangai stopped his jaw from gaping open but shock sat inside his mouth, demanding to be revealed. It bulged behind his eyes, pressed against his ears, and coursed all the way down his spine. His hands became fists.

"You should be grateful." Kamau's voice creamed the air. Slowly, he picked up the forensic file and knocked the edge against his desk, shaking the papers into line. Then he held the file out to Wangai.

"You will also take over day-to-day management of the Kariuki case, but you report to me, understand? No one else."

Shock shuddered into desire. Wangai kept his eyes on Kamau while he accepted the file. He wanted the case very badly. It was worth almost anything, even working under Kamau. It was as if all his years of experience had prepared him for this one moment. He took the case to his heart like a missionary accepting his Bible, thinking also that the case was even worth the risk that solving it could be politically compromising. Yet he saw that this was unlikely. It was Kamau himself who had reminded him. The woman. That sliver of nail polish, that footprint of a woman's shoe; they ran around his mind like a song that would not be shaken loose. They gave him hope, even proof that Kariuki's death had not been masterminded in the upper echelons of Kenyan society. His countrymen were far too chauvinist to allow a woman to come even close to a murder conspiracy.

L ater that day Wangai stood on the bridge looking down over the checkerboard of corrugated rooftops that sprawled around the festering trickle of the Mathare River. Upwards of a hundred-thousand people lived in this sunken ghetto, crammed into shacks made of flattened cans and plastic sheeting, separated by narrow stinking alleys. The main thoroughfare snaking along the edge of the valley was crammed with people, bicycles, barrows, *matatus*, and old cars. The afternoon sun reflected brightly on shining displays of stolen hubcaps and wing mirrors. Barrow boys shouted out sales of *sukumu wiki*, onions and potatoes. Large women wrapped in brilliant *khangas* crouched over minute selections of batteries, candles, matches, individual cigarettes, combs, padlocks, hand mirrors, and toffees, all arranged on newspaper spread over the ground. None of them were doing great business that day. All over the valley men, women, and children were making their way towards the meeting ground beside the New Mathare Amandla English Medium Modern Primary School, where Minister for Energy Muthangu would be addressing his constituents.

Muthangu's singers were warming up the crowd; their ululating song of praise called him hero, teacher, leader, and thinker. Wangai raised his eyebrows, skeptical whether any of those labels really fitted Muthangu, the successful big mouth whose oratorical powers had catapulted him from the ditches of Mathare into Parliament. If Muthangu had been a hero when he made that huge leap, Wangai doubted that the minister deserved to retain the title. He'd become one of the larger land owners in the country (God alone knew how, though no doubt one day, when his political enemies found it worthwhile, all would be revealed). Muthangu's voice had become that of the self-made man rather than of the poor and landless who had originally elected him. As far as Wangai understood it, Muthangu's latest landslide election by Mathare people had been due to their belief in his supernatural powers (how else could a poor man become so rich?), the conviction that his influence might rub off on them, and the powerful incentives offered to his opponents, encouraging them to stand down in his favor.

A scream of sirens and a fleet of gleaming motorcycles ridden by white-clothed policemen heralded the arrival of the politician. The motorcade swung past Wangai into the crowded market, where the motorcyclists blared a path through the traffic, forcing barrows and bicycles off the road. 59

The commotion grew. People yelled, children cried, the sirens wailed, and the speakers beside the primary school sang with feedback that echoed over the shantytown.

By the time Muthangu got down to the school and started his speech, Wangai had switched off, already knowing the familiar political platitudes. At least a hundred people were crowded on the bridge beside him to watch the meeting. When Mwangi squeezed in to have a look as well, no one noticed anything unusual. He was wearing a bright tartan jacket and had a day-glo orange scarf around his neck. Wangai asked him if the cold season had lasted too long this year.

"Eh! I got it in a card game," replied Mwangi.

Wangai sniggered. "And for once you did not gamble your winnings?"

"What is the matter? You do not like it?" Mwangi stood back from the parapet, pulling the jacket proudly over his chest.

Wangai waved his hand for him to stop.

Mwangi sighed. He was about forty, though his tightly wrinkled, purple-black face made him look much older. Wangai had first met Mwangi six years earlier, when the *matatu* driver had been picked up with bag full of *bhangi* stashed among a load of fertilizer on the roof of his vehicle. The "people's taxi" had been stopped for cramming fifteen passengers more than the legal limit into the cramped rear cabin. When the drugs were discovered, Mwangi had been brought to Wangai for interrogation. Wangai had found something indubitably honest in Mwangi's responses to his questions and, subsequently, the *matatu* driver's evidence had helped to convict a couple of much-wanted and well-known drug pushers. Any other detective might have wanted to boost his arrest record by putting Mwangi away as well, but Wangai had let him go. The *matatu* driver had been indebted to the detective ever since.

"What do you want?" Mwangi whispered.

"You got to make me something out of nothing," said Wangai.

Mwangi snorted. "You make me a magician!"

"Like your minister down there," quipped Wangai, nodding towards the meeting.

Mwangi shrugged. "I have got nothing against that man. He has not forgotten who his people are, like some others I know. You look at everyone down there." Mwangi flung his arm out over the parapet, towards the crowd at the meeting ground. "They could be selling beer or parking places up in the town, but instead they leave their bellies empty to come and show respect."

"Okay, okay," said Wangai, unconvincingly. "He's a good man."

Mwangi snorted through his nose. "You know, sometimes I feel sorry for you, Mr. Wangai. All you ever meet are bad people. Eh! It must be very unhealthy."

Wangai smiled. "Yes, okay, Mwangi. Listen to me. I am sorry if I offended your minister, okay?"

"That is better," replied Mwangi, looking proud.

Wangai reflected that he'd not seen Mwangi strut his stuff so much before. Something must have happened.

"Now, Mr. Detective Wangai, how can I help you?"

"I am looking for a car," explained Wangai, "a fancy car, maybe an expensive sports model, judging by the tires. It was on the Mombasa Road on the same evening that David Kariuki was killed. I want to know what car it was and who was driving it." He gave the rest of the details he had, which were precious few, adding that maybe a woman was in the car.

"How many others?" asked Mwangi.

"Don't know."

"Which way was it heading?"

"Maybe towards Nairobi but don't know."

Mwangi shook his head.

"There is also a pistol, like this one." Wangai produced a picture of a Makarov torn out of a brochure and gave it to Mwangi. "Maybe somebody down there has it up for sale," said Wangai, nodding in the direction of the valley.

The sun came out from behind a large white cloud, sending a wave of dazzling light dancing across the tin roofs of the shantytown. The speakers crackled and Muthangu's voice boomed out, almost hysterical.

"You see this!" screeched Muthangu. "You see this sunlight we are blessed with, that shall be our salvation! That shall be the salvation of poor people in all these poor countries like ours. Good people, I have not come empty handed to you today. I have brought you . . . the sun!" Muthangu paused to catch his breath. "Within the next ten years this country will be powered by the sun . . . and I do not just mean rich people. I mean that this government pledges to bring solar power into every home in this nation. We have been asking God, 'Lord, when will you hear the prayers of your people crying out in the wilderness of their poverty?' Let me tell you, He has heard us, He has heard you, and He is giving us His answer!"

Muthangu threw his hands in the air, a signal for the Muthangu choir to unleash a vast wail of joy. The crowd roared with them. Wangai smiled ironically, wondering how many of them knew that Muthangu was the chief share-holder in the solar power production plant, which was already going up in the industrial estate.

Mwangi coughed, signaling that he was about to speak. "This is what I say. I will go and ask questions for you among my driver brothers, though I cannot be sure that they will be able to tell me anything. Whether I get an answer for you or not, there is something you must do for me."

Wangai shot a glance towards Mwangi, who grinned back at him broadly. They'd been dealing together long enough to know where an acceptable request ended and the refusals began.

"Okay," said Wangai. "What is it?"

Mwangi giggled. "It is nothing really. You know there is this girl. Well, she is not a girl really, she is a woman and more like my sister. No, not my sister, my half-sister, if you know what I mean?"

Wangai nodded.

"Her name is Jazeen. She was arrested for prostitution two weeks ago, but it is not true. They have her down at the Central Police Station, and they are treating her bad because they say she is crazy and that she has got 'slim,' the dying disease, and that she has been infecting the whole country with it. None of it is true."

Wangai shrugged. "Maybe she is crazy. Maybe she does have AIDS."

Mwangi shook his head. "She does not. She does not. She is not a bad woman. You have got to get her out of there. She is sick but not with 'slim.' She has TB and they are killing her."

"Good people," yelled Muthangu, "there is more. We have all felt great sadness over the loss of David Kariuki, that famous son of Kenya."

Interested, Wangai looked over towards the meeting ground.

"Kariuki was a wise man," Muthangu announced. "He protected this country's natural heritage so that it could become a benefit for all our people. In Parliament, in a few weeks, we shall be voting on whether to once again start selling ivory. We have millions of shillings' worth of ivory right now in this country. I say to you good people, we are not a rich nation. We need every one of those shillings to build a better place for ourselves and our children. The Bible says that the Lord helps those who help themselves. We shall help ourselves, and I promise you, I shall bring some of those shillings right back here to Mathare Valley, so that we all may share in the bounty blessed to this land."

The Muthangu singers yelled praise and admiration, while Muthangu mopped his face with a large handkerchief.

Wangai thought about it. Kariuki had been definitely opposed to ivory trading. Millions of shillings sounded like a pretty convincing motive for murder.

"What do you say then?" asked Mwangi.

"What?"

"About Jazeen, you will help her."

"Okay," said Wangai, his mind not on the words he was saying. "I will try, okay? I don't know, but I'll try."

Mwangi grinned suddenly. "And I will try and find your car. Now, I have to go because I am seeing the honorable minister at the reception for celebrating the new primary school. You see!" he proclaimed, throwing his hands wide. "Things are really changing for us here. Even I am meeting a government minister. He needs men like me to transport all that sun-catching equipment. You think he won't give jobs to his own people? Next time you won't be seeing me on the street. Eh! Brother! Catch me at the Hilton Coffee Shop!" With a flourish, he chucked the end of his day-glo scarf over his shoulder and sauntered away down the road.

Wangai watched him, regretting making fun of Mwangi's wardrobe, which he must have chosen with care since he was going to meet the minister. The Muthangu singers started up their chorus again and a bunch of kids in school uniforms began performing a dance from the old days. Wangai turned away.

After he got back to police headquarters, Wangai sat in front of one of the terminals and called up the newspaper files. The two local dailies and both Sunday newspapers were routinely screened and saved. Some police stations in the country lacked working motor vehicles, but the computer network linking them all together was among the most sophisticated in the world. With the newspaper file on screen Wangai punched in the key words: "David Kariuki" and "ivory." Within seconds, newspaper articles containing both those references were spewing out of the printer.

CHAPTER SIX

T HE WIND BLEW ACROSS the Amboseli pan drawing up small twisters of white dust, which the Maasai called "women's tempers" because they flare up out of nothing so easily. On the tail of the wind came the rain, falling in great fat drops that thumped into the ground, disturbing the shallow soil. The trees had known for weeks that rain was on its way and had dressed themselves for the occasion in blossoms and awakening buds. Nobody knew why or how the trees knew what no other creature did. In years when the rains failed, trees stood dormant, as if they'd never heard of spring or felt the sap rise.

The failure of the rains was a common occurrence in Amboseli, whose name was derived from the Maasai *empusel*, meaning "salty dust" or "barren plain." Yet, in spite of its name and meager rainfall, Amboseli was no desert. For millennia, underground channels fed by rainfall on Mount Kilimanjaro had bubbled up in the basin, forming pools, streams, and swamps. The water eventually drained and disappeared into that cracked, bone-dry pan known misleadingly as Lake Amboseli. Sometimes this "lake" flooded during the long rains, and a carpet of small blooming flowers briefly covered the rain-blackened earth, but the dry winds and relentless sun that followed soon returned the "lake" to its usual condition, a place of white dust and shimmering heat.

Late in the afternoon, when the clouds had been

driven from the Amboseli sky and a halo of steam was rising from the thorny foliage, Maya Saito was sitting on the roof of her land cruiser in the shade of a flat, spreading acacia. In front of her, a video camera was rigged to a stand that could be raised and lowered through the sunroof of the vehicle. A small monitor fixed to the apparatus told Maya what the camera was seeing without the need for her to keep looking through the lens.

Solo's family of ten were feeding in a sun-dappled glade about twenty yards away. Maya was parked upwind from the elephants so that her scent would not disturb them, but they knew she was there. Earlier on Solo had come close enough to glare at Maya, eyeball to eyeball. The smell of the one-tusked elephant was particularly strong and Maya commented on it out loud, as she did on all aspects of Solo's behavior. She spoke about the way the elephant used her ears, how she raised her trunk more often than the others, seeking hidden scents, and the way she seemed uninterested in eating that day while the rest of the family tore down the glade as if there were no tomorrow. She drew attention to the elephant's streaming temporal glands and her odd walk, suddenly stilted and awkward, her back legs splayed out from the hips. The younger elephants, Star and Jasper, were fascinated. They sniffed and bumped against Solo, who jabbed nine-year-old Jasper, making him squeal.

Maya's commentary was picked up by the microphone fixed to her lapel and saved as the soundtrack of the videotape; the entire recording, visuals and commentary, was logged against time. Meanwhile, a radio-microphone attached to a collar around Solo's neck transmitted her vocalizations to a receiver at the research base located in the center of the park. These sounds comprised a kind of elephant language, communicating a range of emotions and intentions including fear, joy, loneliness, welcome, rejection, the quest for a mate, and successful copulation. Many of the sounds were below the range of human hearing, and this infrasonic quality meant that elephants several miles apart could communicate with each other.

The signals received at the communications center were saved on an infrasonic digitalized recorder, while the mainframe computer filed Solo's

vocalizations as a voiceprint. These transmissions were also logged against time so that the voiceprint could be assimilated with the videotape and reproduced as a subtitle to the visuals. The combination of camera recordings, commentary, and elephant voiceprint provided the basic data for the elephant communication project that Maya led, and which also employed three other women researchers. That afternoon Judith Dreyfus, an American student, was in the western sector trailing another elephant family. Margaret Okech was studying a couple of bulls on the edge of the Enkongo Narok Swamp. Both followed the same videotaping and recording procedure as Maya. Meanwhile the youngest member of the team, Wanja Mugo, was working at the camp, editing extraneous noise from some of the elephant tapes.

The Amboseli Elephant Research Project had been started in the early seventies by an American woman. Long before Maya joined the team, researchers had begun developing a dictionary of elephant signals occurring at humanly audible levels. Various kinds of trumpeting were known to indicate playfulness, silliness, indignation, and great excitement. After Maya joined the project they began investigating lower-frequency sounds, or rumbles, some of which could be felt rather than heard by humans. A long, soft rumble meant "Let's go," a short soft rumble made by a baby elephant meant "I'm lost." Deeper into the frequency register, they found an infrasonic call used by members of the same family to keep in touch with each other. Two loud, long rumbles roughly translated as, "I'm here, where are you?" and an even lower rumble provided the response, "We're over here." The team had come to realize that all the adult elephants in Amboseli's seven-hundred-strong population were probably able to recognize each other's voices. This ability allowed them to meet and avoid each other more or less whenever they chose.

Solo raised her head and the rest of the family stopped feeding. In an almost synchronized motion, they lifted their trunks and spread their ears. Fluid from temporal glands on all the older elephants streamed down the sides of their heads. Solo rumbled loud and low enough for Maya to feel the vibration in her belly.

Offhand, Maya didn't know what the rumble meant. The truth was that every new advance in understanding seemed to expose more of her ignorance. The elephants saw differently, classified differently, heard sounds she did not and could not hear, and detected smells that were full of meaning for them but meant nothing to her. These few square miles of Amboseli translated for them into an entirely different world. It was this great variety in the way different species conceptualized the planet that was the core of Maya's fascination.

The sun poured light upon the glade and the family of elephants stood still, holding their pose until Solo's left foreleg lifted slightly, slowly off the ground. Abruptly, she flapped her ears and began moving away from Maya, towards the southern end of the glade. The others followed. Maya heard heavy feet padding the earth and a rushing sound of vegetation pushed aside. Solo and her family broke into a squealing run, while out of the bush came the matriarch, Astra, and seven other elephants. The two families ran at each other until they were mingling and touching, rubbing their bodies against each other, clashing tusks together, placing their trunks in each other's mouths, urinating and defecating with delight.

Maya was just as pleased. Astra and Solo were old friends, old cousins. In the early eighties they'd been members of the same family. Project records showed that Astra's mother had died during a drought, and afterwards Astra and Solo had formed separate families. The cause for the split appeared to have been insufficient food. An adult elephant needs to consume four hundred pounds of vegetation every day which, with the failure of the rains, had become increasingly hard to find. Since the split, however, meetings between the two families had been recorded on a very regular basis. Also, the scale of the greeting ceremony shared by these families was much greater than they displayed towards other elephant groups.

As the excitement died, most of the elephants moved off to resume feeding while a couple of young males engaged in dominance games. Astra stayed beside Solo for a while, touching the other elephant's face with her trunk, then letting the trunk flop down to the ground. The two matriarchs stood quite still for a moment, then Astra also moved off to feed in the swampy ground on the edge of the glade.

Keeping the camera trained on Solo, Maya sat up and stretched. She wore a loose olive vest and khaki pants. Her face, long and narrow with sharp cheekbones, was shaded by a floppy-brimmed hat. Most of the people who lived around the park were Maasai, like her, except she came from Nairobi. Her father was a successful businessman who had joined the Chamber of Commerce and Rotary instead of passing through the rites of passage of a Maasai elder. Her mother was a teacher at Kenya High School. When she'd come to Amboseli, Maya had brought with her a baggage of prejudice against Maasai who refused to embrace the modern world.

That was before she slept in a *boma*, lulled by the gentle sounds of cattle, which are a Maasai's measure of himself; before she saw the soaring, leaping celebration of circumcision performed by Maasai warriors, which actually mimicked the mating dance of the male whydah bird. She'd understood that for a Maasai the red earth symbolized the blood of man, fertility, life, the cycle of things; they used this soil as an adornment, dressing themselves in their world. They decorated themselves also, with feathers, the stuffed bodies of birds, and the manes of lions slaughtered single-handed in the name of courage. She'd argued with them over these killings of lions and elephants that accompanied the ritual passage of every new Maasai age group from boyhood to warriorhood. But she was also in awe of the closeness of these people to the natural world and its symbols that permeated every facet of their existence.

She knew the Maasai around the park found her strange. Who was she? A woman without a family was nobody, unfulfilled, a ghost of herself. A grown woman without a man was a cause for laughter. She wasn't unappealing; too thin maybe, but there had been offers, a number of cows had sometimes been mentioned (and not always jokingly) as a basis for her dowry.

Maya slipped down inside the cabin of the vehicle, grabbed a bottle of water from the icebox, and took it back to the roof of the cruiser. A couple of bright red-and-black butterflies flitted across the hood and off into the trees. A cattle egret swooped into the glade, landing too close to Solo. The matriarch swirled around, tossing her trunk at the bird, which jumped out of harm's way.

The icy water bathed Maya's throat, and she thought about Sam Hawthorne, knowing that he would be in a foul temper over everything that had happened since Kariuki's death. She would have gone up to Nairobi herself to protest against his detention, but that morning Kariuki's deputy, Elijah Kipkoech, had told her on the phone that Hawthorne was a free man. She was glad, not only because he was free but because she would not have to face him. Her pride was still hurting. She told herself that it was only pride.

Right from the beginning, they'd made it clear that theirs would be a relationship without ties. She'd welcomed it. She didn't want to commit herself to anyone. She'd argued about it for years with her mother.

"You can come back to Nairobi and become a professor at the university, have your career and your husband and your children. You cannot live in Amboseli forever. No man is going to accept that."

Maya had always insisted that she didn't want to work at the university, with its factions and politics, that she didn't want to get married, or have children, because she was perfectly happy the way she was. It was true. She was happy. Except that she'd found herself, after seeing generations of elephants being brought into the world, wondering about herself and thinking about a child coming out of her own body. Then she turned thirty-five and time seemed to be running out.

It had not mattered, in the beginning, because it was all theoretical. There had been no man in her life. Then Sam came along. It was crazy to think of Sam as a father, but she had not been able to stop herself. They suited each other so well. It had annoyed him so much when she teased him about their cultural differences. Really, he had understood her better than any other man she had ever known, African or otherwise. He let her be the way she was, did not try to change her.

But this dream of a child had got out of hand. She began making plans, without saying a word to Sam. She'd thought that for the first year, while the baby was really small, she could go up to Nairobi and they would both live with Sam. She would use the time to write up her research. Then she could come back to the park with the baby and an *ayah*. Sam would come down when he could. She wouldn't have to pressure him. Life would hardly have to change. Besides, Amboseli was a wonderful environment for a child to grow up in. When he was old enough to start school (she imagined him as a boy), he could start off locally. It would be years before she would have to think about being in Nairobi.

She never told Sam about it, never even hinted, but she'd thought that, if she waited, he would soon see how obvious it was. Then, just when she'd expected him to start getting closer, he'd backed off, creating arguments about how hard it was for them to meet, and she'd fought back because that was her nature. She wouldn't let him put all the blame on her. Even when he suggested that they should split up, she'd appeared to agree with him because her pride would not let her do anything else. She could be as strong and hard as he was. She'd smiled when she said goodbye, as if she was just going home after a pleasant lunch.

The gap left by the separation had been enormous. It felt worse because Sam had become a kind of anchor for her, an assurance that she could have her life the way she wanted it and a man she enjoyed being with as well. She did not think of "love" as such, being too aware of the physical urgings of nature to trust that the passion of a few moments should be a guiding principle for life. She didn't want to lose him. She had even been ready to give up the dream, the child, everything, just to continue seeing him.

On a trip to Nairobi soon afterwards she'd bumped into Sam's boss. He was a funny old man, very flirtatious. He'd told her that Sam was in town and she'd decided to go and tell him how she felt, right away, before her pride interfered and told her that she shouldn't go crawling after a man like that.

She'd taken a taxi to his place in Karen a little after five in the afternoon. Walking up the drive, she'd heard music coming from his house. The Dobermans had come across to check her out and padded alongside her all the way to the front door. She'd knocked and waited. A muffled sound came from inside, then the door had been opened by a girl, not much more than twenty, who was wearing one of his shirts. She'd caught a glimpse of Sam as he emerged from the bedroom with a towel round his waist, before she fled back to the taxi and away.

Later, he'd sent a note saying that the girl meant nothing and that he wanted to see her, if only she would call next time she was in town. She never did. She'd been too offended and didn't really trust herself not to break down in front of him and lose all her self respect. Also, these emotions had been interfering with her work too much. She had to shut them away, realize that not all women had children, not all women needed children. Her life was wonderful, rich, and full as it was. Certainly it had been very busy in the last few months, since renewed efforts to ban the ivory trade had got under way. Things had been going well but now, without Kariuki, she wasn't so confident.

Before his death Kariuki had promised he would replace his deputy. Elijah Kipkoech was an ex-army man with a dozen years experience in anti-poaching operations, but Kariuki and Maya had both seen his shortcomings. He lacked the instincts and negotiating skills required to deal with politicans and business people. These abilities were crucial if the trade was going to be stopped. Kipkoech's lack of diplomacy had been all too evident just in the way he'd spoken to her on the phone.

"I can cope with everything," Kipkoech had said. "It is a shame only that they have postponed the parliamentary debate on the ivory trade. If I had that vote today, I know I would win. They would vote against the trade because of Kariuki, out of respect. A month from now, who can tell? They will forget."

In a sense, he was right. Kariuki had possessed an ability to make men feel bigger than themselves; he'd done it with rangers working for him in Samburu. He did the same with politicians, enabling them to think beyond the petty concerns of their individual careers, and to see the ivory issue in terms of "Africa" and "the survival of a species." Kariuki had intoxicated them with his vision, but every day without him was a day in which that vision would fade.

Maya had replied, "Elijah, you have to take every opportunity you can to tell them what is happening. Every day almost, I hear stories about more elephants being killed. There was a whole family wiped out on the Tana River. The babies as well. You must tell people about it. Kariuki would have got photographs and given them out to all the politicians and the press. Do you want me to come up to Nairobi right away? I can help you."

She'd heard Kipkoech sniffing. "I don't think that will be necessary. You have your work to do down there."

"Elijah, we have to work together. We have to win this vote and we have to persuade other countries to support the ban again. If we do not, then poaching may become as bad as it was in the seventies." She had the statistics in her head. During that decade alone in Kenya, they'd lost more than fifty-thousand elephants. "Look, Elijah, Kariuki and I had plans you should know about. I should come and talk to you."

There'd been a silence. Then Kipkoech had said, "Okay, you come up next week, Wednesday. But I have set some things in operation myself already."

It was plain that Kipkoech did not want her around. It was ridiculous because after Kariuki, Maya possessed the strongest contacts with the Americans and the Europeans and others who mattered. She'd been with Kariuki when they'd discussed pressuring the Gulf states into meeting more stringent ivory import regulations. Kipkoech knew nothing of this. Kariuki had said that his deputy was a "solid field man" but he had no imagination, he didn't understand tactics, and he didn't know how to trap an opponent and use him. Maya also had Kipkoech down as a man who had trouble working with women.

She nudged the camera around so that it captured the interaction between the adolescent Star with her baby niece, Ava. Star had draped her trunk over the neck of the tiny elephant and looked as if she were trying to suckle it. Solo meanwhile put her trunk in the air, flapped her ears, and spread her legs.

Back at the camp, where Wanja Mugo was working, the mainframe computer clicked and ran, hummed and paused as it absorbed and sorted incoming elephant signals. When it began emitting a repetitious bleeping alarm, Wanja stopped work, saved and cleared her files, reset the screen in front of her to check incoming data, and ultimately focused on Solo's voiceprint. The pattern was there. The sound was low and strong, repetitive like a song, soundless for human ears but a kind of music for an elephant.

Wanja picked up the radio and called Maya. Solo was summoning a mate.

olo's song was resonant, beautiful, powerful, and demanding. It shimmered in slow waves across the eastern swamp and through a glade of bark-stripped fever trees beyond. It sang across the bone-dry pan, skirting a herd of silent wildebeast, and wrapped itself around the lodge where seventy tourists gossiped over the evening game drive, ignorant of the ancient low music that drifted around them. The notes skimmed the surface of the azure swimming pool and danced through a wall of bougain-villea to the garbage pits beyond, where the maribous sulked over dinner. The song also drifted north, covering three miles of dense bush to finger the thorn-enclosed *bomas* of the Maasai beyond the park boundary. A pie dog rolled over and sat up yawning, not for the song but for the Maasai boy who crawled out of his mother's hut to toss him lumps of last night's *posho*. The boy did not hear the song, and neither did his hump-backed steers, snorting their steamy breath and scraping their toes over the dry dirt. For most of the planet's creatures, the song was barely discernible. It was a fragment of a barely felt vibration with not even the whisper of a feather.

Solo's song ran through the air, covering miles, fed by breezes, relentlessly seeking those who would hear and understand, and for whom it was irresistible. There were ten who caught the song that evening, and the effect on them was devastating. They turned with one head, from the waterhole towards Kimana and the land beyond the swamp, from the weakening stands of acacias and the southern forest that led towards the mountain. They listened and took the song inside themselves, so that their glands bled secretions making them stink with desire. Then, denying hunger and thirst, they went in search of the singer of the song.

Some took longer than others. The younger bulls ran at the sport. They had no experience, no finesse, and not much hope. They tracked Solo by sound and smell and found her surrounded by her family, aroused by the song and the new odors it heralded. Solo backed away from her family, spreading herself wide open, tantalizing the young bulls. Her sister Stroker snorted and tossed her head, rumbling her own low song of warning and excitement. Star, curious and full of adolescent dreams, mimicked Solo's odd walk and spread herself triumphantly between Solo and one of the young bulls. She stood still while the bull tested her orifices with his trunk but, finding nothing, he abandoned her. He tried his luck with Solo, but she bellowed and dodged his advances. Her song would not be appeased by such a creature, who bore none of the ravages of life, with his unchipped tusks and untorn ears. By the time the sun had slipped behind the trees, the novices had all tried, failed, and given up the pursuit, but they hung around the fringes of the family hoping, hopelessly, for the miracle that would deliver them from frustration.

Solo waited. Maya waited, and night fell. She fixed an infrared lens to the camera and pulled up a back shield to give some protection from the evening's predators, though she did not allow that fear to concern her. She'd done this too often. If an elephant under observation was giving birth, or dying, or mating, Maya had to stay with her until the end, night and day or until she was relieved. Right at that moment, she wanted to see Solo mate more than anything else in the world.

The glade rang with the full-throated songs of countless toads, the rattle of myriad crickets. An owl hooted, a hyena cackled, a lion coughed, and Maya chewed on a carrot stick. When Judith, who was now back at camp, called up on the radio to see how things were progressing, her voice sounded oddly remote, from another world.

The bull eventually arrived around one in the morning. Maya was dozing against the backshield. It was his smell that awoke her, and at the same moment a cloud uncovered the moon, flooding the glade with light. Maya murmured into the tape that this was Rameses, a bull of around forty-five years, and that he was clearly in musth.

A male in his prime is aggressive and possessive. Agitated glands, each side of his head, stream in dark rivers down his cheeks, staining his thick, grey hide. His ears waft the scent of his enraged senses. He dribbles incontinently, and his sheath oozes viscous green fluids, creating odors that both warn and seduce. He releases long, low rumblings that spread for miles around, warning other males away. In this temporary state he can overcome any challenger. Females in estrus will welcome him.

Such was the condition of Rameses. He was a massively threatening 75 beast with ragged ears and one tusk half broken. He offered none of the usual displays of non-aggression, such as politely draping his trunk over a tusk. His penis was unleashed, almost scraping the ground. He dwarfed Solo, five and a half tons to her three.

She stood with her back to him, legs splayed, every scent of her body urging his approach. At the last moment she moved, stepping forward awkwardly. He stopped her, laying his trunk flat along her back and lifting his front legs to rest either side of it. She spread herself. The hard S-shaped penis, four feet long, moving independently, found her vagina and he thrust the entire length inside.

They were still for almost a minute before he withdrew, a torrent of semen gushing onto the ground. She released a bellowing cry, loud and low. Her sisters, cousins, children, nieces, and a couple of young nephews ran at her, flapping their ears and joining their voices with hers. They urinated, defecated, and filled the air with low, rumbling vibrations. The cacophony of those voices spread like ripples on a pond. The higher, most audible notes were soaked up by the sponge of the surrounding foliage, but the deeper sounds flowed out over the land. Those who heard and understood this resounding chorus would know that a mating had taken place. Some males would be alerted and might come in search of Solo, but Rameses would remain with the family as long as she was in estrus, which would be for at least three days. He would act as her consort, feeding alongside her, mounting her, chasing other males away and ensuring that his seed was planted. In twenty-two months it would be ripe for harvesting.

Maya laughed. She laughed with joy, amazement, and at the absurdity of her life. She stopped when she saw Rameses turning in her direction. The average male elephant is not particularly aggressive, but the most gentle bull becomes dangerous when he is in musth. Rameses bellowed, shaking his head, the moonlight glinting on the jagged edge of his broken tusk. Maya jumped down off the roof, flipping the catch on the video stand so that it slipped down behind her. She rolled forward into the driver's seat. Rameses was in front of her, his ears spread out, supposedly to make himself look bigger, his head raised and feet scraping the soil. She clicked open the radio channel and pressed the alarm. At the same time, she turned on the ignition and revved the engine.

Judith's voice crackled into the cabin.

"Trouble," yelled Maya. "I might need . . ." She crunched the gears into reverse, and at the same time Rameses made his charge.

"Shit!" she yelled. The vehicle's wheels spun in the mud, releasing themselves; the cruiser shot back too fast. Rameses was bearing down on her. A sentence ran like a mantra through her mind. "Nine times out of ten elephants halt their charge a few feet from the victim." She changed gear to slide forward and along the track to the left. Rameses was gathering speed all the time. He was not going to stop. His trunk was rolled up and his ears were flung back flat against his body. By the time he hit the wing of the cruiser he was traveling at nearly fifteen miles an hour. His good tusk penetrated the bodywork and speared the engine; the pressure of impact sent the vehicle crashing backwards into a clump of thornbushes.

Maya did not know she'd screamed, but Judith heard it and called Maya's name over and over without response. She ran out of her tent, carrying the radio, shouting for Wanja and Margaret, and stood there under the stars praying for Maya to respond. Margaret, dragging on a pair of shorts, half ran, half fell in the direction of the communications center to check on Solo's location. Wanja and Judith followed her and together they climbed into one of the Land Cruisers. They shot off along the rough, rutted road, the sound of the engine shattering the night.

Maya's voice came into the cabin as they drove along, sounding muffled because she was under the dashboard.

"*Wanawake?*" she said, which means "women" in Kiswahili. "I'm okay. Rameses has gone back to the woman of his dreams. The car is a mess, and yes, the videotape is okay."

CHAPTER SEVEN

T

HE HOUSE WAS ten miles outside Nairobi, on the edge of an estate of old, ivy-clad houses hidden behind high brick walls. It was built in hacienda style, with arched doors and windows, whitewashed walls, and trellises stacked with strong-scented jasmine. From the wide rear terrace a stone stairway led down to a small kidney-shaped swimming pool, and below this the garden disappeared into a wild, overgrown gully that was rich with the chatter of monkeys and squawking hyrax.

Silvia lay, unrelaxed, on a sunbed on the terrace among terracotta pots sprouting luscious patience plants. She heard a car approach, heard the wave of canine anger rising and falling with the passage of the vehicle, and knew the guard dogs would be forcing their snouts between the bars of the wrought-iron gates that lined the narrow, pot-holed Langata road. Some of the dogs would break free to charge alongside, snapping ferociously at the wheels. She hated those dogs.

Silvia had chosen the house herself, before killing Kariuki, before Helen Kariuki's face began dominating her dreams. She'd rented it from an English woman called Mrs. Henderson, who had reminded Silvia of her own English grandmother. This grandmother had died long before Silvia was born, but she'd seen photographs of the sweating, blowsy, over-dressed woman. The photos had been kept by her father in an ivory box inside his closet, and as a kid she'd spent a lot of time looking at them, at the source of her own pale brown eyes and full red lips.

When she was a kid, her father had run a shop in the heart of the ivory quarter, where stall after stall was stacked to the roof with carvings, brooches, beads, and earrings. She remembered climbing to the upstairs studio, where fifteen carvers worked in a room shafted with sunbeams of fine white dust, ivory dust. Taking the mottled yellowing tusks, they'd chiseled smooth white statues of gods and goddesses, serpents, and other fabled creatures.

Wu, the master carver, an ancient man with a thin, white beard and narrow, wrinkled eyes, had worked alone in a corner of the room, chipping totems out of the biggest ivories, some of them over six feet long. Wu had told Silvia that the secret of ivory was in its feel. It had the look of something cold and hard, yet when you held it, though it was still cold, it had a warmth that came from its former life. Its hardness was of a pliant kind, giving magic to the touch of the carver who respected its purity. There was no substance like it on earth.

Wu had lived, worked, and tutored his apprentices in that workshop for more than forty years. He'd never married nor had children; the ivories were his only offspring. Silvia had one of his pieces, an ivory girl trapped inside an intricately carved cage of flowers, which still bore the shape of a tusk. A hand shaded the girl's eyes as she looked towards a future she could never own.

One morning the apprentices had arrived to clean up the workshop and found the old master lying in the middle of the room, the sunbeams playing on his motionless, white head. They'd nursed him for a month before he died. She thought later that the soul of the business had died along with Wu, because the following year, 1989, the market had closed down all over Europe and North America, and trading in ivory had been made illegal, as if it were a dangerous drug instead of a business invested in a beautiful and ancient art.

Her father had never recovered, not even after the trade partially re-opened. His fortune was lost, he began drinking more, tormenting her mother more openly. There had always been fights, but now he sometimes beat her mother when he wasn't drunk. They lost their home and moved into a cheap apartment, where he slouched around, hardly changing out of a sarong, watching television, drinking cheap liquor, and smoking foul cigarettes. It seemed as if that whole building sweated in the high humidity. At night, people dragged their sleeping cots onto the communal balconies or even into the street, just trying to catch a breath of air.

Once, Silvia told her father that he was a *wuchanzhe*, a despicable man with no property, and he'd hit her across the face, cracking the flesh open with his ring. The mark of it was still on her cheek. Her mother bowed to him, though, then took her hatred, cooked it up in bowls of noodles and gingered pork, and went off to play mah jong with the neighbors.

Voices approached; Zhu, Sen, and Jimmy laughing about something. She'd told Zhu again that she should get out of the country. It was foolish for her to stick around, especially since the journalist had been released. She'd seen the newspapers; Hawthorne's picture and his face with a twisted, peevish look. Zhu wouldn't discuss her leaving, though, told her she worried too much.

"You wanna fix us some food? We're starved." It was her brother Jimmy speaking; mild, stupid Jimmy. A plump, giggling man-boy of eighteen. When they were kids Jimmy had always tagged along behind her and he was still doing it, only now he liked to pretend that he could tough it out, give her orders. She shot a look at him, and Jimmy grinned humorlessly.

She roused herself off the sunbed anyway, looked round, and saw Zhu come out through the glass doors behind Jimmy. He wore metal-framed dark glasses that gleamed in the sunlight. They were menacing, and she thought, looking at him, "Did you do it, Zhu? Did you sell me out in Macao?"

"Hey babe," Zhu said, softly. He took off his glasses and crinkled his eyes at her. It was a look that sent bolts shooting through her chest and left her feeling guilty. She walked to him, kissed him. He held her softly, whispering, "I got a surprise for you later, see?" He grinned and a flash of gold came from his mouth.

Once she was in the kitchen, chopping onions and garlic, the malevolence returned. She remembered the surprise on his face when she'd turned up after the Macao job, as if he'd not been expecting her. Stupid. Maybe it was nothing. Maybe she was telling herself stories. Zhu had always been good to her, hadn't he? He said he needed her. Why would he do anything to harm her? The trouble was, she knew he had it in him to do just that. He responded to the logic of a moment and, if it made sense, in that moment, to betray his own mother, he was capable of it.

Of course, Zhu hadn't actually seen his mother since he was a kid. She'd smuggled him onto a ship in Shanghai when he was barely nine years old. A sailor had found the stowaway and had promised to help Zhu find his uncle when they got to Hong Kong. Instead, Zhu had been sold to a gangster, who used kids like that for sex and rented them out as well. It had taken Zhu two years to escape, after he'd sliced a bread knife across the gangster's belly.

It wasn't the kind of childhood that was going to make a decent person. Maybe she had less excuse for the way she had turned out. Zhu had told her they were two-of-a-kind.

She'd killed her first man when she was seventeen. It was an accident. She'd found herself in the man's apartment. He raped her and it hurt. He pressed down on her breasts so that she felt as if the air were being squeezed right out of her, and he'd thrown a sheet over her face so that she couldn't see a thing. She'd put her arm back, trying to grab the pillow to throw it at him or something, but he was the kind of guy who slept with a gun under his pillow, and that was what her hand had landed on. His gun. She'd shot him.

He hadn't died right away. Even while she was washing the blood off and dressing herself, he was still breathing, making a harsh, wheezing sound. But when she went across to the bed to retrieve her underwear, she saw his eyes, gaping open and motionless. She'd had no fear of death. The only thought she remembered having was that he couldn't hurt anyone anymore.

She met Zhu a couple of weeks later; a good looking man with wide-boned features and a strong smile. He was a lot older than she, in his late thirties, though he didn't look it. He'd taken her to a party in one of the big hotels for his cousin's twenty-first. This was during the last few weeks of British rule in Hong Kong, when money was flowing like tapwater. Grand parties were going on everywhere, people competing to see who could spend the most on a single blowout.

Zhu had told her to bring her brother Jimmy along, and the kid, being only fifteen, had been overwhelmed by everything; gawping at the women's breasts and jewelry, scraping his shoes through the carpet to look at the pile, staring up at the chandeliers that dazzled like waterfalls of ice. She wasn't much older, but she wasn't so easily impressed.

The party was in the penthouse. Zhu had taken her into another room to look at the view without the dazzle of reflected lights and mirrors. Inside was a king-size bed flanked with dragon-based lamps that glimmered dimly. He pulled back the drapes to reveal all of Hong Kong and stood behind her, kissing the back of her neck. She liked having the attention of this rich, mature man. He was funny, too, made her laugh, and didn't push her around. She let him have sex with her, standing up against the window, the glass pressing hard against her spine while he stared over her shoulder at the bright lights and the ferries pulling out for Cheung Chau or Lamma Island. Afterwards he said it was like fucking the whole city, and she'd laughed because she liked feeling like a whole city.

After they made love, they'd gone across to the bed and he'd curled up behind her, cupping her breast in his palm. Then he'd told her that a few weeks earlier he'd been going to meet this man on business, only when he arrived the man was dead, shot in the belly with his dick hanging out. He'd seen a woman leave the man's room, though, and he'd got a good look at her. He murmured those words softly, like they were words of love, and kissed her neck below the ear at the end of every phrase.

She'd tried to deny it but it was no good. He knew, and it was like he took possession of her at that moment, because he had the power to destroy her life. By the time she realized that he would never have gone to the police, she didn't care anyway. She thought she was in love.

Zhu talked about murder the same way other people might talk about a good ball game. It was all in fun. They laughed a lot and had a lot of sex as well, which with Zhu was usually very spontaneous and happened in weird, often semi-public places. In the beginning it had been okay. It was only later she found herself wishing it could happen in bed. Even when a bed was available, they'd end up on the floor or even with her sitting on the washstand.

One day Zhu had told her about a man who was giving him trouble and threatened to come between him and his uncle. He wanted her to kill this man. At first she'd thought he was joking, but he was serious. He pointed the man out and gave her a pistol to do the job with.

She'd never intended to go through with it, but she made a show of following the guy around. He was grossly overweight and had a thin moustache over thick red lips. Often he was with his girlfriend, a woman in her forties who had a narrow, heavily made-up face. One day Silvia had seen the man hit this woman hard in the head. The two of them were just walking along, side by side, when suddenly *wham!* he lashed out and hit her. The woman staggered against a billboard along the side of the street, then he'd kicked one of her legs, making her fall down. He grabbed her arm, dragged her along, and further up the street he'd put her in a taxi.

Two minutes later the man went down a side-lane to take a leak; he stood between a couple of trash carts. The opportunity was there, lying right in front of her. She moved towards him, light-headed, blood rushing through her veins. He began to turn as she approached, but he remained speechless as the gun shot a silenced load into his plump neck.

This occurred just after nine in the evening. Up on the street car horns were blaring, their fumes filling the spaces between the buildings with a blue haze. Girls stood in doorways heckling customers, music thumped out of the windows, neon lights flashed, street vendors shouted sales of lizard and snake oil, cooking pans at street-side restaurants sizzled and flared up, people talked and yelled and laughed and none of them seemed to have heard a thing.

Silvia carried the tray of food out to the back terrace. The table that Zhu, Jimmy, and Sen were sitting around was covered with newspaper clippings. A glossy magazine on top of the pile showed a photograph of Maya Saito. Sen was studying it, a smile curling over his narrow lips. Silvia had never got used to Sen's face, which was concave; his brow and chin stuck out further than his nose.

"Let me tell you about Elijah Kipkoech," Zhu was saying. "Fifteen or twenty years ago we had a nice little business going. We got ivory from Kenya or Tanzania or wherever and it was smuggled into Burundi, which is a country about the size of a teaspoon. We had people in Burundi who arranged certificates of origin for us, which made it seem that the ivory actually came from there. In fact, that place doesn't have a single elephant, but no one was arguing. We paid everyone real well, including Kipkoech, who was holding down the Kenyan business for us.

"Anyway, with these certificates of origin, the ivory became legal and could be traded on the open market. It was smooth, I'm telling you, but this ape Kipkoech was a greedy bastard. Even then he was in the wildlife business here, and he came over to Hong Kong supposedly to check us out, officially. It was a big joke, you know, and we laughed a bit about that, but then he started demanding stuff. He wanted to stay in a better class hotel, so we topped up his money and put him in the Mandarin. Then he wanted girls, but that was no problem. He had girls. He wanted more money, though, a bigger payoff, he wanted too much. We didn't say we wouldn't give it to him, but as far as I was concerned it was only a matter of time before we squeezed him out.

"Well, Kipkoech must have figured some of this out for himself, because when he got back to Kenya he called a press conference and blew the entire Burundi operation wide open; wrecked that entire beautiful business." Zhu shook his head. "That Kipkoech, he must have had a quarter million stashed in a Swiss bank account from the other deals we did. He screwed me, you know." He paused. "I've been waiting a long time to fix this fucker. Give me a plate of food, babe."

Silvia took a plate and loaded it with chicken, noodles, and mushrooms. Zhu waited until he had the plate in his hand, before saying, "Tell me about Kipkoech's house, then."

Sen leaned over, grabbed a piece of chicken, chewed on it while he spoke. His voice was high and whining. "Single story. Out towards Ngong. Jimmy and me went out there. Brick wall with shit on top. Broken glass, barbed wire. There's a night guard and a couple of dogs. Indian shopkeepers one side, big family, dogs. Old couple on the other." Sen grinned, exposing a row of small yellow teeth. "Every day a government Land Rover with a driver and two guards armed with automatics takes Kipkoech to and from his office, which is also crawling with guards and dogs. They're fucking paranoid." He laughed and threw a look at Silvia.

He went on, "Kipkoech gets home around eight o'clock, and then the driver and guards leave."

Silvia said, "Sounds hard to get to him."

Zhu squeezed her thigh. "We're going to do it, babe. You see this . . ." He dug around the newscuttings and pulled out the local paper. Inside was a headline that read "Muthangu Pledges Ivory Money to Mathare."

"So it's going to happen anyway," Silvia said. "They're going to start trading ivory in any case. That's what I told you. Kariuki was the main man. You don't have to deal with Kipkoech or her." She indicated the picture of Maya Saito.

"Yeah?" said Zhu. "How about this, then?" He turned the page to the paper's editorial, which opposed ivory trading because of the threat from poachers, who were already wiping out elephants in Tanzania. "Like David Kariuki, we say that Africa must stand as one and view its scarce resources from a continental perspective. We are not ready yet to abandon our position as a global leader in the field of conservation."

Zhu tossed the paper down in front of her. "I tell you, Kipkoech is going to get it because he deserves it. Then all these others, like this woman here, have got to go. They've been screwing up our business in the Gulf. They shouldn't do that. This country has been giving me too many headaches with this anti-trade stuff. I just want the business to flourish like it did in the old days. You understand that? This place is the key. If they are trading ivory themselves, then they can't exactly be the leaders of the anti-trade movement, can they? That's our goal. We are going to make these bastards pay, and then we are going to make them trade ivory as well."

Zhu stood up and walked to the edge of the terrace. On the other side of the gully, a monkey family was perched on a rock, prehensile fingers picking fleas off one another. Zhu slung a pebble at them. It landed short, and the monkeys ran off yelping and screeching into bushcover. He turned around and leaned against the wall. "We're all going to come away from this very rich."

Afterwards Silvia went with him to the bedroom. This was an oatmeal-coloured room with rough walls and wooden floors. There was a large bed, a pale-painted closet, and a dresser with a tall mirror. Zhu made Silvia close her eyes before entering the room. When she opened them three assault weapons were lying on the bed.

"I got thirty rounds apiece for each of those. Pretty good, huh? Wong is a big supplier. Gets this stuff for people all over Africa. Brings it in from the Middle East. These two're AK-47s. That's a Heckler and Koch MP-5." He pronounced the names as if they were celebrities at a charity ball.

The night before, Zhu had disappeared for a few hours to meet with Wong. All Silvia knew was that he was a Chinese living in Mombasa, and apparently Zhu had known him for years.

Zhu picked up the MP-5, sighted it at his own reflection in the mirror. "This one's a real beauty. Here, you feel it." He stood behind her, putting the weapon into her hands. "Pretty cool, huh, babe?" he murmured in her ear. "You don't have to worry, though. It isn't loaded. I'm not that crazy. I know you."

He nuzzled his chin into her neck. "You gotta stay with me all the way, babe. I need you. We belong together. You're the only woman that ever understood me, see? You're my lucky charm, you know that?"

"I think you're making a mistake. You should forget about this Kipkoech man. He isn't important."

Zhu snatched the gun out of her hands and pulled away sharply. "Man, you keep on doing that. You don't understand anything. I've got this whole thing figured out. I need your support, you know. Not this shit."

She turned around, putting her back to the mirror and resting against the dresser.

"I understand revenge, Zhu, but not when it gets in the way of something much bigger."

"That bastard isn't five miles from here. I'm not going to get this close and walk away." He laughed. "Babe, you know what? This whole thing is   87 going much better than I'd ever expected. Now there's this idiot journalist involved. Man, it's fantastic." He sat down on the bed, lying the weapon across his knee and caressing the barrel like a baby's head. "I got the psychology all figured out. Look, come and sit here."

She went across, sat beside him on the bed. He set the gun aside and took her hand, kissed the palm, kissed the side of her neck. "Lie down with me, babe." He pushed the weapons across and pulled her down next to him, their heads on the pillows, his arm lying underneath her and his fingers curling through her hair.

"Listen, we are going to make them believe that Kariuki and Kipkoech were killed by a phony outfit who are paying them back for crimes against wildlife. Okay? And this same outfit is going to promise to keep on killing until the government promises that they won't trade ivory. You know what that will do? It will send the whole fucking government into a tailspin. In the end I'll bet that they won't buy it. They'll legalize the trade because they won't want to be seen submitting to terrorist demands, but by the time we're finished it won't much matter anyway."

"How come?"

"Wait and see." He raised himself up on his elbow and looked at her. "I gotta keep a few secrets, you know."

She sighed.

"What's up?"

"I wanna go, Zhu. I don't like this place. I feel uneasy. You can handle everything."

"Babe, you can't pull out now."

"I'm not pulling out. I've done my stuff. You know after doing a job you have to get well out of the area. You know that was what saved me in Macao." There, she'd said it. Ever since the Macao fiasco neither of them had even said the name of the place. It seemed practically taboo.

"That was different," he snapped back.

She watched his eyes narrowing, hardening. What was he thinking?

He laughed suddenly. "Are you trying to tell me you're afraid these monkeys are going to catch us?"

"No . . ."

"Then stop talking dumb."

"I have dreams . . ." The night before, she'd woken in a sweat, and it had felt like the terror in that woman's eyes had bored right into her skull.

He rolled on top of her. "Dreams about what?" He kissed her deeply, warmly. She wanted to dive into that kiss and forget about the doubts, her fears, everything, but he broke off suddenly and murmured, "Now, you know what I need you to do? I need you to call that journalist."

CHAPTER EIGHT

HAWTHORNE WAS FURIOUS that he could not leave for Lumbumbashi. Events had been developing fast, and the conflict looked as if it would blow up into a full-scale civil war. Most of the press corps were there already, but Hawthorne was not allowed to leave the country in case he was needed for the Kariuki investigation. He hung around the WPA office on the fourth floor of the new Kenya Insurance Company building on Wabera Street.

"Take some time off," the chief, Noel Jackman, told him. "Go and relax a bit. You've earned it."

Jackman was in his late fifties, with beady eyes staring out of a heavily lined face and brown-grey hair sprouting up in irregular patches over his scalp. His passions were his wives (four with a fifth on the way), all their children (countless), and entertainers of the thirties and forties, whom he took every opportunity to impersonate. He'd been around Africa a long time.

"I don't need to relax. I need to get the hell out of this place."

"Okay, okay," said Jackman.

Hawthorne gazed out of the window at the jam of vehicles down on the street below. "Well, maybe I'll go down to Amboseli. I want to see Maya."

"Ha," said Jackman, "I thought that was finished."

"Yeah, well, you know."

Jackman said nothing. Hawthorne headed for the door. 91

"Sam? I have to say that I don't think it's a good idea for you to see her right now."

"How come?" He turned around.

Jackman raised his bushy grey eyebrows. "It's up to you, but I really think you should stay right away from the whole Kariuki thing. She's too close." He paused.

Hawthorne raised his hands, palms to the ceiling.

Jackman sighed, "Look, just give it a couple of weeks. Okay? She's not going anywhere." He broke off to flip through a stack of letters in his in-tray and pulled one out. He scanned the letter, then slammed it down in front of Hawthorne. "If you want something to keep you busy, you could try this."

Hawthorne scanned the letter, which came from the United Nations Environmental Program. "Desertification?" His tone barely disguised his contempt.

Jackman said, "Right. This is the hottest thing going down in the Northern Frontier District. Believe me, one day the planet will be so green they'll be preserving little pockets of desert just so we can remember what it used to be like."

"Jesus, man," said Hawthorne.

"Take your choice. You can mope around that kennel of yours in Karen or get busy."

Hawthorne spent the rest of the afternoon at UNEP headquarters. Jackman's letter had come from a field officer who had not received permission to contact the press. There was plenty of bureaucratic in-dignation over who was claiming credit for the project's success. The source of all the excitement was a tough little grass plant. Over a cup of coffee in the UNEP canteen, Hawthorne was lectured on the subject of grass by an earnest Spaniard with winged glasses, pointed breasts, long brown hair, a great pair of legs, and the worst taste in clothes he'd ever seen. She had a brutal accent but spoke slowly enough for a chimpanzee to understand.

"Mr. Hawthorne, people do not realize that the single most successful visible life form on this planet is grass." She paused to adjust her spectacles and leaned across, resting her ample bosom on top of the table. Hawthorne grinned with his teeth and concentrated on his notebook.

"I don't know if you knew this, but in volcanic grit, which may have a surface temperature higher than fifty degrees Celsius, grass can still grow!" She laughed, showing a row of perfect white teeth. "It is a truly marvelous plant. Existing with the minimum of life support, the searching roots of the plant . . ."

She waggled her red-painted fingernails in imitation of the plant's searching roots. ". . . break down the particles of soil and add to the organic content of the new soil when they die. In this way they modify their habitat, changing it so that it gradually becomes suitable for other kinds of grasses, eventually small bushes and trees. In the end, these tough little grasses may alter the environment so much it becomes too rich for them to survive there any longer. They move on, leaving behind an enriched habitat, while they continue pushing back the frontiers of the desert." She pushed the hair off her face in imitation of the receding desert.

She continued. "This new strain we have developed is a voracious little thing. It has an accelerated growth pattern; it spreads, grows, dies, and decays more rapidly than any other grass in the world. It is extremely hardy, capable of withstanding high temperatures and surviving through long periods without rain. It is also incidentally unpalatable for nomadic domestic livestock occupying the region and will therefore have the opportunity to become properly established. What we have achieved here is a quite brilliant acceleration of the perfectly natural process of habitat mod-ification. You have heard of fast-growing trees? This is fast-growing grass."

Hawthorne was impressed. "It really works?" he asked.

"But of course," beamed the Spaniard, smoothing an elegant hand over her perfect knee.

"Is Yolande spinning her fairy tales again?" The voice was Canadian and came from behind Hawthorne. He turned to see a short man with a wide, beaming face and lank blond hair falling over a bald spot on top of his head. "Mind if I sit in? Hello, Yolande."

The Spanish scientist waggled the fingers on one hand. "Ciao!" she said, unsmiling and clearly minding the intrusion.

The newcomer held out his hand to Hawthorne. "My name's Bill Derren. They told me you were speaking to Yolande here and I just thought I should share a few points with you that Yolande has a way of omitting. She sees the world through green glasses and has a way of missing the people standing in the foreground."

The Spanish woman stood up. "Mr. Hawthorne, I am sure you will find Dr. Derren most entertaining. I will be in my office should you wish to contact me further."

Derren was brisk and to the point. The new weed, as he called it, was so virile it was overcoming every other kind of grass in the district. There was a risk it would necessitate a major evacuation of people and livestock from the area. He conceded that everything might eventually happen in accordance with the theory, but the trials had been inadequate and inconclusive.

"These are hard times," said Hawthorne. "Don't you think a few dramatic moves are called for? I mean, if it works, it might be worth shifting a few thousand people."

Derren drummed his knuckles on the table. "That's the trouble," he said. "Everyone wants results right now and it just isn't going to happen that way. So what if we uproot a few thousand people, what does it matter? They're only a bunch of primitives living centuries out of step with the rest of the planet. What right have they to stand in our way? Especially when we are trying to do what is best for them! Is that it? No way. You tell me any community of several thousand people in North America who would willingly give up their homes and livelihoods for the sake of an experiment no one has bothered to explain to them. Christ, those people won't even cut down on their gas consumption. Why should the Rendile be any different? Those guys are not idiots. What I'm talking about here is consultation and planning, setting things out on the line for the people involved." He thumped the table with the tip of his finger to emphasize the point.

"The Turkana, Rendile, and Samburu know the way things work up there," he went on, "and they have things to say about it. Get their cooperation and exercise some control over experiments that we really don't know the consequences of. You can't have fascists like Yolande marching in, flicking people aside like they were specks of dust."

Derren stood up. "I've got a meeting. I hope you understand what I'm getting at. We aren't going to solve environmental problems by compounding them with unnecessary human catastrophes. The solutions have to work together." Derren hesitated, swinging his head around as if searching for the exit. "By the way," he said softly, "I saw your picture in the paper. Who couldn't? I'm sorry about the Kariukis. He was a good man. It must have been tough." He touched Hawthorne's shoulder and left.

Hawthorne drove away trying to balance his hope that some kind of breakthrough had been made against his innate skepticism. He did not doubt that Derren was right and people living in the NFD should be properly consulted, but even if the Turkana, and whoever else, were brought into the act, what then? Hawthorne could not help believing that something would have to go wrong. Every giant leap forward in Africa landed in the mire. Educational expansion could hardly keep up with population growth, agricultural development was unaffordable due to the cost of oil imports, economic growth was built on international bank loans with interest rates impossible to repay, and health systems that had been proud of their ability to deliver vaccinations to every infant were now overloaded with people dying from AIDS. It made an utterly depressing litany.

He swung off towards the small day and night bar that was the unofficial hangout for foreign correspondents. The bar was not busy because so many of the journalists were out of town, but Vanna Deacon was there and a few others. Hawthorne was greeted as a kind of local hero and did not buy a drink all night. He got home a little after eleven.

Hawthorne lived in Karen, the suburb ten miles out of the capital named after the author Karen Blixen, where he rented a small cottage on the estate of a much larger residence. He swung into the long drive, greeted by the flashing torch of the *askari* guarding the gate. The Dobermans came lumbering out of the darkness to gallop alongside his vehicle until it pulled to a halt. The dogs were not Hawthorne's. They belonged to the big house, but they were friendly enough. They padded behind him up the path to the cottage and would have followed him right inside had he not shooed them away. The front door opened straight into the living room. He clicked on the lights, but not before he saw the small red dot on his answerphone flashing through the darkness. He went to the kitchen and poured a glass of ice water. Drinking it, he came back into the living room, sat down and ran through the calls.

The third call made him sit up.

"Mr. Hawthorne," said a woman's voice, edged with an unfamiliar accent, "I have information for you. Kariuki was punished for killing hundreds of innocent creatures. Someone else will die tonight. A corrupt man who enriched himself by trading ivory."

That was all. He ran it back again and listened, copying down the words as the woman spoke.

"Holy shit!" he murmured.

He called Jackman first. The bureau chief was concerned. "You better get onto the police right away, Sam, but do me a favor, call your lawyer first? Let me know what happens."

It was Hellman who told him to call Detective Wangai. He also said that there may be nothing to worry about. Perhaps it was just a crank call.

Maybe it was, thought Hawthorne, but he did not feel any better.

CHAPTER NINE

WANGAI WAS DREAMING. A chameleon the size of a dog was lying on his doorstep, and he could not get past. He wasn't afraid, which was surprising because chameleons bring bad luck. This chameleon had not changed color though. Instead of blending into the doorstep, it was a bright, lurid green. Not a nice color, but not a frightening one either. So there was Wangai, the door, and the chameleon, which was just lying there, like a dog, and he couldn't get around it. He didn't want to step over it, so he had to wait for it to move. He'd been waiting for hours.

The phone called him out of sleep, dragging him through layers of consciousness in which he tried to shrug off the chameleon, banish the doorstep, relieve himself of the dilemma. The phone was right beside the bed. Wangai clamped one hand over it and, still with his eyes closed, still with one thought on the chameleon, he mumbled into the speaker.

"Is that Detective Wangai?" said a voice in English. Nobody from the office would call him in English, except maybe Kamau, but this wasn't Kamau.

"Huh," grunted Wangai.

"Detective Wangai?"

"Yes," said Wangai, his mouth chewing on itself, eyelids stuck tight. Couldn't place the voice. Didn't care anyway. The chameleon was still hovering somewhere, faint, but still there.

"This is Hawthorne, Sam Hawthorne," said the voice.

The American, thought Wangai. Americans called people in the middle of the night. He'd seen it in a movie. Hawthorne was probably drunk or something. "Call me at the office," murmured Wangai, fighting off the wakefulness that was finally beginning to stir. If he woke up now it would take hours to get back to sleep.

"This is important, Mr. Wangai," said Hawthorne. "I've rung fifteen different Wangais in the Nairobi phone book trying to track you down. Something has happened."

Wangai sighed. His eyes opened. He was lying on his side looking straight into the mirror of a massive wardrobe, barely two feet from his nose. It was too dark for the mirror to reflect much except his wife, who was groaning in her sleep, and the looming shape of the dressing table beyond.

With some effort he hauled himself onto his elbow. "Okay," said Wangai, "what happened?"

"There was a surprise waiting for me when I got home tonight," Hawthorne said.

Wangai made no comment.

"There was this strange message on my answerphone. Listen . . ." The journalist read out the words he'd written down.

"Huh," said Wangai. He sniffed. The message sounded crazy to him.

"It was a woman," Hawthorne went on, "weird accent . . ."

"What?" said Wangai. He felt a prickling along the back of his neck, a sensation he experienced when faced with a distinct, important truth. It would be a woman, of course. "What did you say?"

"I said she had a weird foreign accent, kind of Australian or something."

"Why did she call you?" blurted out Wangai.

"How the hell should I know?" Hawthorne snapped back.

"Look . . ." said Wangai. "Just stay where you are. What is your number?"

Wangai wrote it down on the pad of paper next to the phone.

"Stay where you are," he repeated, "I will call you back."

Wangai hung up the receiver. He rubbed the bridge of his nose, then dragged both hands down his face, feeling the thick flesh of his cheeks, the stubble of his chin. He checked the luminous dial of the clock. It was after midnight. Getting out of bed, he padded barefoot into the living room and clicked the switch. His eyes wrinkled under the glaring strip lights. The living room had pink emulsion walls, a deep crimson sofa, and two orange armchairs draped with white lace antimacassars. A polyester rug in pink and green lay on top of the black-and-grey checkerboard linoleum. There was also a large bureau, a tall cupboard, and three coffee tables. It tested your navigation skills just to cross the room.

Next to the front door, which led straight out of the living room, there was a second phone set on a wrought iron table with seat attached. His wife called it her "gossip chair." The phone was draped with another lacy antimacassar. Wangai tossed the cloth aside, sat down, and dialed police headquarters.

He got hold of the duty officer, asked if anything was going on that night. The man ran through a list of incidents, none of which struck Wangai as especially significant. A few muggings, a rape, a suspected homicide outside a bar on River Road; it was just another normal night of crime in Nairobi city.

He hung up, thinking about Hawthorne. Why would anyone call the journalist? Was Hawthorne involved in this business after all? Perhaps it was a hoax. Wangai shrugged. He wasn't all that used to hoaxes. They didn't often happen. It didn't matter anyway, he thought. He had to treat the matter seriously, just in case. He called Hawthorne back.

"I'm coming over. Where are you?"

Hawthorne gave him directions.

Wangai went back into the bedroom to dress. His wife raised her head for a moment, looked at him, said nothing. Her head fell back on the pillow with a thud.

Wangai went through to the bathroom, splashed his face with water, and gargled noisily, frowning at the lime-green shower curtain that dominated the room. The bathroom was the size of a peanut, even without the shower curtain. He thought about Kamau up in his Spring Valley mansion, with yards of corridors to stride from bedroom to living room, and space to stretch his feet out when he was sitting on his sofa, a house where you could get some exercise just going to the kitchen for a beer. Of course,

Kamau would have stairs in his house, balconies, gardens, and servants to bring his beer. What must it be to live like that? Wangai looked at himself in the mirror, thinking that he looked old, wondering also why he did not envy Kamau. Yet he didn't. He knew Kamau was only a shell of a man. He smiled suddenly, imagining that his wife would always fill a room with furniture, no matter how much space she had.

Wangai's ancient reconditioned Volkswagen was parked in the road right outside his house. The deserted street was dead straight and full of bungalows identical to his own, all of them owned by middle-ranking government employees. He climbed into the VW, the worn fabric of the seat sighing under his weight, and pulled the choke out full. The engine turned over three or four times before it finally caught. It took twenty minutes to cover the distance to Karen.

Hawthorne's *askari* had been warned to expect a visitor but the Dobermans had not. The dogs pursued the car all the way up the drive, trapping Wangai after he stopped outside Hawthorne's cottage, one monster on each side of the car, perched on their back legs, clawing at the windows. The journalist had to come out and rescue him.

Once inside the house, Hawthorne turned on him. "Listen I called you because I thought . . . I didn't know who I could trust, okay? Hellman told me you were okay . . . but I don't want to find myself in trouble again . . ." The journalist broke off, went into the kitchen, and came back with two cups of black coffee. He handed one to Wangai.

"I'm probably crazy, you know," Hawthorne said, laughing at himself as he sat down. "Hell, I know this place and yet, I still get surprised by it."

"Can I hear the tape, please?" said Wangai, who was still standing, since Hawthorne had not invited him to sit. He also hated black coffee and did not know where to put the cup. Hawthorne's place was quite spacious, he noted, even if it was small. The living room wasn't much bigger than his own, but Hawthorne had a fireplace. It was unnecessary to have a fireplace, but Wangai liked it.

"Right," said Hawthorne, springing up, almost running to the phone. He glanced at Wangai as he wound the tape back. "Er . . . sit down if you want."

Hawthorne did not have a sofa. He had three mismatching armchairs. One of them the journalist had been occupying. The others contained an assortment of clothing, books, and newspapers. Wangai chose the least crowded and sat gingerly on the edge of the seat. There was still nowhere to put the cup, no coffee table, so he set it on the floor.

While the tape played, Wangai tried to concentrate on the woman's voice, trying to feel his way inside it, penetrate her mood, get a sense of who she was, where she was.

"I have information for you. Kariuki was punished for killing hundreds of innocent creatures. Someone else will die tonight. A corrupt man who enriched himself by trading ivory."

There was something empty about the tone. Rehearsed, perhaps. She was reading it, maybe. It did not come across as spontaneous speech, anyway. He listened to the tape a couple more times. There were no clues to location that he could hear.

"D'you know her?" he asked Hawthorne, studying the journalist, still not quite sure where he fit into all this.

Hawthorne sighed. "No. Look, I'm being straight with you. I don't know who the . . . who she is."

"Why do you think she would call you?"

"I don't know," Hawthorne said quietly.

"Huh," grunted Wangai. "Foreign."

"What?" asked Hawthorne.

Wangai looked up. "It is most unusual for anyone in Kenya to claim responsibility for a murder, and unlikely that a local woman would be implicated in a crime as violent as Kariuki's murder."

Wangai said this with such certainty it made Hawthorne laugh briefly in a derisory way. "That sounds like something produced by your public relations division."

"It is the truth, Mr. Hawthorne," Wangai replied simply.

Hawthorne shrugged. "Well, maybe. But what could they have against Kariuki? Since when has he been responsible for the deaths of hundreds of—oh!" he broke off.

"Yes?" asked Wangai expectantly.

"The cull in Amboseli a year or two ago."

Wangai looked at the journalist with suspicion.

Hawthorne held his hands up as if warding off a demon. "I know something about it. Okay? I knew someone . . ."

Wangai raised his eyebrows. "You are very defensive, Mr. Hawthorne."

Hawthorne laughed. "You're not bad, Wangai." He threw his arms wide. "I hate cops, all right?" he said, grinning. His arms retreated and he dragged a hand through his hair. "I'm sorry. This is not easy." He clapped his hands together. "Okay, Kariuki ordered the cull in Amboseli. A few hundred elephants were killed, don't you remember? It was very controversial. Plenty of people objected to it. Maybe that is what they are talking about. Maybe this is some loony, radical environmental group chasing revenge. Huh? Happens all the time these days in the States. A couple of lumberjacks were assassinated last year. Assassinated! Some woman called a radio station claiming responsibility, and that is what she called it."

Wangai sat dead still, thinking. It was far too soon to grab hold of a motive like the one Hawthorne was offering. Believing in a motive like that this early in a case could shape everything and leave you, in the end, with nothing. Even so, if the phone call had any truth in it, if anything did happen, Hawthorne might have a point. "I need to make a call," Wangai said.

He rang the duty officer at headquarters again.

"Yeah, we have a homicide," the voice on the phone said in a lazy tone. "Elijah Kipkoech, deputy director of Kenya Wildlife Services, lives on the Ngong Road. Ah . . . I think they said it was an attack by, ah, three men."

"When did this come in?" snapped Wangai, feeling his forehead break out with sweat.

"The local Ngong station were called in at, ah, nine-thirty this evening, but they were unable to respond for almost an hour. They called us at eleven-thirty-three, but it didn't get on my desk until ten minutes ago."

Wangai took a deep breath. He was angry, too angry to speak. He waited a moment, then said, "Has Superintendent Kamau been called in?"

"What?" said the duty officer.

"Superintendent Kamau. This is a Special Ops. matter. I think it is important that . . ."

"We don't call him out," the duty officer said, as if Wangai were a fool. "That isn't Special Ops. procedure."

Wangai breathed out heavily. "What is?"

"What is what?"

"What is the procedure?" asked Wangai, exasperation invading his voice. Slow down, he told himself.

"Detective Mbitu is in Ngong now. Speak to him." The duty officer hung up. So did Wangai.

He turned to face Hawthorne. "I have to go. I'll take the tape with me."

"What is it?" asked the journalist.

"You'll find out," replied Wangai. "The tape." He held out his hand.

Hawthorne went over to the answerphone, took out the small tape, held it up. "I think you owe me," he said.

Wangai took the tape out of his hand. "I don't owe you anything. I am just doing my job. I think it would make life easier for you if you keep the phone call from the woman quiet for a while."

Hawthorne emitted a false cough. "Hey! You know, that's difficult."

"Listen, as far as I am concerned you can write anything you like about it. I'm only saying that life will be easier for you if you don't. If you do, everyone will be breathing down your neck, my colleagues, your colleagues, everyone."

"That's my problem," Hawthorne replied.

"Do me a favor Mr. Hawthorne, keep the answerphone running and record all your calls," shouted the detective, heading for the door.

Wangai went outside, climbed into his Volkswagen, and pulled off down the drive. While he waited for the *askari* to open the gate, another car pulled up behind him. It was Hawthorne. The detective got out of his car and went back to speak to the journalist.

Hawthorne wound his window down. "Like my new car?" he said to the detective, "On loan from the office."

"Where are you going, Mr. Hawthorne?" asked Wangai.

"I thought I'd take my new car for a drive"

"Are you following me?"

"You? No, course not."

"Where are you going then?"

"Just driving, driving around. But you better be careful."

"Why?" asked the detective.

"The dogs are coming."

Wangai looked up. Hawthorne was right. He could hear their great feet pounding down the drive. He didn't have time for this. If Hawthorne followed him to Kipkoech's house, so what? Hurriedly, he ran back to the VW and got the door shut just as the Dobermans bounded up. He shot the car into gear and pulled out fast through the gate.

Wangai remembered Ngong as it had been in the old days, as a sleepy frontier village. He'd been sent there on his first posting, as a raw cop who'd felt he was being sent to the back of beyond, because it was at Ngong that the twenty-mile stretch of road from the capital came to a dead stop at the plummeting edge of the Great Rift Valley. The Maasai used to walk into Ngong, bringing their trinkets and goats to exchange for the few items of the modern world they deemed valuable. Ngong's dirt streets had been lined with wooden sidewalks and cement hovels. Josiah's General Provision Stores had sold flashlights, batteries, tools, insect spray, matches, vegetable seeds, and condoms.

In those days, Ngong had been separated from the nearest settlement at Karen by several miles of bush, where giraffe and lions occasionally roamed. Gradually, though, plots had changed hands and a few isolated homes had appeared. Kipkoech had been one of the first to build. The high walls and heavy iron gates had been impressive. Wangai had been inside them once, had seen Kipkoech's luxury bungalow, which nevertheless had a porch overlooking a small *shamba* of maize and beans, a chicken run, a goat keeping the grass trim, and a couple of scrawny bottle brush trees.

Others had followed Kipkoech, eventually filling the entire roadside from Nairobi to Ngong with houses, neighborhood shops and workshops, banishing the wildlife for good. The Asians who erected a three-story cement dwelling next door to Kipkoech opened a variety shop in Ngong that sold such luxuries as bedside lamps, saucepan sets, and lingerie. The town also lost its frontier image since the tarmac road now descended right into the Rift Valley, taking progress right to the doorsteps of Maasai *bomas*.

Wangai found a crowd of people and four police cars parked outside Kipkoech's gate. Inside, Banabas Mbitu had divided his team into two or three groups that were sweeping the area inch by inch. Mbitu was running between one group and the next, chivvying them along like a mother hen guarding her chicks. He did not look surprised to see Wangai.

"They couldn't reach you," he said.

Wangai waved his hand. "What did you find?" He knew Mbitu's reputation for being a reasonable detective, thorough if uninspired, but then thoroughness was sometimes more important.

"Nothing," Mbitu replied gloomily. "No prints. The gang was masked from head to foot. They were driving a Land Rover. Looks like the *askari* opened the gate for them. They shot him . . ." Mbitu indicated the blanket covering the *askari*'s body, ". . . and the dogs. Someone across the street said they thought the vehicle had GK plates, but there is some disagreement over that. Neither the wife nor daughter could tell us anything, not even the color of their skin. They think they were all male."

"How many were there?"

"Two or three." Mbitu spat on the ground. "You want to see inside?"

Wangai followed the other detective to the back of the house and entered the kitchen. Kipkoech was lying on the floor, which was splattered with his blood and brains. One of Mbitu's men was trying to draw a line around the body, but the chalk would not work through Kipkoech's blood.

"Who called us in?" asked Wangai.

"People next door. Asians," sniffed Mbitu. "Mr. and Mrs. Singh. They heard gunfire and Mrs. Kipkoech scream. It took the Ngong station awhile to respond because they only have one vehicle and it was out on another call. They should have called us in right away, but they didn't understand the extent of the attack." Mbitu gave Wangai a look. "Apparently the Singhs are always complaining about something. Anyway, after the Ngong police got here, they took another hour to call us because Mrs. Kipkoech was . . . well, crazy, they said. The daughter, too. Then they had trouble with the Singhs, and . . ."

Wangai held up his hands. "Okay, okay," he said. He did not need to hear everyone's excuses blaming everyone else. He wasn't surprised about the Ngong police taking so long to respond anyway. It was amazing that they actually had a police vehicle these days. When he'd been stationed at Ngong, they'd only had bicycles.

"Where is Mrs. Kipkoech now?" asked Wangai.

"In the living room with her daughter. They're both in a bad way."

"Okay," said Wangai, "I have to make a call, and then I want to interview them."

"You'll have to use the phone next door. This one is dead."

Wangai went out of the compound and found Hawthorne arguing with two policemen who were preventing him from going inside. He seized on Wangai.

"Okay, tell me what happened," he demanded.

"There isn't anything to tell, Mr. Hawthorne, just go home," said Wangai.

"Kipkoech is dead?" asked Hawthorne, trailing Wangai as he walked towards the Singh's house. "This is Kipkoech's house, Kariuki's deputy. This is what my phone call was about, isn't it? Was Kipkoech involved in ivory deals?"

"I don't know," replied Wangai, thinking the same thing. He remembered when Kipkoech had been putting up his luxury bungalow, years ago; the talk about where he'd got all the money.

"Who was it? Did anyone see them?" Hawthorne persisted.

Wangai stopped and faced the journalist. "No questions, okay? None."

"Oh, that's fine," said Hawthorne. "I give you information and you give me nothing."

"That's right," snapped the detective. "That is your duty as a citizen of your country and a visitor to mine. Believe me, there is nothing I can tell you right now anyway. Go away."

Hawthorne shrugged but continued following the detective.

106   The Singhs' dogs barked convulsively at Wangai and Hawthorne until

Mr. Singh appeared on the porch. He was a rotund man with a shining face and straight, greasy hair, wearing a vest and baggy pyjamas. Inviting the two men into his home, he embarked on a lengthy round of introductions. There appeared to be at least four families living in the house, and all of them were gathered in the enormous living room, the women wearing cotton floor length nightdresses and the men in baggy pyjamas like Mr. Singh. Although it was the middle of the night, several young kids were running around. Everyone looked at the visitors expectantly, hoping for fresh news of events next door.

Wangai asked to be directed to the phone, which was located inside a cupboard next to the kitchen. He abruptly closed the door on Hawthorne, Mr. Singh, and Singh's brother, all of whom had come along in the hope of learning something new.

Wangai called Kamau at home, waking the superintendent up. He thought Kipkoech's murder was just too important for Kamau to sleep through, but after the detective had finished describing the events of the evening, Kamau said, "I'll be in my office at 7 a.m. and want to see a full report on my desk." Then he hung up. Wangai should not have been surprised, but he was. He'd had a fantasy that Kamau might suddenly turn into a decent cop.

Wangai pushed open the door of the cupboard and saw Hawthorne still waiting outside. He sighed, realizing he had to deal with the journalist or else something worse might happen.

"Come," he muttered, and stormed out into the night. He stopped in the narrow lane between the two houses and faced the journalist. "I don't want to hear that you have received another phone call from this woman by seeing it on the evening news. It just occurred to me that you might do that."

Hawthorne shrugged. "Did I say I would do that? I'm a good citizen, aren't I?"

Wangai ignored this. "If you hear from her again, you let me know right away, you hear? Otherwise I will have you kicked out of this country so fast you will not have time to pack your toothbrush."

Hawthorne grinned. The flashing lights of the police cars bounced off his teeth.

"I am not joking," said Wangai.

"Okay, what are you doing?"

Wangai took a deep breath. "Kipkoech's *askari* was shot once, point blank, straight in the heart. Kipkoech was hit by automatic gunfire. Mrs. Kipkoech was found bound and gagged lying next to the body of her husband. The daughter had also been gagged and tied up. Both are in a deep state of shock." He went on in brief staccato sentences describing what had happened. Hawthorne jotted down some notes on a pad.

Finishing off, Wangai said, "Right, I've told you what I know. If you hear from that woman, call me, okay?"

"I always intended to," Hawthorne said with a smile.

"Get out of here," said Wangai and pushed off through the crowd still gathered around the entrance to the compound.

The detective found Martha and Esther Kipkoech huddled together in the living room. Mrs. Kipkoech had bloodstains all over her clothes. Her face was swollen and had been bleeding. She'd been hit hard. Wangai sat in front of them and spoke softly.

"I need you to tell me everything all over again. I know you have been over it already with my colleague, but you have to try once more. You might have forgotten something. I'm going to try and help you remember."

It was not easy to get them to talk. Martha Kipkoech was in shock. Her eyes were unfocused and her speech unclear. Esther, the daughter, said she'd tried to hide in a cupboard but the man had found her there, tied her up. He'd threatened her in a way that made her think of kung fu movies, the kind that played nonstop in at least three cinemas in the city.

Wangai had asked if one of the assailants was a woman, but neither of the witnesses could say for sure.

He got back to the office close to four in the morning. Slamming a coin into the tea machine in the corridor, he took a scalding cup of the brew into his new office on the sixth floor, which in the daytime he shared with three other "Special" operatives. Switching on a computer terminal, he started throwing onto the screen everything he knew about the case so far. His last line read, "Suspect radical foreign group, environmental terrorists."

CHAPTER
TEN

BACK IN LANGATA, Jimmy Chi gulped glasses of scotch so fast his eyes stuck out like a couple of wet marbles. He paced the living room from one end to the other, filling his glass every time Silvia came by with the bottle.

"Man, that was something!" Jimmy spat the words at the ceiling, stretching his neck back and hooting. "You should'a seen us, Silvie."

"Kipkoech arrives like clockwork," Zhu told her. "Everything was like clockwork. His driver plays this tune on his horn, the guard opens the gate, Kipkoech goes into his house, car drives off . . ."

"We come along," interrupted Jimmy, "in the Land Rover that Sen 'borrowed' from the Kenya government this afternoon, and I play the same tune on the horn." Jimmy grinned at her, looking proud. Silvia smiled weakly.

"But the guard didn't like it," added Zhu. "He opens the hatch in the gate and shouts some garbage that no one understands. So Jimmy plays it again, you know, like we are gettin' impatient or something . . . and then," Zhu laughed, "the fucking guard just opens the gate!"

He grabbed hold of Silvia and dragged her down to sit next to him, putting his arm around her shoulder. She could feel the heat of his palm through the fabric of her blouse.

Sen leaned forward, his elbows resting on his knees. He said, "Zhu took out the dogs, and I fixed the guard 109 while Jimmy parked the car." He laughed at the joke, parking a car while a killing was going on, showing his tiny teeth.

Zhu pecked her on the cheek. "We cut the phone lines, right, and go around the back of the house, and you know what we find?" He laughed.

"The fucking door was wide open," said Jimmy.

Zhu said through the laughter, "Babe, Kipkoech had all that shit, guards, dogs, wire, broken glass . . . but there's his wife in the kitchen cooking dinner with the door wide open. She screams when she sees me, and that brings her husband running in. I waste him. The woman went crazy. She was down on the floor trying to put the brains back in his head, I think." He laughed and Sen and Jimmy joined in. The three men carried on, fueling each other with what had happened. Going over it again and again.

"I got that bastard," Zhu muttered. "I got him real good. I just wish that Kipkoech had known it was me. I would have liked that, y'know, to see the look on his face when he saw it was me."

Silvia eased Zhu's arm off her shoulder, poured herself another scotch and took it out onto the terrace. The moon hung full overhead, dousing the gully and house with a grey pall. The woman's face still had not left her. She saw the terror in the woman's eyes, pleading with her over Kariuki's shoulder. She remembered how she'd wanted to let the woman live. She wasn't like Zhu and Sen. She felt guilty about it. She'd never killed a woman before. She felt as if she'd crossed a line and could never go back.

Zhu came out to the terrace. "You want to take a moonlight swim with me?"

"No."

"Sure you do, come on."

"I don't want to, Zhu. I'm going inside." As she moved for the door he grabbed her hand and put it to his lips, but she took it back. "I'm tired, Zhu. I haven't been sleeping good, okay? Please?"

"I had a thought about you, when I was over there at Kipkoech's house," he said. "I thought you might just take off, you know. You wouldn't try nothing like that, would you, babe? You know I'd have to come and find you if you did."

She smiled. "Sure, Zhu. I'm not leaving town. I'm just going to bed."

Her lips quivered, though. While they'd been at Kipkoech's place she had hunted everywhere for Zhu's stash of money, which he kept in a leather satchel. Of course, he'd had it with him but if she'd found it, maybe she would have taken off.

"Goodnight then," she said and started moving towards the house again. For a moment it looked as if he might let her go, but he grabbed her elbow, pulled her to the steps, and took her down to the pool.

The night seemed much louder down there; the gully shrieking, whooping, and whistling; the undergrowth rustling with unseen creatures. Zhu cantered around the pool on all fours while she stood by the steps, hugging herself. She laughed a little, watching Zhu. He pointed his face at the moon and howled.

The moon dazzled the water into liquid silver. She watched him undress, then let him remove her clothes and lead her naked into the pool. She stood in the shallow end, the cool black water licking around her waist while he kicked across the pool, sending splashes into the air. He dived under the surface and she lost sight of him; then she felt something brush against her ankles. Startled, she jumped back, but he held onto her feet and she felt him nibbling and caressing her legs as he rose to the surface. Breaking the water, he kissed her belly, breasts, and neck, then lifted her body, buoyant in the water, pushing her legs around his waist. His mouth closed on hers, the tongue pushing inside while he maneuvered her body in the water, until she felt his prick poised at the entrance to her womb. She gasped as he thrust inside, as a wave of water splashed up between their chests. With every thrust, water surged in and out of her vagina and she began to lose herself, feeling a part of the gully, the pool, and the crazy noise of the night. Even then, she did not loose Helen Kariuki's face from her mind.

That night her dreams were dark, insensible; shadows without substance, shadows of jagged coal. Pain was present everywhere, like a physical being, something she could touch, embrace. She hovered on the edge of consciousness so that the two became confused, the dreaming world a reality. She thought she was out of bed, on her knees, could feel the hard tiles underneath, was aware that she should run except movement seemed impossible. A voice called out to her and she could not answer.

In the morning she woke up when he brought in her coffee. "We've had a change of plan," he told her, sitting on the bed. He was wearing a royal-blue Japanese kimono and his hair was still wet from the shower. She sat up, took the coffee.

"You have to come with us to Amboseli," he said.

He wasn't looking at her. She could only see him in profile; a strong face, freshly shaved, perfect in a way.

"Why?" she asked. Originally, the plan had been that Silvia would fly ahead to Mombasa and meet up with them at the Wongs' place. She knew the answer to her question already, though. Zhu was worried that once she got in the air she would just keep on flying. Funny, it hadn't occurred to her to do that until that very moment. The night before, she'd thought of leaving if she could get her hands on some of his money, but now the money didn't seem to matter. She could have gone anyway. She had the credit cards still, in a variety of names. She had three different passports.

He didn't look at her as he patted her thigh and said, "I just want it that way. We've got to keep the team together."

"I don't want any part of this Amboseli thing, Zhu."

He looked at her then and smiled distantly. "You don't have no choice, babe." He stood up and left the room.

Later, they watched the morning television news. Superintendent Kamau was introduced as the man in charge of investigating the Kipkoech and Kariuki murders. He explained about the anonymous call of the night before and quoted from it. Kamau said the suggestion that Kipkoech had been involved in ivory dealing was spurious.

"I'll lay the fucking proof out for you!" Zhu muttered at the screen.

The reporter asked the superintendent to comment on rumors that the killers were members of a foreign group of environmental terrorists.

Kamau smiled smugly. "We know who these people are. We know where they are and we are coming to get them. They will learn the meaning of the word 'justice'."

112   Zhu smiled. The MP-5 lay on his lap. He picked it up, pointed it at

Kamau. "See that?" he said, with Kamau in his sights, "That's the best they can come up with. Look at it. The man is a joke." He lowered the gun, leaned across, and crooned into Silvia's ear. "That's the bastard who's looking for you."

Zhu sent Jimmy off with an envelope to run an errand for him, and Silvia went all over the house wiping their prints off doorknobs and drawers. When Jimmy got back they piled into the Daihatsu and took the highway out of town, the same road Silvia had followed when trailing the Kariukis. At Athi River, they turned right and headed across the Maasai rangelands, driving towards Namanga and the Tanzanian border.

Still feeling hung over from the night before, Silvia dozed in the back of the vehicle, her head lolling against the window frame. In her dream she was on that other road, to Tsavo. Standing in the middle of the highway, she was distressed because her dress was already bloody. The car that shimmered towards her, white, ethereal, floating above the ground, hovered to a stop. She realized she'd forgotten the gun, which was still in her car, but if she went to fetch it now, she would be too late. She smiled at the white car instead, approached it, intending to ask for directions. The blood was suddenly gone from her dress, and she was happy. There was no driver, no one in the front seat at all, but when she looked in the back she saw her own mother smiling at her helplessly. The man whose head lay on her mother's lap was a stranger and he was dead. Her mother held up her hands as if to say, "What can I do?"

Silvia shook herself awake. Zhu was driving, Sen was sitting up front next to him, and Jimmy was sleeping in the back. The dream rode with her. She could see her mother's face as clear as a picture. Then she thought about the woman hiding underneath Kariuki, hiding behind a dead man. What had she expected? That he would come back from death and save her? It was pretty desperate if a woman was so dependent on a man that she hoped he would protect her when he was dead.

Silvia had a flash of insight then. It grabbed her so acutely that she jerked physically in her seat. She saw how extraordinary it was that everything in her life should have led to this moment, to her riding in this car with these 113 three men. It was odd because this was definitely nothing she would ever have wanted for herself. She hated Sen. He never referred to her by name, treated her like an object. She had no feeling for Jimmy, even if he was her brother, or maybe she did have feelings but they were all negative. He was weak and bullied and had only got around it by sucking up to the biggest guys around, doing anything they wanted him to in exchange for their protection. The first time Silvia saw him with a gun, she knew Jimmy would never want to put it down again because it was plain that at last he felt like a really big guy. He was still impressionable, though. He laughed when Sen laughed. He even stood like Sen and used the same kinds of gestures. She wanted to shake Jimmy; shake him until his brain rattled free in his head so that he could see what a jerk he was.

Then there was Zhu. She thought how the night before she'd not wanted to go down to the pool, but she'd gone; how she'd watched him howling and even laughed at it; and had let him undress her and had sex with him, when really she hadn't wanted any of it. That was the problem with Zhu. He was overwhelming.

She remembered how ecstatic Zhu had been after she killed the fat man. He'd taken her to Tokyo, and they'd partied and got drunk and had the kind of sex that left her feeling legless most of the following day. He'd been so attentive, so constant, and she had never laughed so much. He said that he'd been waiting all his life to find someone like her. She'd felt special, chosen. It was hard to associate the man who'd made her feel that way with the one who'd betrayed her less than a month ago. Ever since then, despite her suspicions, she'd not allowed herself to think the thing through. She'd just been trying to avoid it, to pretend that she might be mistaken. Now it burst right over her, and she knew Zhu must have given her away. Only he had known the alias she was using in Macao, so only he could have given it to the two men who came looking for her.

She closed her eyes. She did not want to deal with this now; she couldn't do anything about it yet anyway. She had to set it aside and wait until the right opportunity arose.

114   The road was smooth and new looking. Gradually the terrain became

hillier and they reached the Namanga township, which hugs the toe of a sacred soaring rock known as Ol-Doinyo Orok. They fueled the vehicle and passed through the gate into Amboseli National Park, driving along twenty miles of baking roads that crossed the chalk-flats. As they reached the center of the park, the vegetation became more lush, and they saw elephant, buffalo, and Thompson's gazelle, though the most common species in view were the zebra-striped minibuses bristling with tourists and cameras. One of these flagged them down, and a gaunt American woman with a heavily lined face told them about a cheetah kill she'd just witnessed.

"If you go over there you might catch the cheetah still eating the gazelle. Harry here got the whole thing on camera, didn't you, Harry?"

They didn't wait for Harry's reply. Zhu had a map which showed the location of the Amboseli Elephant Research Camp. They drove around until they found it. It was close to dusk by then, and the park gates were already closed for the night. They drove off the track into the bush to wait until dawn.

CHAPTER ELEVEN

S HE CAME TO OL TUKAI OROK, which means "place of the dark palms," a marshy woodland fed by springs from Kilimanjaro, where yellow butterflies flit among the trees and succulent grasses sprout from the springy soil. Rumbling deeply, trunk raised to test the wind, she flapped massive ears against her back. Some time ago she had been parted from the others. They had young appetites, young compulsions. These last few months she had always trailed behind. Now they had gone too far, too fast, and she could not keep up. She did not seem concerned, though previously she had been matriarch, making all the decisions about where to feed and when to bathe. These days she was driven by greater needs; backbone sticking out like the ridge pole of a sagging tent; gaunt skin exposing every curve of her skull. The rains had been good, there was plenty of food, but the sixth and final set of teeth were worn out. Now all but the softest, greenest shoots were beyond her. She was suffering from old age which, for an elephant, usually means starvation.

Ol Tukai Orok was a place of gentle shade and soft fodder. If she could eat anywhere, it would be here. Finding some shoots at the base of a palm, she wrapped her trunk around them, tugged against the slightly swampy earth and pulled them free. Her mouth, already hanging open in anticipation, closed upon the grass, leaving strands protruding on either side. Awkwardly, she moved the grass around, trying to crush its resistance with sheer pressure. Eventually, she took a slow, unsatisfying swallow.

Lying down during the hottest time of the day, one great ear flapped languidly over her sagging frame; then even this ceased. The glade was silent but for the faint trilling of insects. She released a deep sigh, a tremor shivered through that ancient body, and all was still.

Later that afternoon the others burst into the glade at a run, as if expecting to find her there. They slowed, and were unusually silent as they approached and surrounded the massive beast. Trunks searched every part of her, tusks nudged the unresponsive frame. Then many of them began tearing down palm fronds and flinging them across the dead creature. Others dragged up tufts of grass and soil, tossing them onto the mounting grave. Occasionally they stripped a slice of bark from one of the tall, yellow acacias and feasted on the soft under-flesh. Then they resumed the tugging and digging, until a mound of debris smothered the dead animal.

As soon as the elephants had departed, a couple of bush vehicles bounced between the trees, approaching the dead elephant. Maya emerged from one vehicle. Moving steadily towards the mound, she studied the palms, dirt, and grass, catching glimpses of the elephant hide beneath. She videotaped, photographed, and measured the buried animal. With the help of rangers from the other vehicle, she dragged aside the palms and grass to expose the corpse. She took blood samples, skin samples, more measurements and, with some difficulty, retrieved a massive collar from the beast's neck. Carrying it to the land cruiser, she slung the collar inside and climbed in after it to unclip the transmission device and detach the solar power cells, stashing these in metal compartments. Turning back to the battered collar, she gazed at it a moment. It had been a lifeline between her and the elephant. Removing it gave a definite finality to their separation. Maya had not allowed herself to be emotional about the elephant's death, particularly since it had been so perfect, but she had been trailing the creature for so long that she did feel the loss.

She returned to find the rangers slicing the belly of the elephant from one end to the other so that the carnivores could feed more easily on the flesh within. A full postmortem was impossible, but Maya inspected the guts and took more samples. Once the scientific tests were complete, one of the rangers raised a massive chainsaw, its jagged teeth catching the orange rays of dusk. The air was shattered by its screeching whine as he went to work on the tusks.

She drove slowly back to camp, through the hordes of fat, flying insects flapping into the sharp path cut by the headlights. Once she startled a dik dik, whose eyes shone momentarily in the glare before it bounded off into cover. At the camp, she pulled up next to a line of sentinel fever trees, their stripped bark hanging in dark shards. Night sounds enveloped her like a drowning sea as soon as she stepped out of the vehicle. Opening the rear door, she unlatched the video camera and monitor and slipped them into the carrying case with the cassettes. She locked the vehicle and, carrying the gear, headed into the camp.

Straight ahead was the kitchen and common room, a rambling structure of bamboo and elephant grass where the team usually gathered in the evenings. On the right was a collection of old green tents pitched under thatched frames where the researchers slept. Left of the kitchen was a brick building, bristling with antennae, that housed the communications center and at the far end of the camp was a small shower and latrine block. The entire camp was surrounded by an eight-foot-high mesh fence to discourage predators and to protect the valuable communications equipment.

Maya stowed the gear in the communications center and locked the door. She found Wanja, Judith, and Margaret already in the common room, sitting around a large trestle table on canvas camp chairs. They knew already about the death of the matriarch whom they'd called Cassie, and the atmosphere was morose as they consumed Solomon's meal of rice and chicken with a salad of tomatoes and chives.

A television and VCR were set up in one corner of the room, and after supper they sat in the two lumpy sofas and watched the extraordinary footage of Cassie's burial. This led to a discussion of the way elephants responded to death. They knew of mothers who refused to leave the side of their deceased newborns, of female elephants who returned repeatedly to the place where their mothers or other close family members had died. If they discovered the bones of dead elephants, they might pick them up in their trunks and carry them for a while. Skulls had a special fascination. A number of elephant skulls that had been collected over the years by members of the research team lined the entrance to the camp. One of these came from a known matriarch who had died miles away, on the other side of Longinye swamp. Three years later, when the family of this old matriarch passed by the camp, the skull had caused them some excitement. The son of the matriarch, who was then close to fourteen years old, had been particularly intrigued by the skull and stayed close by, touching it with his trunk and nudging it with his tusks. The team had no way to explain the phenomenon except that it seemed as if that young elephant had known that this was the skull of his mother.

They broke up soon after nine. Maya went across to her tent. It was rudimentarily furnished with rush matting on the floor, a camp cot, desk, stool, and a noticeboard that contained clippings and some of Maya's favorite photos. Among them was a picture of Sam Hawthorne, which she glanced at briefly before flopping down onto the cot. She picked up a scientific journal and tried to read, but the text swam in front of her eyes and she was soon asleep.

She awoke just before four the next morning. It was still dark outside, but she threw off the layers of exhaustion, glad to be getting an early start. She wanted some computer time to complete a paper she was writing on the different family management styles of three matriarchs, of whom Solo was one. She preferred writing while it was dark in order to save the daylight hours for observation.

Gathering her clothes and a towel, she slipped on sandals and stepped out of the tent into the soft, predawn air. Heavily dewed grass licked her ankles as she walked across to the shower block. Yawning and shivering, she clicked on the glaring strip lights inside. The grey cement shower stall was plain, ugly, and uninviting, but she stripped off the long t-shirt she'd slept in and turned on the spray. The shock left her gasping, stamping her feet, and wishing that she'd showered the night before, when the solar-heated water would at least have had some warmth left in it. The torrent spilled down her back, and with a great effort of will she tipped her face back under it. Water bombarded her forehead like hundreds of fine needles.

The strip lighting attracted battalions of flying insects, so Maya switched it off as soon as she'd finished washing. Her eyes slowly adjusted to the soft moonlight filtering through the large, mesh-covered window. Rubbing herself dry, she crossed over to the bench under the window where her clothes lay.

The roar of a vehicle shattered the murmur of predawn song. At first, Maya thought it must be a tour group getting an early start, but no trained tour driver would use a vehicle in a way that would scare any animals they might have a chance of viewing. The vehicle approached from the southern end of the camp along the trail she'd taken the previous evening. She looked out of the window and saw the headlights coming towards the camp like the monstrous eyes of an agonized cat. Perhaps it was a ranger. Something had happened and they were coming to fetch her. She began throwing on her clothes. The vehicle pulled right up to the camp and the headlights died. She could only make out the dim shapes of men jumping out of the vehicle; the sound of doors slamming. Pushing a foot into her shorts, she heard a shout, an odd thudding noise, and a cry. She pulled a shirt over her head, but wet hair became entangled round a button. Struggling, her face buried in cloth, she heard the creaking camp gates opening and feet running hard. Then there was a scream. It was Wanja.

Maya pulled her face free. She saw Wanja being dragged out of her tent and thrown to the ground. Margaret and Judith appeared and she saw them forced to the ground beside Wanja. One man ran into Maya's own tent then re-emerged shouting something in a language she didn't understand. For a moment no one moved, and then he started walking towards the shower block, towards her.

There was a moment in which Maya felt ill with betrayal, because to run was a kind of betrayal of her friends, but escape was the only weapon she possessed. Slipping out of the door, she edged round the building and charged for the northern boundary fence. In the far corner was a small gate. She heard a voice call out, footsteps pounding the earth. She rushed for the corner, her hand stretching out to grasp the metal bolt. The voice called out again. Seizing the bolt, wrenching it along the dull rusted slot, tugging against the complaining hinges, she flew through the gap and slammed headlong into the wall of dark bush beyond. Brambles snagged her skin; the rough ground stung her naked feet. She fell to her knees, half crawling, half dragging herself through the foliage, tearing her hair as she bent her head down against the thorns and needles, trying to protect her eyes. The ground gave way and she tumbled into a narrow, swamping ditch. Grabbing a branch as she fell, her body twisted, wrenching her back; her feet slid around, slapping into soft mud that oozed up over her knees.

She heard the man thrashing around above her, shining a powerful flashlight that lit the bush like day. She buried her head in the bank, to quell her thumping heart and gasping lungs. Some other creature, not six feet away, must have been disturbed from sleep and scampered away through the bush.

Leaves rustled; a twig snapped.

"Come out and you won't be hurt," he shouted, an American twang in his accent. Seconds later he zipped the bush with gunfire.

CHAPTER TWELVE

AWTHORNE WAS AWAKENED by the phone a little after six. The answerphone invited the caller to leave a message, then a man's voice came on the line.

"Hawthorne? Pick up the phone or else I'll take my story someplace else. You've got three seconds."

He snatched the phone. "Who the hell is this?"

The man laughed. "Hey, it's good to talk to you at last, but I have to say that I am very disgusted about Kipkoech. About none of you believing me. You'll find the evidence outside your house."

"What the fuck are you telling *me* for?"

"You know, Sam—d'you mind if I call you Sam?—I will call everything off as soon as I hear that the Kenyans are not going to start trading ivory again. I can't allow that, Sam."

"Where do you come from? What do you call yourselves?"

The man laughed. "We are the Enemies of Man, Sam. We are defenders of the fucking planet. By the way, you know I have a problem when wild animals are treated like circus performers like that business down in Amboseli. See you there, Sam." He hung up.

Amboseli. Maya. The thoughts crashed together like a couple of trains inside a dark tunnel. Hawthorne grabbed the phone book and found the number which Maya had written on the back. It would put him through to the 123 ranger station in Amboseli. His heart was thumping in his chest. He tried to tell himself that it wasn't her, it couldn't be. Why should they be interested in her. She was against ivory trading, but then, Kariuki had been against it, too. Hawthorne pressed the digits hurriedly. The phone clicked a couple of times and then fell silent, as if the signal had slammed into a dead end. Frustration threatened to suck him under, into pure rage. He searched for Wangai's house number, dialed it, got an engaged tone, and swore again.

He tried the Amboseli number again and listened to the lines connecting and was relieved when it finally started ringing. He waited ages, and then when someone finally answered, the line was bad. He could hardly hear the man on the other end. He did pick up the word "attack" and the fact that someone had been hurt. Then the line went dead.

Hawthorne slammed down the receiver, picked up a book lying next to the bed, and threw it hard across the room. Uttering a succession of expletives, he got up, stormed across the room, and out of the house.

The garden at dawn was peaceful. The sweet smell stung his nostrils. Dew hung heavily on his landlady's rosebushes and on the brilliant bougainvillea growing wildly along the hedge opposite. The hills of Ngong in the purplish distance rose into a helmet of mist. Hawthorne noticed little as he strode down the damp driveway to the wrought iron gates. Excited by this early morning activity, the Dobermans bounded after him, tripping his heels with their great paws. Hawthorne shoved them aside. Anger and fear clouded his vision, Maya's name ran like a mantra through his mind.

The *askari* blearily unlocked the gate and watched Hawthorne hunting the ground outside, until he pulled an envelope from the rocks beside the "Mbwa Kali," sign which meant "fierce dog." The envelope was damp and had clearly been there for awhile. He held it uneasily with the tips of his fingers, at arm's length since it had occurred to him that the envelope might explode. For a moment he knew the panic of the paranoid. After all, why were they calling him? What had he done? Perhaps they were out to get him, or else those he cared about. He fled back to the house.

He dialed the home number for his boss, Noel Jackman. When Jackman picked up the phone, Hawthorne could hear songs from a fifties musical playing on the bureau chief's CD. He explained what had happened.

Jackman sighed down the phone. "Sounds dangerous, Sam," he said. "These guys are using you for something."

"There's nothing I can do," replied Hawthorne. "I have to go with it."

"Guess you're right. Talk to that guy Wangai again and then get down to Amboseli. Call me, okay? And be careful." Jackman also promised to hurry up Hawthorne's request for background on environmental extremists.

Hawthorne tried Wangai's number again. A woman answered the phone.

"He is in the shower," she said. "He can call you back."

"Look . . . er . . . can you get him out of there?" said Hawthorne. "This is serious. I mean, please."

There was a pause. He heard voices on the other end, and then Wangai came on the line. After he'd finished delivering the news, Hawthorne said, "There's a friend of mine down there, you know. She's . . ." He dragged his hand over his mouth. He was losing it. "Look, I'm going down to Amboseli right away. Are you coming? Are you calling out the fucking army or something?"

"All right, Mr. Hawthorne, let me try and reach the police at Namanga. They might have a better idea about what has happened. You stay there for now. I will be in touch."

Hawthorne went into the kitchen and tried to make coffee. Fine arabica grounds spilled over the counter as he filled the machine. He started to clean them up but only half completed the job, and sent the sponge flying into the sink. He was too personally affected by what was happening and knew he had to extricate himself, to pursue it methodically, deal with it like one of his stories. He backtracked over the events of the last week. This man and woman, others as well, were responsible for at least five deaths, all of them somehow connected to the Kenya Wildlife Service. Who would be their target in Amboseli? Maybe it was the warden. Perhaps this was still to do with the cull that Kariuki had ordered. They'd mentioned circus animals. He remembered Maya saying that the two- and three-year-old elephants who had been orphaned by the cull were sold off to zoos and circuses. Maybe that was it.

The coffee machine began to do its job. He poured a mug of the black liquid, tossed in three spoons of sugar, and took it into the living room. Sitting down with the phone book, he searched for the number of one of the Amboseli lodges. He dialed it and heard the phone ringing at the other end, but no one picked it up.

Wangai called back about fifteen minutes later. "Okay, I spoke to Namanga, but they do not know much themselves. There has been an incident at one of the research camps, but they cannot say which one and don't know if it was just a fire. They think someone was hurt, but they are not sure. I am going to Amboseli anyway. I cannot judge the situation from here. Do you want to meet me at Wilson Airport?"

"Sure," Hawthorne breathed.

"Bring the tape with you," Wangai added.

"Okay. What about the envelope?"

"Right," said Wangai. "What's inside it?"

Hawthorne put down the phone and found a paper knife, thinking that he did not want to sacrifice his life to an envelope. On the other hand, maybe the contents were important. He had to find out. He sniffed the envelope first, trying to detect the scent of marzipan, which was sometimes an indication of a letter-bomb. He also bent it between his fingers but it felt like nothing much was inside except paper. Carefully, he slipped the knife into one of the lower corners and slid it up the side. It contained a photocopy of a statement from a Swiss bank account, apparently belonging to Elijah Kipkoech, that revealed a succession of deposits made in the seventies and eighties. Another page contained photocopies of deposit slips revealing the Hong Kong Ivory Emporium as the main depositor to the account.

Hawthorne described them for Wangai. "You think this is real?" he asked.

"I don't know," replied Wangai. "Bring it with you. I'll see you at the Sasa Airways hangar at Wilson."

At his home on the other side of the city, Wangai hung up the phone and went into the kitchen. His wife ladled porridge into a bowl and dropped a lump of margarine in the middle. The detective perched on a stool, eating as fast as he could. The porridge was hot and burned his tongue.

"You will give yourself heartburn," his wife said.

"Yes, I know. Look, I don't know when I am going to get back."

"Is it dangerous?"

He swallowed. "Maybe."

She picked up the porridge pan and sank it in the sink.

"I will try and call you," he said.

She shifted her head slightly to one side. From the back he saw her shoulders rise and fall.

Wangai got into his VW, burping porridge and pressing his scalded tongue against the roof of his mouth. He drove too fast to Wilson. The sidewalks were busy because it was close to the end of the month, and family budgets could no longer stretch to the *matatu* fare. Wangai hardly noticed them. He was too absorbed.

The previous day he'd unexpectedly been given complete control over the case. It happened after Kamau appeared on breakfast television and announced that he was personally leading the hunt for the terrorists. Afterwards, when they were riding in the lift up to Special Ops., Wangai had commended the superintendent for taking such a public stand.

"There's no other way," Kamau had breezed.

"I mean these people seem to be real professionals," Wangai had said. "Look at the way they dealt with Kariuki. Look at how they took Kipkoech. Nobody saw anything. They didn't leave any prints. They were in and out of that place so fast it was unbelievable. I don't doubt at the moment that this gang could do just about anything they set their minds to."

"Don't be ridiculous," Kamau had said.

"This is not ridiculous, sir. We have never come up against anything like this before. There been groups like this running around Europe for years, and there are special anti-terrorist squads and whole networks of undercover agents out there fighting them. And you know something else, every one of those anti-terrorist officers is a marked man."

Kamau coughed.

Wangai went on. "What you did this morning was to tell these terrorists that you are the very man who will bring them to justice. I hope you don't   127 mind, but I think you should do something about your personal security and take care of your wife and children, because you could all be in danger."

Kamau had made no reply.

A couple of hours later Wangai received a call from Kamau's deputy, Inspector Mbaya. Apparently the superintendent had been taken ill suddenly and had gone home for the rest of the day. He'd left instructions that Wangai was to be given complete control over the Kariuki and Kipkoech cases until such time as he was able to resume work.

Hawthorne's vehicle was already parked outside Sasa Airways. One of the young officers from police headquarters, Jenkins Odenge, was also there. He'd brought a radio unit for Wangai to stay in touch with the roadblocks that were being set up on every route out of Amboseli. So far, none of them knew what they were looking for, but they'd been instructed to search every vehicle and to report anything suspicious.

Within the hour, Hawthorne and the detective were airborne over Nairobi National Park heading due south for Amboseli. The journalist was glad that the loud droning of the engines prohibited any attempt at conversation. He'd tried to shake off the fear that Maya had been hurt, but the Namanga police had said that a research camp had been hit. Maybe it wasn't the elephant camp, he prayed it wasn't. He slumped in the narrow seat, face pressed against the window, and thought only of her.

It was two years ago. They met on the night train to the coast. As usual, he arrived at Nairobi station only minutes before the train was due to leave. He checked his name on the berthing chart posted on the platform and ran along outside the train searching for his cabin. An extraordinary looking African woman had been leaning out of a window, long neck, strong cheekbones, incredible eyes, talking animatedly to someone on the platform, laughing. The whistle blew and Hawthorne leaped on board, realized he'd gone too far along the train and had to double back.

He lugged his gear along the narrow corridor, checking the cabin numbers and name tags until he came to one which listed "Mr. S. Hawthorne and Dr. M. Saito." The African woman was inside reading a journal. Hawthorne checked the names again, pulled back the door, and said, "Dr. Saito?"

She looked surprised. "Yes."

"Hi!" he beamed at her, dragging his bag in behind him.

Ordinarily, single women traveling first class on the train either had a cabin to themselves or shared with another woman. The booking clerk had made the assumption that Dr. Saito must be a man. The inspector came around, and she requested a change of cabin. The train was full. There was no other berth available unless she cared to downgrade to third class. She glanced at Hawthorne. He laughed. The journey was twelve hours long and he had no plans to spend it sleeping on his feet.

The cabin was arranged in its daytime mode, the top bunk lying down flat against the wall and the bottom bunk available as a seat on which they sat side-by-side, facing the fake wooden wall. Dr. Saito was next to the window. As the train pulled sluggishly out of Nairobi and onto the Athi plains, Hawthorne stood up and leaned over to look outside. He brushed against her knees. She jerked backwards and brusquely shuffled along the seat, out of his way. Outside, Hawthorne saw zebra, wildebeest, and a few giraffe standing in the fading red glow of sunset. It was a pretty scene.

"You should look at this," he told his cabinmate. "Look."

She looked at him, glanced out of the window, smiled briefly, and went back to her magazine.

He shrugged and even had a biased thought about how most Africans did not appreciate their environment. He tried to see what she was reading, but the print was too small to interpret upside down. She glanced up, caught his eye, and pulled the journal higher as if it gave her some protection.

"I'm going to get a beer. You want one?" he asked her.

She frowned and shook her head.

He slid back the door and turned around. "I'm just being friendly, okay? I'm not giving you any trouble."

He spent the rest of the evening in the more convivial atmosphere of the bar and restaurant. He saw her come in to eat and waited a good hour after she left before returning to the cabin. The shades were drawn and the beds made up. She was sleeping on the top bunk. He lay down on his bed and let the rocking of the slow moving train send him to sleep.

He awoke around three. The train was stationary, and he could hear voices shouting on the other side of the train. He stepped out into the corridor to look, but could not see anything. When he came back into the cabin, the shades were raised, and she was standing at the window. He lay down on his bunk quietly. The moon cast a strong silver light, giving her silhouette a breathtaking aura. She was wearing an oversized shirt. Her legs were naked.

"Did you find out what was wrong?" she asked him.

He coughed. "Er . . . no. I mean, they always wait here to let the up train go past. There's only a single track."

She climbed back up to the bunk, and the frame shook slightly as she slipped under the covers.

"I can't sleep," he said. "Can you?"

There was a silence. Finally, she said, "No," quietly.

They talked, haltingly at first, but it carried on long after the up train chugged past and their down train took off at its soothing, slow pace. Perhaps there was something about the darkness of the cabin that made her feel secure. She told him about Amboseli, where she was director of the elephant project. Hawthorne had heard of it, of course. He told her he was going to interview American sailors and hookers in Mombasa for a feature he was writing on the sexual dangers of shore leave. He told her stories of Africa that made her laugh or brought her close to tears. He was a good storyteller. In the darkness he gave her his best tales, the ones that sometimes seduced women right into his bed.

She was going down to a meeting at Shimoni where zoologists and biologists from all over Kenya would be trying to work out a more rational distribution of funds for environmental research.

"It is a very insecure business," Maya told him, "and highly competitive. You never know what will happen. Most of our sponsors come from the U.S. or Europe. We have no control over what happens there."

Hawthorne knew what she meant. His own job was also precarious and dependent upon decisions that were made thousands of miles away.

He said, "Living out of a suitcase so much, I never really get to unpack. Not my clothes or my emotions." He laughed, partly from embarrassment.

She laughed as well, to help him. "Oh, I know what you mean. In the bush you don't meet the kind of solid citizens my mother would like me to marry. Not many of them want to live even part-time in a tent."

Against the racket of the wheels and carriages thumping into buffers, the conversation became more personal, revealing the isolation which lay behind their careers. Like most African women who chose to shape their own lives, Maya seemed very strong, direct, ready to speak out. Everything was against such women: tradition, their families, the modern state that was still so male-oriented.

He found her directness and strength very attractive. She was different from most of the women he was used to, who seemed to be lost or searching for something to fill a vague emptiness. He wanted an excuse to look at her, see her face, her eyes. When the train came to another grinding halt, Hawthorne took the opportunity to get out of bed, ostensibly to discover the cause of the delay. But when he returned to the cabin, hoping to stand next to her bunk and continue the conversation, she appeared to be sleeping.

They were embarrassed over breakfast the next morning because of the mental intimacy of the night before. She was beautiful, Hawthorne realized, not just because of her eyes or her mouth, but the way she challenged him.

"I study animal behavior," she said to him. "I know exactly what you are thinking."

"You do," he commented, laughing, pushing a hand through his hair. "I'm supposed to be a fairly decent observer of the human condition myself." He laughed, giving her his best laugh. He wasn't used to attempting seduction this early in the morning, but she would be getting off the train in half an hour and then she might be gone for good.

She played with the spoon in the sugar. "This is called displacement activity," she said. "Elephants do it all the time. They want to fight but they pick up a branch and toss it around instead."

Hawthorne leaned across the table. "Would you have dinner with me some time?"

She laughed. "In one of your suitcases?"

"Well, I don't mind. If you prefer a tent, I can go along with that."

She stopped laughing. "I don't know."

"Why?"

"I don't know you."

"I'm only asking if we could go to a restaurant."

"Is that all?" she said. "As an expert in body language, I'd have to say that your physical posturing does not exactly match your words. It implies something else as well."

He threw himself back in his seat, laughing, but also slightly annoyed that she was making fun of him.

"Do you go out with many African women?" she asked.

"Some," he said. "It isn't really an issue, is it? I like you, that's all. I'd like to know you."

"Okay," she smiled.

They met in Nairobi two weeks later and went for dinner at an Indian restaurant. Things progressed much faster than he'd expected. She must have made some decision about him, because they went straight back to his place after dinner and were naked in bed before they'd even kissed.

She seemed much more vulnerable in bed. It was a long time since she'd slept with a man. She laughed when he touched her. He caressed the panic out of her, enjoying the feel of her firm, slim body that was almost as long as his own. He could sense the woman at war with herself, struggling to keep control, yet wanting to relinquish it. He gave her time, held back his own powerful desires. They kissed gently at first, tasting, testing, before sharing their mouths and tongues, bodies pressed together, limbs coupled. The kiss broke, and he moved all over her, tasting every part of her, until she pulled his face back to hers, kissed him deeply, rolled on top, and demanded urgently that he provide the condom. She helped him to put it on, then eased herself down, sitting on top of him, moving slowly at first. He held back, thought of something—anything—to make it last. Finally, he pulled her towards him, rolled on top and thrust deeply until she was crying out and he was crying out with her, joining, sharing, loving, trying to fill the only space left between them.

The lovemaking was always good. In fact, thinking about it, he could hardly make sense of why they'd ever parted, except that he knew it had been his fault. He had been afraid of digging into that suitcase and dragging out an emotion that would have committed him to Maya in a much more serious way. They had reached that point when either they had to become closer or fall apart, and he had moved away, out of habit and out of fear. Flying in that plane down to Amboseli, he felt the emotion being drawn out of him. He could not shut it down any longer. He did love her. He'd always loved her. He wanted her more than he'd wanted anything else, ever. Wanted her safety, her life to prosper and survive, wanted desperately to hold her again. If she was dead or injured he thought he would go crazy.

"You okay?" shouted Wangai as the plane started dropping towards the Amboseli airstrip.

"I'll soon know," he replied.

The strip was right in the middle of the park. It was no more than a stretch of grass where a herd of Thompson's gazelle were grazing until the pilot buzzed low overhead, scattering them in a fan-shaped stampede. As soon as they landed the plane was subject to another stampede, of frightened, angry tourists, most of them Americans, clamoring for seats on board. Hawthorne heard the words "maniacs" and "terrorists." A highly powdered and lipsticked woman in her fifties, dressed in a jungle jumpsuit, was screaming abuse in a thick New York accent at the man next to her.

Wangai headed over to the landing shed while Hawthorne pulled one of the less demented tourists aside for an explanation. The traveler was a skinny man with a long face and the kind of expression one associates with priests who have grown weary of the world and its sins. Hawthorne introduced himself, and the man immediately brightened. It was like that with a lot of people once they knew they were talking to a journalist. Unfortunately, the man did not know very much. Some place in Amboseli had been attacked during the night. People had been killed and buildings burned. Everyone wanted to get away, but nobody wanted to risk the journey by road because the terrorists were still at large.

Hawthorne glanced over at the pilot of the plane, who was dealing profitably with the situation. He heard sums of money mentioned that were outrageously high, but credit cards were being chucked around like confetti. He turned around, intending to join Wangai, and saw the detective running full pelt towards him, like a ball with legs. Hawthorne ran to meet him.

"Who did they hit?"

"An elephant research project. They killed the cook and raped an American girl."

"Oh, God," said Hawthorne.

"They destroyed the place," said Wangai. "Burned everything. Let's go."

CHAPTER THIRTEEN

T

HE ZEBRA-STRIPED tour vehicle carrying Hawthorne and Wangai pulled up alongside the burnt-out wrecks of the project land cruisers. The communications center was reduced to rubble. The kitchen was nonexistent. A couple of the tents were more or less intact, but ashes and charred timbers were all that remained of the rest. A ranger jeep was parked in the middle of the destruction, and its driver was leaning against the door smoking a cigarette.

"Jesus," whispered Hawthorne, jumping out of the vehicle and walking fast towards the ranger. Even before he reached the man, Hawthorne was yelling, "Where are they? What the fuck . . ."

Hawthorne felt a tug on his arm and saw Wangai beside him. "No, Mr. Hawthorne, I will talk to him first."

The journalist stopped dead in his tracks. "Yeah," he breathed. "Only . . . find out where the people are."

"Of course," replied Wangai, who began moving off.

"Maya Saito," Hawthorne called after him. "She was the director of this project."

Hawthorne took a couple of deep breaths and lifted the Nikon. Through the camera lens the scene looked no less devastated, but, professionally speaking, the scene wasn't unfamiliar. He took a few long shots and then went over to the trashed remains of the tent that had been Maya's. The metal frame of her camp cot stuck out of the ash pile. The mattress was gone. One of the 135 thatched frame posts was still standing, but there was no longer anything for it to support. On the ground beside the camp cot he picked up a couple of curled-up photographs. One was of the elephant she called Solo, the other was of himself and Maya. An almost intolerable weight of sadness fell on him. His hand rose as if to push back his hair but stopped part way and hung in the air, as if it had forgotten the instruction it had received.

Wangai shouted, breaking the moment, and Hawthorne spun round to see the detective heading back fast towards the zebra-striped minibus. Slipping the photos into his pocket, he ran to catch up.

"What did he say?" Hawthorne asked as he fell into step alongside Wangai.

"Your friend is at the warden's house with the others. She is not hurt."

Hawthorne felt like he'd shed a skin.

"The cook was murdered. A bullet through the head. The warden had the body taken away. A couple of the scientists were hurt, but Dr. Saito escaped during the attack. Apparently, she went for help on foot, at night, through this!" He held up a hand as if it cradled the entire Amboseli wilderness.

Wangai pulled himself into the minibus beside Hawthorne and sighed as he fell into his seat. "It's bad, very, very bad," he said, taking out a handkerchief to wipe his face.

"What is?" said Hawthorne.

"There was an American student staying here," Wangai said, "Judith Dreyfus. They raped her." He stuffed the handkerchief back into his pocket. "At least we have some more witnesses."

Hawthorne shook his head. "You don't have the first idea what you're doing, do you?"

Wangai looked at him but did not respond. "They also stole some research equipment, that's what the ranger said. We will have to ask Dr. Saito. By the way, what is your connection to her? Why are you both involved in this?"

Hawthorne answered as well as he could. The pattern of attacks just did not make sense. When Kipkoech had been killed, he'd thought that Kipkoech, maybe even Kariuki, might have been involved in secret ivory deals in the past and that the Enemies of Man was a freaky extremist environmental group taking revenge. It was impossible, though, for him to see how they could have anything against Maya.

The trip to the ranger station took less than twenty minutes. The driver pulled up at the entrance to the compound and hailed the man on duty. Wangai introduced himself, waved his badge, and asked for the warden. The vehicle was signed in, and they were directed to a bungalow at the far end of the station. They entered the compound and drove past garages, workshops, a barracks, and a couple of other dwellings before reaching the flower-lined path to Hari Ngweno's house. Hawthorne and Wangai got out and followed the path around the side of the house to the wide-screened porch, which looked out towards the cloud-covered peak of Kilimanjaro.

The warden came out of the house as the two men approached. He was a slight man with a thin face that made him look older than his thirty-five years. Wangai introduced himself, but Ngweno was antagonistic towards Hawthorne.

"Why have you brought him here?" he demanded, gesturing at the journalist. Hawthorne understood. The newspapers had printed his photograph a lot in the last week or so. They'd also written some pretty harsh things.

Wangai took Ngweno's arm and led him towards the veranda. Hawthorne saw the detective murmuring in the warden's ear. Once or twice Ngweno turned to look at him, but he appeared slightly mollified. When he was done, Wangai clapped his hands and rubbed them together as if he was getting down to business. "Now, I would like to interview Dr. Saito and her colleagues. They are here?"

Ngweno shrugged. "Inside, but they are not in good shape."

"Right, and the deceased?" continued Wangai.

Ngweno's eyes shifted. "In one of the garages. I could not leave him there. A couple of lions got to him."

Wangai froze for a moment, then he clapped the warden on the back. "No problem," he said, inviting Ngweno to lead them into the house. Hawthorne followed.

They went inside the porch door to the living room, a gloomy place   137 furnished with oversized government-issue furniture. A woman, who looked like a Luo to Wangai, was standing beside the window, staring outside. Maya emerged from the back of the house carrying a tray of cups and a teapot. She stumbled when she saw Hawthorne and the tray slipped. Two of the plastic cups fell and bounced over the floor, but she steadied herself and saved the pot.

She had not expected to see him, not at all. What was he doing there? He was walking towards her, taking the tray out of her hands, looking at her face, wincing at her red swollen eyes, her cracked lips.

Ngweno pushed in front of Hawthorne. "I'm sorry, Maya. This man is with the detective from Nairobi, he's . . ."

"It's okay," said Maya, quietly. Hari did not know about her and Sam. He'd only been warden of the park for two months.

"Hi," said Hawthorne, his eyes pouring into her own.

She looked away. His soft voice shocked her. It made her shake and feel cold. "Hello, Sam," she said, trying to keep steady, not wanting him to see.

"Are you okay?" he asked.

"Ah . . . no," she said, moving over to the sofa. How could she be okay? She felt strange, a little dizzy. Her back was painful; her arms and legs were a mess of weals and scars.

Wangai picked up the cups that had bounced across the floor and set them on the tray, which Hawthorne put down on the coffee table.

She wished he hadn't come. He could have come any time before, but not now. She couldn't deal with him, did not have the energy to cope with how she felt about him. She had Judith to take care of, and Wanja and Margaret. They needed her. They were her family, what was left of it. Solomon was gone. He'd worked at the camp longer than any of them and now he was lying out there under a piece of tarpaulin. She'd seen them bring in his body.

Ngweno said, "These men have to talk to you, I'll . . . er . . ."

"You could leave us for a moment," said Wangai, like he was issuing an order. Ngweno shrugged and pushed through the screen door, letting it bang behind him.

138   Maya leaned forward and picked up the teapot. "My mother always said

it was a good idea to drink tea in a crisis. It was something she picked up from the colonials."

"Dr. Saito?" said Wangai gently.

Maya let go of an almost-smile and nodded. "Oh, I am sorry," she said. "Would you like tea as well? I'll fetch the cups." Hawthorne stopped her from standing up and went to find the cups himself.

"Margaret," Maya said softly, "do you want to join us?"

The woman standing next to the window turned around, her round-cheeked face streaked with tears, mumbled a "No," and went back to the window.

Hawthorne sat beside Maya, placing the cup on the tray. He wanted to touch her, to hold her hand, or put his arm around her. He couldn't bear not to.

"Maya," he said, quietly. "I'm so sorry, I . . ."

Wangai interrupted him. "Mr. Hawthorne, please."

Hawthorne shut up. He could see the rigidity in Maya and sensed her resentment. He didn't expect her to fall into his arms and pretend that everything would be all right because he was there, but he wanted a gesture from her, a look that would let him in.

"I need you to tell me what happened," Wangai said.

"I know," replied Maya, sipping the tea. It scalded her lips. "The trouble is I don't know very much and neither does Margaret." She let go of an empty laugh. "We both had our faces in the mud. Wanja and Judith might tell you more maybe, only neither of them have been making much sense. Judith is worse." She broke off. "I suppose we were all very frightened, and it stops you from seeing the things in front of you." She described the things she remembered. Then she added, "I didn't go back to the camp this morning. I should have gone but I couldn't face it. Everything is wasted." She could hardly bear to even think of it. Everything was gone. Years and years of work and effort wasted.

"Did you see any of them?" asked Wangai. "Their height? Skin color? Voices? The car? How many were there?"

"Four," said Margaret from the window. "There were four of them.

They had masks on but they were not Kenyans. I don't know what they were." Tears brimmed in her eyes. "I kept saying to myself that I had to look and remember. Look and remember. You know, all I can remember is their shoes. Isn't that stupid! I can only tell you about their shoes. I was too scared. I was lying in the dirt listening to Wanja and Judy screaming. They practically shoved their feet in my face." Her words drifted around the shabby walls, filling the room with pain.

"What about the car?" Wangai persisted.

"It . . . er . . ." Margaret stammered.

"What," coaxed Wangai, crossing the room to her. "What can you remember?"

"I think it was a Daihatsu. I have a friend with a vehicle just the same. I think it was."

"Thank you," Wangai murmured.

No one had seen the license number, but Wangai got on the radio and passed the information to HQ, who would in turn pass it on to the police roadblocks around Amboseli. It was doubtful whether the Daihatsu would still be in a vulnerable location, but there was always the hope.

He asked about the equipment that had been stolen, so that he could pass that information on as well. The stolen items included four-hundred-watt speakers, an infrasonic recorder and amplifier, cables, a solar powered generator, and a tape of a female elephant in estrus. Wangai wrote it all down. "What use would anyone have for all that?" he asked.

"I don't know," Maya replied.

"What do you use it for?"

"Communication experiments, to test calls and responses."

Wangai looked blank.

Hawthorne said, "What she means is, when they play this estrus tape, it has the effect of . . ."

"Sam!" She turned on him, intending to protest because it was presumptuous of him to explain her project. He fell silent. They looked at each other, and she saw that he spoke with his eyes. Wanting her. Demanding. He distracted her from everything she needed to think about.

"Why is he here?" she said, accusingly, turning to Wangai. Hawthorne had no right to be there. It made no sense that he was here with the detective. She couldn't understand why she hadn't seen it before.

Wangai explained about Hawthorne's connection to the killings of Kariuki and Kipkoech, and the phone calls he'd been receiving. Maya did not even know about Kipkoech. She listened to the detective, head bent forward, holding the bridge of her nose, hearing him but also worrying about Judith, Wanja, and Margaret and about the terrible destruction of all her work.

"Tell me," Wangai said eventually, "why would anyone want to steal that equipment."

She shook her head. They used the estrus tape to help indicate patterns and differences in the signaling devices of females who were ready to mate. "I don't know," she whispered.

Judith and Wanja were both sedated and resting in a couple of bedrooms. Wanja was knocked out, but Maya took Wangai to see Judith. The American girl had been tormenting herself with fantasies that her attackers were still out there; she could hear them, smell them even. Maya eased open the door of the cramped room. Rose-patterned curtains billowed in the soft breeze coming through the mosquito-netted window. Judith looked pale and drawn, with sunken eyes circled by grey shadows, and her brown hair, matted and tangled, spread across the pillow. Maya sat beside the bed and took her friend's hand. Judith opened her eyes, saw Maya, and sobbed. Maya held her close, so that grief flowed between them, opening both their hearts, making them weep harder. Wangai had been hovering in the doorway. He moved into the room slowly, sat down on the other side of the bed, and asked Judith softly what she could remember.

Judith mumbled phrases that often died before they were complete. Her eyes flitted constantly around the room. She would not let go of Maya's hand and squeezed it hard. She couldn't tell them much, except that she thought the one who raped her had been Oriental, perhaps Chinese or Japanese or something. Then she said, "There was a woman with them. I heard her."

"What did she say? Did you see her?"

Judith shook her head. "I don't know, but there was some kind of   141 argument. I don't know what. I couldn't . . ." and the tears came again.

Wangai took Maya onto the porch. She sat in a cane chair while he leaned against the wooden railing, his back to Kilimanjaro. "I want you to tell me about Kariuki," he said.

"What do you want to know?"

"Tell me, what was he like as a person? Did you like him?"

She shrugged. "Yes . . . no . . . he was a very hard man."

Wangai studied her. "You know, the phone message said that they killed Kariuki because he was responsible for killing hundreds of animals."

She gave no response.

"Tell me about the cull."

She shook her head and said nothing. She was already numb from violence. She did not want to remember the cull as well, but the whip of helicopter blades invaded her memory. For a second she saw the dust thrashed by the blades as the elephants were driven in front of the army vehicles. Two-hundred-fifty animals had been shot. Kariuki had made her witness the cull because only by being there had she been able to prevent elephants being killed who were part of the study.

"Did you agree with it?" asked Wangai.

"No."

"Why not?"

She shook her head again. "I don't want to talk about it now."

"We have to," Wangai insisted. "I am trying to understand the motives of these terrorists. If the cull was their reason for killing Kariuki, I have to know about it."

She looked at him.

"Why did Kariuki think the cull was necessary?"

She sighed. "The elephants were doing too much damage to farmland around the park. Claims for compensation were too high. But by fencing the park, we cut off the wet-season migration routes for the elephants. Many of them used to spend several months each year outside the park. Kariuki thought the cull was necessary because there would be severe environmental stress if all the elephants remained here year-round."

"You didn't agree?" asked Wangai.

She shrugged. "I thought they should be given a chance. Elephants can adapt to overcrowding, through disease, starvation, even by reducing their birth rate. The park was too profitable for Kariuki to risk those kind of experiments." She sighed. "Tourists do not want to see starving animals, but any kind of natural death is preferable to a life that is cut short by a bullet." She did not bother explaining to Wangai that the animals that survived those difficult times also enriched the gene pools of their species because only the strong survived. A cull did not make that distinction. Strong and weak were wiped out together. Whole families were destroyed and their genes lost forever.

"Was there any backlash against Kariuki at the time?"

"Many people disagreed. A lot of people agreed with him as well. It is one of those perennial debates of wildlife management."

"Did anyone lose money because of it, or gain money? Was anyone hurt so badly by it they would want to kill him?"

She thought about it. "No. But I think it was a turning point for him. You know, in places like Zimbabwe where they cull elephants regularly, whole industries have grown up. They process everything, not just the tusks but the hide and the meat, which is canned. Even elephant feet are made into wastebaskets. Some people wanted to do the same here but Kariuki saw that once a business like that was created, it would be necessary to continue culling elephants, just to keep it going. He did not want to create a market for elephant products, and wanted to destroy the tusks for the same reason, but he was stopped."

"Who by?"

"People in the government. Many politicians supported him, but not everyone did."

Wangai said, "Like Minister Muthangu."

"Muthangu?" She remembered him as a politician who had once said that he wanted to divide Nairobi National Park into *shambas* for squatters.

Wangai said, "He has promised to use funds from ivory sales to develop Mathare Valley. Where does all this ivory come from?"

143

She told him that it had been collected over the years from culled elephants or those that had died naturally or had been confiscated. A lot had been discovered up in Lake Turkana by an archaeologist. The tusks had been buried. She said, "In the early nineties we were still burning most of it, but then, like most other countries in Africa, the government saw that the trade would become legal again someday, and that the tusks were money in the bank. That is the thing. We legislate against the ivory trade, but it doesn't make the tusks go away."

"What did Kariuki want to do about this ivory?"

"We wanted to destroy it or at least make sure that nobody sold it. We want to keep the trade banned in Kenya and persuade other countries to agree to a further fifteen-year ban on all ivory trading. At present, for every legal ivory transaction going on in southern Africa, there are ten or more illegal deals going on."

Wangai said nothing. He was puzzled. Why would the terrorists attack her and Kariuki, when they all wanted the same thing? He left her and went across to examine the body of the the cook killed in the attack. Afterwards he went back to the elephant camp to meet Michael Odile, who had come down from Nairobi to conduct the forensic exam.

After Wangai had left, Hawthorne joined Maya on the veranda. He handed her the photographs he'd picked up at the camp. She held them loosely on her lap. They were too powerful a reminder of all that had been lost.

"I need to talk to you," he said.

She put a hand on the side of her head. It ached badly.

"Please," said Sam, standing over her.

This didn't sound like Sam. They might shout at each other, argue over politics or something some idiot had done, but they didn't say, "Please, I need to talk to you."

She sighed. It was a mistake, a sign of weakness, and he picked that moment to drop to his knees and reach out for her hands.

"Don't, Sam," she said, looking away. "I can't."

"God, I'm just trying to . . . you don't know what . . ." He stood up, took a few paces away and then swung around. "I miss you, Maya." He didn't mean to say that, but it seemed to fit the moment, express the loss he'd been afraid of.

"I was just here," she said sarcastically. He could have seen her anytime. He need not have "missed" her at all.

"Look, I know this is hard, and this isn't the right time . . ."

"No, it isn't," she said.

". . . but I wanted you to know that . . . that . . ."

"What?" she said stonily, refusing to look at him or help him in the slightest.

He sat down heavily in the seat next to her. "Shit!"

She might have laughed another time, but she couldn't. "You don't know how much . . ." she began. Her voice tailed off, caught in her throat. She thought it might break into a cry. "I just can't deal with this now, Sam. There's too much going on." She fell silent, feeling that she did not have the strength. She seized herself, sucked air into her lungs, and the words poured out. "Look, I know it is a shock for you to find me like this, but please don't say anything, Sam. Don't do anything. I have enough to cope with as it is."

She walked into the house, leaving him there.

CHAPTER
FOURTEEN

ZHU, SILVIA, AND THE OTHERS had left Amboseli via the Kimana Gate shortly after dawn. Zhu had driven like a maniac. He'd taken a couple of amphetamines and was flying by the time they pulled up outside a small hotel, where he'd made the call to Hawthorne. Soon afterwards, they'd entered Tsavo West National Park, and by eight-thirty they were parking outside Kilaguni Lodge.

"What you stopping here for?" demanded Sen.

"Breakfast," snapped Zhu, flinging the door open.

"Come on, man," said Sen, "let's get right away."

"I'm hungry." Zhu grinned. "Come on, babe." He held out a hand towards her.

Silvia looked at the hand. She hadn't said a word in hours, not since the rape. Sen had dragged that poor girl into the bushes. The girl had screamed, and Sen had hit her. He'd come back afterwards, ostentatiously zipping his fly, grinning with his small teeth.

"Your turn," he'd said to Jimmy, and Jimmy would have done it. He'd put his gun inside the vehicle and gone after the girl, who was on her hands and knees, crawling out of the bush. Silvia had grabbed Jimmy's gun and fired it close to his feet. He yelled, "What the f . . ."

"Don't touch her, you hear me. Don't you . . ."

Sen shouted, "Hey, Zhu, your woman's gone nuts!"

She swung round on Sen then. Pointed the gun at his belly. She wanted to do it.

147

"Hey, Zhu, man!" Sen shouted.

"Put the gun down, babe."

His voice came from behind. She knew he too had a gun and that the trigger would be tickling his forefinger. Could he do it so easily?

"Put the gun down, babe."

"You tell Jimmy he should leave the girl alone."

"Leave the girl alone, Jimmy," he mimicked her. The other two men laughed. "Now put down the fucking gun."

She'd lowered it, and Sen had grabbed it.

"Come here," Zhu said, his voice as quiet as a birdwatcher's.

She'd gone to him, around the back of the Daihatsu. He put her against the vehicle, his hands leaning against it either side of her head.

"You embarrass me, babe."

"I didn't like what he was doing."

He stared at her. She couldn't see his eyes clearly, but she could feel the force of them. She opened the door and sat, eyes averted.

"I don't want to see you with a weapon in your hands. You understand? From now on you don't touch one without asking me first. You're a danger to yourself, babe. I'm only trying to protect you."

The hand was still there, waiting for her to get out of the vehicle and go inside Kilaguni Lodge for breakfast. He said, "Babe, if you don't come now, I'll have to dump you out there somewhere. Move it."

She heard the aggressiveness in his tone, and for the first time she was truly frightened. She'd not imagined what it would be like to face up to Zhu's disapproval. Whatever had taken place in Macao had happened from a distance. Once she'd returned, after he'd recovered from the apparent shock of it, things had not been so different between them. It had seemed as if he still loved her, and that was probably why she'd been so willing to disbelieve the evidence in front of her.

The evidence, she thought now. For instance, that the two men who'd come to the Estoril Hotel in Macao asking for her had not only known her alias, they'd known where to find her as well. The fact also that the telephone message on Zhu's answering machine had indicated that he was going to meet with Joey Han, and Han was partners with the man Zhu had sent her to kill. She breathed in sharply.

"I'm going to die of starvation waiting for you, babe," Zhu said, smiling now.

She tried to smile back, stepped down from the vehicle, and took his hand. There was no exchange of affection in the way their palms touched; there was only the grip of control. He was still smiling, though, nodding at people inside a tour bus pulling up alongside after their morning game run. "See that?" he whispered to Silvia. "They don't look any different from us." He laughed, pulling her towards the restaurant. Sen and Jimmy dragged along behind, looking furtive, but Zhu marched right up to the maitre d' and demanded a table for four.

There was a sumptuous buffet of tropical fruits, eggs, sausages, bacon, pancakes, waffles, and five varieties of cereal. The restaurant was packed with excited tourists: Japanese, Americans, Germans, Swedes, even a few Chinese. It was awash with khaki and soft boots, gold jewelry, silk scarves, casually expensive hats, stylish holdalls, the stench of a hundred perfumes mingling with the scent of breakfast. There were also cameras of all shapes and sizes, draped around necks, slung from shoulders, standing on tripods, and lying on tables like exotic condiments; cameras pushed in front of squinting eyes even while the mouth below was chewing; lenses turned and twisted and tested and exclaimed over, passed around, bragged about. It was the only thing that made their group stand out, Silvia thought. They had no cameras.

Zhu was still buzzing. He drew attention to himself, imitating people in the buffet queue and then knocking over a jug of passion fruit juice and making a scene about it. When he got back to the table, Sen was livid.

"You have to cool down, man. You look crazy. People are watching you, you are out of control . . ." He paused for breath. "I don't know either why the hell we had to bring all that stuff from the research camp. You're going to get us caught, man. I say we should dump it, and fast."

Silvia watched Zhu, who studied Sen while he finished chewing and then exclaimed, "You've got no imagination, you know that? You don't understand. This is going to be beautiful. Ha, you know what, we switch on that stuff and it brings horny old elephants running right at it." He 149 laughed. "Then one of them runs into the machine or someone tries to switch it off and boom! It's amazing."

"It's crazy."

"Exactly. We want them to believe that we are total crazy lunatics. The more crazy we are, the more angry they're going to be when we tell them they must ban the ivory trade. They'll just do the opposite to spite us. See? You don't understand, do you? None of you do." Zhu hit the palm of his hand against his head, demonstrating their stupidity.

Silvia saw Sen and Jimmy exchange looks. They finished eating in slience.

Afterwards, they left Kilaguni and drove through Tsavo West, crossed over the Mombasa highway, and entered the less popular reserve of Tsavo East. This was a retreat for the privileged few who paid expensive prices to experience the wilderness in virtual solitude. None of the economy tour buses went there; there were none of the manufactured tourist attractions of the West and only one very expensive lodge. The East was uncompromisingly wild, harsh, pristine, and extremely hot.

Elephants were the gardeners of this wilderness. They trimmed the bush and carried seeds in their bellies which were deposited, ready fertilized, in their feces. The elephants pruned vigorously, rooting out acres of scrubland, creating new grasslands that gave birth to hundreds of new springs. During the seventies, when elephant numbers declined and the bush grew high, Tsavo had become unpopular with tourists because the animals had been too hard to find. Chunks of the park might have been lost altogether, to mineral prospectors and the land hungry population, if the situation had not been turned around during Kariuki's era. The park, both east and west, now made its way as one of the most important preserves of truly wild populations in the world. There was no talk of culling here, as there had been in the late sixties. Tsavo was considered to be a large enough wilderness to stand on its own feet.

Clouds of red dust flew up in the wake of the Daihatsu, and the dry air caked their mouths. Silvia felt drugged by the motion and the heat soaking through her clothes. Zhu had calmed down, at least, during the last hour and had surrendered the wheel to Jimmy, who drove more sedately. Finally,

Zhu directed him off the road. They drove for half a mile across rocky terrain, then stopped. The equipment was unloaded and set up. Zhu gave instructions from the magazine article by Maya Saito. There was even a diagram showing the linkages between the various items of apparatus. It took them about forty-five minutes to get everything organized. Zhu checked the volume, checked the angle of the solar panels used to charge the batteries, and clicked the switch which started the tape turning. From the way the dials on the infrasonic recorder flickered, it was clear that some sound was coming out of it, though none of them could hear it.

He looked up from his handiwork. "Pack it," he told Sen.

Sen attached a small plastic explosive to the on-off switch and, the trap complete, they departed, driving onward through Tsavo East, taking the track that had once been a highway for slavers and ivory traders, and which ran alongside the great swath of sluggish red water marked on the map as the Sabaki River. Soon after passing Lugard Falls, they encountered an old bull elephant with a pair of massive tusks. He was standing motionless in the shade of a thorn tree, apparently dozing. The noise of the vehicle's engine disturbed him enough to glance in their direction, but he obviously did not consider them a threat. He rubbed his rear against the thorn tree, making it shake to its topmost branches.

"Stop," said Zhu. He got out of the vehicle and walked a few paces towards the bull.

Sen muttered "Fuck," under his breath. He leaned out of the window and shouted, "What you doing now?"

Zhu turned round and got back inside the vehicle. "You know, that bastard over there is walking around with about twenty-thousand dollars worth of extended teeth." He shook his head, watching the beast. "I guess I was hoping I could perform some dentistry." He laughed at himself. "Another time," he promised.

They left the elephant behind and drove for the park exit at Sala, and once they were free of Tsavo, they ate up miles of dusty sandy roads, heading for Malindi and the coast. During that journey, everything seemed to unravel for Silvia. She'd opened the floodgates of suspicion and now she 151 couldn't stop the torrent that came pouring through. It wasn't only the things that happened in Macao. There was also the question of why Zhu had given her the most dangerous job in Kenya, of dealing with Kariuki. Certainly she had plenty to feel resentful for over what Kariuki had done. He was virtually responsible, or else men like him were, for the destruction of her family's fortune. People like him had stopped the ivory trade and ruined her father, her mother, and her own life. Yet Zhu had hardly given her time to plan the job properly. He'd sprung it on her only days before. It was all wrong. As if he had wanted her to fail.

Zhu was sitting in the front passenger seat, and she studied the back of his head, thinking how short his neck was and how his skull seemed to rise out of it like a blunted club. She had no love for him. It was all gone. He must have sensed her eyes upon him, because he turned around and looked at her. She gave nothing back.

CHAPTER FIFTEEN

HAWTHORNE FLEW UP to Nairobi with Maya and the other researchers. He drove them to Nairobi Hospital, where Wanja and Judith were admitted for observation.

Hawthorne was feeling fairly bruised himself, emotionally speaking. He'd hung around in case he was needed, but most of the time felt worse than useless. He wanted to be close to Maya, but she didn't want him. He couldn't stand the resentment or whatever it was in her eyes whenever she looked at him. He didn't know if he could do anything to remove it.

They came out of the hospital and walked across to Hawthorne's car. "Where do you want to go?" he asked.

Maya didn't speak until they were sitting inside. "I cannot deal with my mother right now," she said, quietly. She knew her mother would be hysterical, would blame everything on her lifestyle. "I need somewhere quiet where I can think."

Hawthorne's hands were resting on the top of the steering wheel. He felt sucked down by her mood, depressed, exhausted. It was completely understandable that she should feel that way, only he hated being infected by it. He sighed. "I don't know. What do you want? I'll take you anywhere you want to go. Personally, I have to get home and file a story."

"My God!"

"I'm sorry, Maya. That's what I do. It's my job."

She lay her head back on the seat and closed her eyes, looking for peace. At least the people she cared about were safe. Judith and Wanja were not badly hurt. They would mend. Margaret had gone to stay with an aunt. She could let go a little. Tears started welling up behind her closed lids. She quickly dragged a hand across her eyes, wiping them away.

"I need to go somewhere and rest," she said.

"Do you want to come to my place?" Hawthorne regretted it as soon as the words were out, didn't even know why he'd said it. She would react badly. Besides, he wasn't sure he could cope with her in this state. He didn't really know this Maya. Even so, he said, "You can have my room all to yourself, okay? You'll have all the peace you want." Part of him wanted her to reject the idea. She must have girlfriends in town she could stay with. On the other hand, he felt like he owed it to her. If she wanted his room, it was the least he could do.

When she didn't reply he said, quickly. "You just tell me where to take you. Anything is fine by me."

She thought, he has to do this. He has to feel . . . necessary. She wanted him to be close, was glad he was there, she just didn't want him demanding anything from her. There was one good thing about the offer, though. At least she wouldn't have to explain anything to anyone. Anywhere else she would be asked questions about what had happened, she would have to go over it all again. Sam wouldn't ask her to do that. Maybe she could just stay at his house for one night, give herself time to rest and feel stronger. She felt so tired.

"Okay," she said.

"What?" he asked, looking at her. Her eyes were closed.

"I'll have your room."

He put the car in gear and she felt it moving forward. She dozed off on the drive over there, but woke up when he pulled up outside the gates, the same old gates, same *askari* grinning at her, same dogs tearing down the drive to greet them, and Sam's little house with its arch of crimson bougainvillea framing the entrance. This was a friendly retreat, at least. It felt a little bit like home.

Inside, she wasn't so sure. The living room was a mess. She stood in the middle of it while Sam rushed around, searching for clean sheets to put on his bed. She went into the kitchen. Coffee grounds lay all over the counter. She felt trapped, claustrophobic, because of the mess and because the house was so small. Where was he going to sleep anyway?

Hawthorne found her in the kitchen. "I've fixed the bed for you, if you want to lie down. I still have some cleaning up to do . . ." He pushed a hand through his hair. He wanted to hold her so much. The urge was overwhelming. To rid himself of it, he snatched up the sponge from the sink where he'd tossed it that morning and started scooping the coffee grounds into his palm.

"Spilled them this morning," he said, hurriedly. "After I got the call from those bastards." He paused. "I was so worried." He slammed the sponge back into the sink. "There!" he said. "Okay, can I show you to your room? D'you want something to eat or something? You want coffee?" He sounded businesslike, matter-of-fact.

"Sam, where are you going to sleep?"

He breathed out, audibly. "In the living room. I have a sleeping bag. It's okay. I won't disturb you. I said you could have my room and I meant it." Only he wished he could be in there with her.

"Fine," she said, walking by him. "I'm going to lie down."

He checked on her an hour later. She was fast asleep, her beautiful face relaxed and calm. It was great. He felt like he'd accomplished something. It was good for her to sleep like that. She'd feel better afterwards.

Hawthorne went back to the living room, stacked some wood in the fireplace, and watched the flames crackle through the twigs. It was a soothing sight, and, with Maya at peace in the room next door, he almost felt relaxed. He began to smile to himself, but not for long. The events of the day came tumbling back into focus. It had begun with the phone call and the envelope. The envelope! How could he have been so stupid! Had he really forgotten that the Enemies of Man, or whoever they were, knew where he lived? What if they were watching the house? Had seen him arrive with Maya?

He stood up, pacing the room, trying to decide whether to wake her up and insist on taking her somewhere else. Somewhere safer—her mother's, maybe. Yet, if they were watching the house, they could follow him wherever he went. It was no good. He should have demanded police protection from Wangai, but the police weren't usually armed with anything except their *rungus*. What good would that be against people as well armed as the Enemies of Man? He needed the army.

He laughed at himself suddenly, realizing that if they really did need protection, it was already too late. If they didn't, he may as well stop worrying about it. He tried to settle down to write the story, finished it within the hour, and sent it to bed down the phone line. Then he grabbed the file on activist environmental organizations that Jackman had delivered earlier.

The file contained a selection of computer printouts and faxes from various bureaus of the press agency. A decade of environmental fervor had spawned a multitude of societies and affiliations that made Greenpeace, the mother of them all, look about as extreme as a pensioner complaining about overly loud rock and roll. Hawthorne scanned the who's who of planet-activists. The more reasonable among them were categorized as "rationalist" groups, which advocated a gradual approach to environmental reform. The "radicals," however, demanded revolutionary action and the immediate suspension of all environmentally damaging activities. Some of them appeared willing to return man to the Stone Age. Within both categories were groups dedicated to single-interests such as the anti-nuclear movement, Canadian seal protectors, or the small Dutch cell of vigilantes dedicated to protecting the habitat of a particularly rare butterfly. There were also multi-interest organizations which claimed planet-wide concerns, like People for a Perfect Planet, a radical California-based organization with which Hawthorne was familiar. The female director of PPP had been indicted for attempted murder earlier that year, accused of spiking the coffee of the foreman of a logging company with the chemical used to kill the roots of trees before they were felled. Hawthorne went through descriptions of over a hundred organizations. None of them were called the Enemies of Man.

Later, he lay down on the rug beside the dying fire and forced himself into sleep by focusing on the back of his eyelids, diving into the blackness and driving thought from his mind. A little after one he was awakened by the phone. He heard the answerphone click on. The man spoke.

"Hello, Sam. You know that scene in Amboseli? We don't like these zoologists fooling around with nature in the name of science. It's dangerous. We're going to prove it to you. If man, or woman for that matter, rapes the planet, we take the planet's revenge. We are the Enemies of Man." He chuckled softly and hung up.

Hawthorne ran the tape back and listened again. It was insane, every word. Hawthorne called Wangai's home. It rang five or six times before Mrs. Wangai picked it up and mumbled that her husband was out and she did not know when he would be back. Hawthorne left an urgent message for him to call. He tried reaching Wangai at the police headquarters but had no better luck there.

Setting down the phone, he heard Maya sobbing. Hawthorne went through to the bedroom and clicked on the bedside light. She was crying in her sleep, her face shining with sweat. He sat down, stroking her forehead.

"Wake up," he urged, "it's okay. Wake up."

Her eyes jerked open suddenly and she shivered. He could see that whatever monsters had disturbed her sleep still hovered behind her eyes.

"It's okay," he said again, softly. "It was a dream, that's all."

Slowly her vision cleared. She tried to laugh but could not quite make it.

"Do you want some water?" he asked.

She nodded, and he went to the kitchen to fetch it. When he returned she was staring up at the ceiling. She rose up on one elbow to take the glass and sipped the ice-cold liquid, which cut a path all the way to her stomach. She was wearing one of his shirts, and it slipped off her shoulder as she set the glass on the table next to the bed.

He touched her face, then leaned over to kiss her forehead. He hadn't intended to take it any further but, being so close, found it hard to pull himself away. He kissed her naked shoulder, hovered there, aware of the tension in her body. He wanted to love the fear right out of her. He moved closer.

"This isn't fair, Sam," she said.

He pulled away abruptly. "God!"

"I am too vulnerable, right now. You have no right."

"I know. Okay? I know."

"You keep on pushing yourself at me."

"Don't be ridiculous."

"It is true."

"You didn't have to come here."

"You invited me, remember? You said I could have a room to myself. That I could have all the peace I wanted."

"Yes."

"Well?"

"What?"

"So what do you think you're doing now?"

He sat on the bed, his back to her, shaking his head. "I don't know, okay? I'm sorry. I'm sorry. It's just so damn hard. You're crying in your sleep, and you look so incredible . . . and those bastards called again and . . ."

"What happened?" she demanded.

"They called again, just before you woke up." There was a silence. "I have it on tape," he said. "You want to hear it?"

They went through to the living room, and he replayed the tape.

"Sam. When he says it's dangerous?" she said urgently.

"What is it?"

"You know what you were trying to tell Wangai in Amboseli? When he asked what the equipment was for? I stopped you, but . . ."

"What?"

She shook her head as if she could not believe herself. "I only told him what we used the tape for most of the time. I did not tell him that the tape could also be used to attract bull elephants. Sam, that could be what they mean. What shall we do?"

"Don't know," he replied. "Tell Wangai." He crossed the room fast. "I feel so . . . helpless, you know. I can't do anything about any of this." He snatched up Jackman's file and gave it to Maya. "Here, look through that, see if any of these guys ring a bell."

He made coffee while she went through the file. She'd heard of some of the organizations but had no idea that the environmental movement in the industrial world had become so diffuse. She shook her head. "It is unbelievable."

Hawthorne said, "Not all of these organizations are particularly efficient. Some of them are probably phony moneymaking scams. Others might have less than a dozen members."

Maya put the file aside and picked up the coffee. She felt more comfortable. This was more like the way things had been before between her and Sam. She liked him best when he was concerned with some problem, outraged about some injustice, then he became animated, excited, and the relationship between them just flowed naturally.

"It is terrible," she said, "but I don't think we can do anything. What about Mr. Wangai? Do you think he knows what he's doing?"

Hawthorne shook his head. "Unless he's holding back, I haven't seen any indication that says he knows who or what he's looking for."

Hawthorne was sitting on the floor, his back to the fireplace, facing her. "I'm sorry," he said. "About what happened in there."

She smiled at him. It was her first real smile. "The coffee's good," she said, willing him not to spoil things.

He laughed, shook his head, "I won't bother you, okay? Scout's honor." He coughed, putting an end to the laugh. "You can stay as long as you want."

"I don't know, Sam. It's not fair you sleeping on the floor . . ."

"Damn right it's not fair. But there again, it's fine by me. Seriously. I'm glad."

She knew he was trying really hard. She just couldn't unravel what she felt about it, though she didn't want to shut him out altogether. She stood up. "Let's just take it one day at a time," she said.

He stood up as well, came close to her. "There's just one thing," he said, quietly.

"What's that?"

"I just want to give you a hug, that's all." He almost laughed.

She smiled. "If this is a trick . . ." she said.

159

"It's no trick." he said, sliding his arms around her waist, burying his face in her neck.

"There. That's not so bad is it?" he murmured.

"No," she whispered.

"Now I could get carried away just standing here, but I've given my word." He pulled away from her, looked at her face. Her eyes wouldn't meet his. He bent over, softly kissed her head, put his hands on her shoulders, leaning his forehead against hers.

"Anytime, huh?" Maya said.

He laughed. "You got it."

"I'll let you know," she murmured gently and went alone into the bedroom.

He was awakened by the phone again around nine-thirty, surprised that he'd slept so late. It was Wangai. "You were trying to get hold of me?"

"Yeah," said the journalist, "the man called again." He recited the message left on the answerphone. "Maya also had some ideas about the equipment they stole."

"Meet me in town, at the Thorn Tree," said the detective.

"You're sounding pretty pleased with yourself," said Hawthorne.

"I know who killed Kariuki."

CHAPTER SIXTEEN

THE DAY BEFORE, Wangai had come up to Nairobi soon after Hawthorne and the others. He'd gone over to HQ and found the place in an uproar. Crowds of police officers were standing outside the building, shouting, throwing their arms around each other. More lined the corridors, laughing, slapping backs and hands. Wangai discovered the cause of the disturbance. At the ten-thousand-meters final at the Olympic Games, Kenyan runners had taken all three medals. The winner was a policeman who'd got onto the Kenyan team after a spectacular performance during the annual Police Games.

Wangai shut his door on the racket and found the ballistics report on the Kipkoech killings which was lying on his desk. He'd been partially right about the *askari*'s wound. It had been caused by a bullet from a Makarov, though probably not from the same weapon that had killed Kariuki. Kipkoech had been the victim of an AK-47, which told Wangai practically nothing. The Russian weapons were almost as common as cattle in Africa.

Wangai also found a message waiting for him from Mwangi, the *matatu* driver from Mathare Valley. Mwangi wanted to see him right away. Wangai set off for River Road on foot. This was the quickest way to get across town, since it was late afternoon and the roads were choked with homebound traffic. Exhaust fumes had turned the air purple. Wangai bought a hot dog from a cart outside the office and joined the pedestrian flow, mustard and ketchup dribbling down his wrist as he fought for a space on the pavement and room to get the hot dog into his mouth. In the end he was forced to run along in the gutter where the fumes induced instant headache. Wangai took a handkerchief out of his pocket and held it over his mouth and nose, removing it only to bite chunks out of the hot dog.

By the time he reached River Road, the sweat was streaming down his face, making it shine like a polished walnut, and he felt like he'd been living on the streets for a week. He located Mwangi in a small bar, where Zairois rhythms jangled their insistent beat and the *matatu* driver hung moodily over a warm bottle of Tusker.

"I thought you were not coming," Mwangi said without greeting him. "I missed a trip to Thika this afternoon because of you. I hope it is worth it."

Wangai devoted the next ten minutes to coaxing information out of the wizened little man. Eventually Mwangi downed the last drop of Tusker and carelessly informed the detective that one of his brother drivers, who was a regular on the Mombasa-Nairobi route, had noticed a foreign woman in a red Mercedes sports car parked at a gas station near Voi on the day Kariuki was killed.

"What was she, European?" asked Wangai.

"Maybe," replied Mwangi. "He didn't say. He said foreign. Does it help?"

"I don't know," replied Wangai, "but it might."

"Then you tell me what you have done for Jazeen."

Wangai blushed a deeper shade of brown. "I will, I promise."

"You have forgotten her!" protested Mwangi, slamming a clenched fist onto the bar.

"No . . ."

"If you have forgotten, then that is you and me finished, I can tell you this."

"Cool it, Mwangi my friend, just slow down. I have to get these villains, you know that. I have hardly had time to breathe since I last saw you. This case is just running away with itself." Wangai sighed. "You know I am like a dog chasing his tail."

Mwangi smirked and then laughed. Wangai smiled as well, but he also knew that the words had some truth in them. For the last few days he'd done nothing but follow the trail laid by his adversaries. If he continued doing that, they would never be caught. One day the trail would smash into a dead end, and he would wake up and find them gone. He had to do something, seize the upper hand, take the initiative. The only way he could accomplish that was by following the clues they'd left behind by mistake, rather than the ones they kept ramming down his throat.

He stood up and clapped Mwangi on the back. "I don't forget my promises," he said. "I will try and help your sister. Just give me some time."

Mwangi shrugged.

Wangai ordered him another beer and left. He ran back to the office, which was even harder going since he was battling against the tide of humanity. When he got to headquarters the time was pushing six-thirty. Inside the office he grabbed the phone book and started dialing car hire firms, beginning with those located in Mombasa. It took a long time. Connections did not always succeed and he got several wrong numbers. Some companies had closed down for the night, though others remained open twenty-four hours, ready to pick up custom from the tourist arrivals who flew into the coastal resort day and night. Finally, he got lucky. A small up-market company called South Coast Rentals had leased a red Mercedes sports car to a young woman the day before the Kariuki killings. The car had been handed back in Nairobi the day after. The car, as far as the woman at South Coast Rentals knew, was still in the Nairobi area. She'd taken the booking herself and was able to describe the leasee as a dark-haired woman with Oriental features called Denise Soto, who'd given her address as the Hilton Hotel in Nairobi.

Wangai put Jenkins Odenge, his young assistant, on the task of tracking the car down. It took most of the night. Michael Odile from forensics then inspected the vehicle and confirmed that the match with the tire prints at the scene of Kariuki's murder was close, though as a piece of evidence it was slim. Unfortunately, the car had been spring cleaned since Soto had used it, so they were unable to pick up any prints or other evidence.

163

Wangai, meanwhile, contacted the Hilton and came up with a negative on Denise Soto. No one of that name or matching her description appeared to have stayed at the hotel recently. He turned to the yellow pages and started calling every hotel in town, asking if they had any guests called Soto or who looked like her. He got lucky again when he called the Norfolk. Denise Soto had stayed there for a couple of weeks, around the time of the Kariuki murders.

Wangai called Dennis Forsythe, general manager of the Norfolk. Forsythe was about to retire for the night and wasn't pleased about being disturbed or about Wangai's request for access to visitor records, staff names, and duty rosters.

"Mr. Forsythe," the detective said, coaxingly, "you can either be known as someone lending his full cooperation to the police, or else I can call the Daily Nation right now and let them know you are hindering our investigations."

"But you don't have a warrant," protested Forsythe. "You are supposed to have a warrant."

"A warrant takes time, Mr. Forsythe," said Wangai. "I don't have time. Of course, I can get a warrant, but I can also ask friends of mine at the Immigration Office to investigate whether you truly deserve your work permit."

"This is outrageous!"

"Please, Mr. Forsythe?" said Wangai.

In the end, Forsythe was charm and helpfulness embodied (he'd spent half a lifetime perfecting those traits in his personality). He met Wangai at the hotel, put a desk clerk at the detective's disposal, threw open his record books, and ordered that Wangai should be supplied with as much coffee and sandwiches as he could consume.

"I really appreciate this," Wangai told him.

"Glad to be of assistance," beamed Forsythe, without the slightest trace of resentment in his tone. A true professional, Wangai thought to himself.

Examining Soto's hotel booking form, Wangai noticed a scrawl on the back, which said, "occupancy extended during client absence." The desk clerk explained. The guest had left the hotel for three days in the middle of her stay. The break coincided exactly with the Kariukis weekend trip to the coast, from which they'd never returned. Apparently, Soto had called the hotel and said she'd decided to take a spur-of-the-moment journey to Lake Baringo in the north of the country. It took Wangai a while to get confirmation that no one called Denise Soto, or answering to her description, had checked into any of the Baringo hotels during that weekend. Wangai knew anyway that Soto had been in Mombasa. The car rental proved it.

He obtained the address of the woman responsible for cleaning Soto's room and sent a police car over to bring her in for questioning. The big woman arrived in a state, her hair in curlers covered with a plastic bag, her ear lobes tied up in knots for the night.

"I haven't done nothin'," she snapped in Kiswahili. "I don't take nothin' from the rooms, and they's lying if that's what they's sayin'."

"Relax, mother," Wangai told her, sitting her down in an armchair and asking the desk clerk to fetch some tea and cakes.

"Humh," snorted the woman, shuffling back in the armchair, holding her handbag close like it was a precious child.

"Young cops don't know politeness," Wangai said, sitting on the edge of the desk.

"They come in an' snatch me up. People talking," she said.

"You did nothing wrong," said Wangai.

"That's what I said."

"But I need your help, mother," said Wangai, watching her closely. Her eyes flicked towards him, then shot back gloomily to the clasp of her handbag. "You clean Room 54," he said, and went on to talk about Soto.

The cleaner remembered her well. Skinny. Hardly left the room.

"Mother," Wangai asked, "would you know this Denise Soto if you saw her again?"

The old woman bit into an angel cake and chewed slowly, moving the flesh of the cake around her mouth. Swallowing, she said, "I know that woman. I always know her."

Wangai went to the door and called the desk clerk over.

"Have you got any rooms free?" he asked.

"Two or three," replied the clerk.

"Could you put the old woman in one. I'm going to need her later."

The clerk breathed in sharply, gazing beyond Wangai to the maid who was noisily slurping her tea. He looked back at the detective. Wangai smiled, raising his eyebrows expectantly.

The clerk laughed. "Right. I'll give her a room."

"Good," snapped Wangai, clapping his hands together. He swung around to the old woman. "Mother, tonight you are a queen. You go and rest yourself." He bundled the woman to her feet and pushed her and the tea trolley out into the corridor.

The clerk was waiting. "Madam," he said, "if you would follow me, please." He took the trolley, and the old woman followed, clutching her handbag to her chest, the other fat hand patting the plastic bag that covered her hair curlers.

Wangai shut the door and clapped his hands together again. He was onto something. Soto could have been following the Kariukis. Why would she change her plans so suddenly and then lie about them? And, if she'd had the Wildlife Service boss under surveillance at the coast, she must have been staying somewhere close by. He started calling hotels on the south coast, beginning with Trade Winds where the Kariukis had stayed on their last weekend. He struck out with Denise Soto. No one of that name had stayed in the hotel. He asked to speak to the desk clerks who'd been on duty that weekend, but they worked the day shift and would not be at the hotel until six the next morning. He would have to call back later. He spent the next hour calling other south coast hotels, with no better luck.

Frustrated, he put a call through to the Deputy Director of Immigration. Everyone entering the country was recorded by video cameras positioned at all the immigration booths, and the DDI, a man called Joseph Kasigi, had responsibility for the tapes. Wangai could tell from Kasigi's tone that he was not used to being disturbed with official matters at home in the middle of the night. He was anything but helpful. Wangai tried the same tactic he'd used on Forsythe and suggested that he would have to let the press know that the DDI was personally holding up investigations into the murder of David Kariuki. After this Kasigi backtracked fast.

"Of course," he told Wangai, "we are always very happy to help the police, only you must understand that we cannot be held responsible for the incompetence of others."

"What others?" sighed Wangai, waiting for the usual cartload of excuses and blame-laying that every government official dragged around.

"These fools at the airport," hissed Kasigi. "They do not check their equipment." Apparently, the airport had been afflicted by a series of power cuts lately. Although the generator usually kicked in to supply essential services, the videotaping system had not been linked to the emergency circuit. Whole flight-loads of visitors had been missed.

Wangai checked the date Denise Soto had booked into the Norfolk, and asked Kasigi if there had been a power cut that day. Kasigi didn't know, but he promised to send someone over to Immigration right away to check it out.

Wangai thought about calling his wife but decided to leave it until morning. He snatched an hour's sleep on the office couch until he was awakened by the desk clerk. A call had come through from Immigration. They had something for him to see. Wangai went over to Haile Selassie Avenue, taking the old maid with him. It was just after 4 a.m.

The airport tapes were complete for the day that Soto had checked into the Norfolk. But according to the computer record, no one of that name had entered the country that day. Wangai considered that she might have come into the country through another port of entry or on a different day, or maybe she'd used an alias. He asked for the records to be searched for all ports of entry for the preceding week. Meanwhile, Wangai took the maid to a small room equipped with a television and VCR, and slotted in tape after tape of endless lines of visitors, hoping that she would eventually ID one of them as Soto. Three hours later, at seven o'clock, the woman let out a thin, high-pitched yelp of recognition. Wangai, who'd been dozing in an armchair beside her, leapt to his feet with a start.

"It is her," shouted the maid, "I know her. I know her anywhere!"

It took a few minutes to link the video image to the computer record, which identified the woman as Janice Lee, a citizen of Singapore. Wangai

167

queried the old woman. Perhaps she'd become so bored watching the tapes that Janice Lee had been picked out of convenience. The old woman was adamant, however. It was definitely Denise Soto up there on the television. Wangai began to believe her after he called back to Trade Winds Hotel and found that a Janice Lee had checked into the hotel the same weekend as Kariuki and his wife.

Wangai felt good, really good. Janice Lee-Denise Soto, or Lee-Soto as he came to call her (like the African country Lesotho), felt close enough to smell, all the way down to the expensive perfume he was sure she must be wearing. He wished he felt the same about the men who had helped her attack Kipkoech and the Amboseli camp. They were still completely invisible.

Wangai wanted to get a photographic print of Lee-Soto from the videotape right away. It was a setback to learn that the Immigration Department's own video-photo printer was out of action, and the only place where the job could be done was at a small film studio, out in Banana Hill, that was run by an eccentric expatriate. It would take at least half a day to get the print from him, even if he was at home and sober enough to deal with it right away. In the meantime, Wangai had to get roadblocks set up, circulate Lee-Soto's description, and, as soon as they were available, distribute the photographs to police stations and border posts throughout the country. He went back to police HQ to work out a plan, checked in with his wife, and called Hawthorne.

CHAPTER SEVENTEEN

ONG'S JUICE FACTORY was situated on an apparently ordinary residential street in the heart of Mombasa's Chinese Quarter. The main entrance was via a massive, solid double gate that led to an enclosed yard and warehouse. The warehouse contained the bottling plant for blended passionfruit, pineapple, and orange juices. Wong had twenty legal employees, most of them women from the neighborhood, who overlooked the three production lines. From dawn to dusk, six days a week, small clattering bottles jiggled along the droning, thumping conveyor belts to the carousels, which pumped them full of sweet nectar, then slapped the caps on. They were packed by hand into wooden crates, most of them stamped for export to the Middle East.

The warehouse was situated on the right of the yard, inside the main gate. On the left of the gate the factory wall merged into a line of terraced houses. Wong owned half a dozen of these, and the facade was misleading. Walls inside had been knocked down, creating a warren of dusty rooms and hallways that stretched from the factory as far as his own house, halfway along the street. A hidden door on the upper floor led directly into Wong's bedroom. He'd shown it to Zhu and Silvia, the first day they arrived in Mombasa.

Gerry Wong was a short, stocky, moon-faced man of around forty. He'd been living in Kenya five years, ever 169 since he'd purchased his citizenship at one of the Hong Kong emigration fairs which had been commonplace towards the end of British rule. He said he'd made a pile of money in Africa and one day soon would be checking out of the place. In the meantime, he had to keep a low profile to avoid exciting the envy of his fellow Kenyans. He appeared to live simply. Even his wife, he told them, had to wear rubbishy polyester clothes, when upstairs she had a closet stacked with designer dresses she used whenever they traveled abroad. Mrs. Wong giggled when he told them this. She was a plain woman with a curved spine and low self-esteem, evident in her frequent, fleeting smiles, which were mainly directed at the floor.

The night that Silvia's picture was first broadcast, she was alone in the Wong's living room watching television. Like the rest of the house, the room was simply and cheaply furnished with plastic furniture and a linoleum floor. The walls were pale blue, and the ceiling fan did little to stir the stifling air. Silvia had been drinking. A bottle of scotch stood next to her glass on the coffee table. She'd been drifting in and out of the movie, hardly following the plot. Nothing had changed between her and Zhu. There was the same hard distance between them that she'd been sensing ever since the rape incident. He seemed to be watching her constantly and even now, when he was in the next room playing poker with the others, she could feel his malevolent presence, as real as if he were right beside her.

Her mind clouded with drink, she did not realize at first that the movie had been replaced by a newsflash or that she was looking at her own face on the screen. Then she heard the voice telling anyone who saw or knew the whereabouts of Denise Soto or Janice Lee to notify the police immediately.

"Do not approach this woman yourself," the voice warned. "She is extremely dangerous." Then the whole thing was repeated all over again in Kiswahili.

She jumped up, upsetting the glass, and slammed the Off button as if that would shut the voice up for good. She swung around, searching for anyone else who might have seen it. The murmuring voices of the men drifted across the hall. She heard Jimmy laughing at something. She was alone, but the living room felt like a trap and she fled to the kitchen.

She pulled a jug of ice water from the fridge and, hands shaking, poured herself a glass. How could they know? How had they found out? Her first thought was that Zhu must have been responsible; maybe he'd given her away again. She drank the water, but her throat was too tense and she almost choked over it. She stood over the sink, chest heaving, not realizing that Zhu had followed her and was standing in the doorway, watching. When he said, "Hey, babe," she dropped the water glass. It bounced on the drainer and crashed onto the floor, showering the place with thousands of tiny fragments.

"Huh . . ." he said, half a laugh and half a question, looking at the glass. "What are you doing? I thought you were watching a movie. I heard the TV switch off."

"I . . . it was garbage, you know. I . . . er . . . better get this cleaned up." She stared at the floor.

"What's wrong?"

"Nothing." Sharp eyes, looking up.

"You look funny."

She smiled, lips quivering slightly; she felt them and tried a laugh to disguise it. "What do you mean I look funny? I'm up to my ankles in glass."

"You going to come through and give me some luck around the table then?"

"I'm feeling tired. I've got a headache." She pressed her lips together, then said, "You always win anyway, don't you?"

He grinned. "Sure, babe, and don't you ever forget it." He slapped the door frame and left. She listened to him cross the living room, footsteps tapping across the linoleum and into the hall beyond.

She found a broom to clean up the glass, her thoughts muddled by drink and fear. It wasn't possible, she told herself, that Zhu had given her away this time. He would not purposely draw the police to himself. She was still here, wasn't she? Furiously, she shoved the broom over the floor and for a moment she thought that maybe she'd been wrong about him. She'd been behaving badly, hadn't she? If she just made up to him he'd probably get her out of this mess. After all, she'd killed Kariuki for him.

171

She stopped sweeping, leaned on the broom, and realized that she'd virtually had a premonition that things would go wrong. That was why she'd been trying to get out of Kenya ever since the Kariuki hit, but every time she'd tried to save herself, Zhu had blocked her.

Her stomach rolled over. So why did she think he would help her now? Could she really ignore everything that had happened in Macao? Was she a fool or something?

It was pathetic. It was almost as bad as hiding behind a dead man.

She pushed the brush against the glass, shoving hard, sending fragments flying into the air. She had to escape and she had to do it alone, but she hated to think of stepping outside the door when her picture was everywhere. She wanted to hide, crawl inside a hole, but it couldn't happen here. She couldn't hide at Wong's. As soon as Zhu found out about the newsflash, he would see her as a threat, wouldn't he? She was the only one identified by the police.

She remembered what he'd said once. "Why trust a man when you can kill him? It gets rid of all the aggravation." Zhu would kill her. He would not risk "the aggravation" of even allowing her to attempt an escape.

That was the moment the panic began to subside. She got on with the job of sweeping the glass into a neat pile, pushing it into a pan and dropping it into the garbage can under the sink. She walked back through the living room, not looking at the blank-faced television that sat like an enemy in the corner. She was the same way before she did a job; numb and set apart from everyone, walking the edge of a precipice that was a line between life and death, only this time it was *her* life and *her* death. She moved into the hall, not looking through the open door to the room where the men played poker, though she felt Zhu's eyes piercing her back.

Upstairs, she entered the Wongs' bedroom. Mrs. Wong had gone out hours ago. Gerry was downstairs with the other men. It was in this room that the Wongs embraced their secret lives. The place smelled of sweet perfume. The walls were covered with red brocade, the floor with a dark red carpet, and the bed draped with a black satin spread, a dragon embroidered in its center. There was an antique dresser, a tall bookcase,

172

and a large wardrobe. The windows were closed, but the air conditioning made it an icebox in comparison to the rest of the house. She shivered, crossing the room to the massive wardrobe, pulling open the doors and finding rows of Gerry Wong's suits inside, some of them expensive. She found also Mrs. Wong's designer robes, but she ignored these, hunting through the closet until she found the polyester dresses, which were folded up in one of the drawers. She took one of them and also a nylon blouse, a faded flowery skirt, a headscarf, a pair of worn sandals and stuffed all of it into a plastic bag.

She moved to the dresser, hunting for scissors which she found in one of the side drawers. At the back of this same drawer she discovered a roll of shillings, which she took. She opened the next drawer and pushed her hand to the back, thinking more money might be hidden in there. There was none, but her hand closed on the barrel of a small gun. She gasped, pulling out the gun. It was no more than a kid's plaything really. Zhu had not let her anywhere near a gun since Amboseli. She dragged the entire drawer off its runners, setting it on the ground, hunted through it, and found a small box containing five bullets. She smiled as if she'd met an old friend. Then she replaced the drawer, closed the closet, grabbed the bag of booty, and slipped onto the landing.

Men's voices floated up through the stairwell, wrapping around her like a sticky web. She fled into the bedroom she and Zhu used, which lacked the furnishings of the Wongs' room but shared its claustrophobia. She tossed the plastic bag onto the lumpy bed, grabbed the scissors, pulled a pin out of her hair so that it tumbled loose down her back, and was already hacking wads off it as she crossed the room to the mirror. This was badly tarnished and sent back a speckled image, but she studied her eyes, pouring prayers into them as locks of her hair fell all around until her head was as scrawny as a chicken's. It was a mutilation, a cleansing. She removed every trace of make-up, slipped out of the soft cotton shirt, and removed her bra so that her breasts, large and slightly pendulous, hung free. She put the bra into the plastic bag with her shirt, shoes, make-up, and skirt, then stopped for a moment. There was one more passport with an alias she hadn't used yet, 173 but Zhu had that, kept it in his leather satchel. He even slept on that satchel, putting it under his pillow at night, and right now it was with him downstairs. She would have to go without it.

Wearing the polyester dress and sandals, clutching the plastic bag, and smelling slightly of Mrs. Wong's sweet perfume, she moved to the door. She opened it a fraction and was preparing to move onto the landing when she heard footsteps on the stairs. She clutched the gun, now loaded, and the piece sweated in her palm. If it was Zhu, she might be lost, but at least she could get him first.

It was Mrs. Wong, which was just as bad. Silvia had been planning to go back to the Wongs' room and escape through the hidden door into the warehouse warren beyond. Leaving by any other exit meant passing the room where Zhu was playing poker, and that door was open. Of course, he might only catch a glimpse of her and think she was Mrs. Wong if she tied the headscarf over her head, but he might not.

She watched Mrs. Wong enter her bedroom. The gun sat in her hand. She could exit through the hidden door anyway, though maybe she'd have to kill Mrs. Wong on the way. She fell back against the wall. She didn't want to do that.

It was hard descending those stairs, the voices getting louder, the threat of discovery filling the hot hallway. She stepped cautiously, carefully, and sank back in panic against the wall when Jimmy stepped into the hall and crossed over to the bathroom. Even with her pores oozing fear, even with the way he'd been behaving with Sen, with his weakness and failings and the trouble in Amboseli, Silvia was suddenly filled with remorse over Jimmy. She'd brought him into this and she was abandoning him. She felt bad, too, that she couldn't trust him. It hadn't even occurred to her to go to him for help, and she could not risk him seeing her now.

She heard the toilet flush and saw the shadow of Jimmy crossing the hall. He reentered the game-room, and she realized, as she moved down the stairway, that he'd closed the door behind him, as if he'd known that she needed him to do that. Quickly she moved down the hall, turned the handle, and stepped out into the street.

She practiced an anonymous walk, shoulders slumped, eyes cast down, resisting the powerful temptation to look around and see if anyone was watching, only glancing up occasionally to check the path ahead. A couple of young African men were hanging around outside Wong's factory doors, and she thought they probably worked for him. They might have seen her leave Wong's house. She steeled herself as she passed them, but they said nothing. Why should they? She looked like nobody.

At the corner she turned left, following the road that led up the side of the factory. It was around nine, and people up here, away from the somber presence of Wong's factory, were sitting on the streets, their doors and windows wide open. Some of them even watched the television from outside, leaning in through the windows. She heard the newsflash repeated and shrank deeper into the polyester dress.

She walked out of the Chinese Quarter and into an Indian neighborhood, where children drove remote-control cars across the streets and the night was flavored with cumin and coriander. Old men and women dressed in white sat on dining chairs on the pavements. Some of them greeted her. She had no idea where she was going, but when she reached the main road and found a small guest house, she knew she had to go inside. She needed a place to think about what to do next.

The guest house proprietor was an Indian. He was watching television and hardly glanced at her when she asked for a room. She handed over the money, signed his book, and took the key. He nodded towards the stairs. "Second Floor, third door on the left, bathroom at the end of the hall," he muttered and turned back to the screen.

The room was pitiful, smelled stale and damp. She opened the windows and drew the sheets off the bed to air it. She emptied the plastic bag, hung up her clothes, and put the gun in a drawer. She took out the rest of Mrs. Wong's money and counted it. It came to just less than ten-thousand shillings. It wasn't a lot. She should have been more worried. She should have felt crazy about all the people that were looking for her—the police, Zhu, the Wongs—but she didn't. She was free.

CHAPTER EIGHTEEN

I T WAS RAINING the following morning when Wangai and his wife left their house to attend the memorial service for the Kariukis. At the Nairobi Baptist Church they were mobbed by reporters. Rain-soaked faces shouted at them through the windows of the Volkswagen. His wife looked alarmed.

"What do these people want?"

Wangai shook his head. "Ignore them. I have nothing to say."

With Lee-Soto's picture plastered all over the morning newspapers and broadcast hourly on television, he'd become a celebrity. Wangai had tried to play down the apparent motives of the Enemies of Man, but the newspapers were full of it. Local editorials raged against outside interference in the ivory trade vote coming up before Parliament.

Wangai edged his way out of the car, raising his hands in protection, as if he were fending off blows rather than questions. Raindrops splashed all over his Sunday suit as he struggled to put up his umbrella.

Vanna Deacon was standing under a vast candy-striped umbrella. She shouted, "Any progress in the case?"

He shook his head, moving with difficulty around the car because of the flashbulbs and questions and crush of people. He pleaded with them but it didn't have much impact. He held the umbrella up while his wife stepped   177 out of the car in her funeral clothes. Huddled together, they walked to the church. Wangai thought, if this is the kind of attention Kamau relishes, then he can keep it.

The choir was already singing a slow, moving hymn of regret and praise. Clad in deep purple from throat to floor, they swayed gently from side to side to the mournful rhythm. The church was packed. He escorted his wife to a pew at the back, aware of people turning in their seats to look at him. Some of them smiled, others looked downright aggressive. He tried to be unaffected and concentrated instead on the large photographs of David and Helen Kariuki, suspended on each side of the pulpit and draped in black cloth.

A blast of motorcycle sirens cut through the singing of the choir, which subsided into a gentle murmur as the president and his wife entered the church. Once they were settled in a front pew, the service began. Kariuki's pastor led the prayers for David and Helen, and then the eulogies began. While people stood up to pay tribute to the Kariukis, Wangai realized he felt a lot better knowing he was closer to catching the person who had put them in their grave. No matter what, she would not escape.

The choir launched into a resurrection hymn that left their faces glistening with sweat and their bodies moving frantically to the rhythm under their flowing robes. Their voices rose to the roof and even convinced Wangai for a moment that there had to be a God out there somewhere. He was brought down to earth by the hiss of Jenkins Odenge whispering in his ear. Wangai turned round. Odenge beckoned. Wangai leaned towards his wife. "I have to go." He handed over the keys to the Volkswagen.

When Wangai stood up it caused a stir. Whispers spread around the church, eyes turned on him. He pulled himself erect, forcing himself to walk sedately; once in the porch, the two policemen had to shout over the din of the rain, which was still thundering on the tin roof.

"There is a woman who has been calling to talk to you," Jenkins spluttered. "She has called a dozen times this morning, a real *memsahib*. She will not speak to anyone else."

They drove in Odenge's vehicle to police headquarters. Wangai called the woman. "Mrs. Henderson?" he enquired.

"That is correct," she replied, plums in her voice.

"This is Detective Wangai. Could you give me your address?"

"The Ivies, Loresho," she said primly.

Wangai could imagine it. An English house with a gabled roof and a garden of watered lawns and rosebushes.

Mrs. Henderson explained that she also owned a house in Langata. She was sure she'd rented it only ten days ago to the woman suspected of killing Kariuki, though the woman had used a different name, Silvia Tianshui. Wangai took down the Langata address and the new alias.

"Listen," said Mrs. Henderson, "I don't want you people going in there and making a mess of the place. If you do I shall hold you personally responsible, Wangai."

Henderson's tone was very condescending and revealed a massive superiority complex. Wangai might have cared, except he knew people like her were dinosaurs. Once, their kind had ruled the world, and that had been a very trying experience, but they were a dying species, all but extinct.

It was possible that Lee-Soto and her gang were still occupying the Langata house, armed with their Makarov pistols, AK-47s, and whatever else. They'd even used explosives to wreck the Amboseli camp. Such weaponry far outranked the tools of the police department. Wangai spoke to the chief of the Special Forces Unit on the phone. The chief asked for a reconnaissance of the house before sending his men in, and Wangai agreed to organize it.

Within the hour, two men equipped with a Nairobi City Council cart tended the roadside verges outside the Henderson house. A female operative, apparently a maid in the house across the street, set up a flirtatious conversation with the weeders slowing their work and giving them plenty of time to observe the house. Another man went in as a gardener next door, with a brief to keep the rear of the Henderson house under observation.

After a while they were able to report to Wangai that the place was completely quiet, probably empty.

Wangai was depressed. Lee-Soto had already flown but that did not stop 179 the SFU, which went into action assuming a "worst possible" scenario. Men were despatched to the far side of the gully and approached the house from the rear. A second group dodged behind walls, gates, bushes, and giant plant pots, creeping up on the front door. A shout came from inside and the front door slowly opened. In the entrance stood the rear assault team, their weapons hanging limply at their sides.

Maya was sitting on the porch of Hawthorne's house. Yellow streaks of light cut the sky beyond the Ngong Hills. The rain had finally stopped and left the garden glistening in the dusk light. Water slipped from leaf to leaf before dropping onto the ground, giving the atmosphere a soothing, liquid feel.

She'd returned to the house after the memorial service for the Kariukis. Hawthorne had remained in town to follow up on some work at the office. It was the first time she'd been alone since the attack on the Amboseli camp.

Since that first night Sam hadn't pushed himself on her, though she could still see the demand in his eyes and feel it in the way he sometimes took her arm, as if he were taking possession of her. In the old days things had been different. He'd just been glad of her presence, but now, he seemed to have a need of her which was almost intimidating. She felt that she lived on shifting ground, where nothing remained constant, especially her own feelings. Sometimes she felt like throwing herself at Sam, and was unsure what held her back, except that she hated herself like this, hated the vulnerability, hated whatever it was in her that made her feel so desperate.

She'd had more nightmares; dark, surreal visions that didn't quite make sense, that left her feeling anxious because something vital had been left undone, and she was the only one who could fix it, yet she didn't know what to do or where to begin. The dreams were about the elephants, of course, and everything that had been lost, years of data destroyed, years and years of effort wasted, no camp, no equipment. There was nothing to go back to.

She wanted everything to be the way it had been before, but did she have the strength even to imagine starting again? Even if she tried, it would take thousands of dollars and it would never be the same. Judith wouldn't be there. She was going back to the States. Wanja was back at her mother's home in Jamhuri. They'd spoken on the phone that day. Wanja had tried to joke, but her voice had betrayed her as a very frightened woman. Margaret Okech had taken the train back to her parent's farm in Nyanza Province, and Maya had heard nothing from her since. Solomon's family had taken his body home to Loitokitok for burial.

The phone rang inside the house. Maya was glad, hoping it was Sam. She wanted him to come back, distract her from this depression. She'd had enough of her own company. When she heard someone else on the line, a man, she became intensely suspicious, so much so that her hand gripped the receiver and her heart began to beat faster.

"When do you think he'll be back?" said the voice.

"I . . . er . . . any time now. Who are . . . what is your name? I can tell him you called."

"You tell first. What's your name?"

She didn't answer. She couldn't even think fast enough to lie.

"Is that Maya Saito?"

She swallowed. It was the way he said her name.

"That is Maya, isn't it?" He sounded triumphant. "I'm so glad to talk to you. Listen, I was so sorry about your camp. All that work wasted."

"What do you want?" she whispered.

"Well, now, I have a message."

Silence. She didn't speak either. She couldn't.

"Don't you want to know what it is?"

"Who are you?" she screamed.

The man laughed. "Have you ever thought what could happen if that tape fell into the wrong hands?"

She caught her breath. "Why are you doing this?"

"Oh, I'm just going to teach you a very serious lesson, Dr. Saito. I guess I'll be seeing you in Tsavo East. By the way," he laughed again, "we are the Enemies of Man."

She was too shocked to speak. She could hear his breath on the line.

"Do you hear me?" he asked.

She swallowed with a dry mouth. "Who are you?"

He laughed and hung up.

For a moment she did nothing, just stood there, holding the phone, until she sensed its contamination and dropped it. She felt invaded, abused; the man had dug right inside her. She felt sick. Grabbing the phone again, she quickly called Sam's paging number.

Hawthorne picked up Wangai on the way. The detective was still wearing the suit he'd put on for Kariuki's memorial service, and it was now looking crumpled and stained. He'd been at the Langata house much of the day. They had one set of prints, which matched those found on Kariuki's Peugeot. He also had news for Hawthorne. His jeep had turned up in Voi. It had been stripped down and abandoned, but at least it was there.

They found Maya pacing the floor, and furious. She swung round on them as they walked in the door.

"What the hell is he talking about? I cannot stand this. You have got to do something. *We* have got to do something!"

"We are," Wangai replied. "I called the warden of Tsavo East already. There have not been any incidents there yet, but I have sent down an SFU force, which should get there in about three or four hours. What did this man sound like? What did he say exactly?"

The conversation had not been recorded, but she went over it carefully and remembered a lot. As a professional observer, Maya was used to studying and analyzing everything that went on around her, whether it was a sound, a smell, or something barely glimpsed.

Afterwards, she said, "I just can't stand sitting here waiting for something to happen. I want to do something. I want to go to Tsavo myself, right now." She stood up, ready to leave.

"Hold on, Maya," said Hawthorne.

"I don't think you should . . ." said Wangai.

"I'm going. You can't stop me." Her eyes widened. "You are going to Tsavo, aren't you?" The two men exchanged glances. "Shit!"

"It isn't a good idea," said Wangai. "Maybe they have something personal against you. You could get hurt."

"I could get hurt anywhere, here as well."

"I didn't think you were ready," said Hawthorne. "You've been through a lot. It's better you get stronger before . . ."

"Listen to you!" she shouted at them. "Just listen to the two of you! This is my neck, my project, and listen to you two . . ."

Hawthorne smiled; he could not help himself.

"What are you grinning at?" she yelled at him. "It's time we left."

CHAPTER NINETEEN

T HERE WAS ONLY one airstrip in Tsavo East, the one that served the Sutcliffe Institute. The people there had been warned to expect a night flight. The police Cessna bounced over the grassy strip between the flares. Hawthorne, Wangai, and Maya stepped out of the aircraft into a cacophonous celebration of the night. The sound shook Maya to the bone. It was so familiar, so necessary to her existence. She stood still beside the aircraft, just listening to the night, her eyes welling with tears.

"Maya?" said Hawthorne. "Are you okay?"

She nodded.

Owen Sutcliffe and the Park Warden of Tsavo, a beefy Kikuyu with military bearing called Kinyanjui, had driven over to meet them. Maya had not seen Sutcliffe for a while. She stiffened as he approached. Zoologically speaking, they did not get along. He was too much of a showman, he'd supported Kariuki over the Amboseli cull, and he was a known ivory trade sympathizer.

He came straight at her, ignoring Wangai and Hawthorne, throwing his arms wide open, wanting to commiserate. There was no way to back off. She let him embrace her, smelt his overstrong after-shave, and heard him whisper, "You and I have to talk."

She shrugged him off. There wasn't much she wanted to discuss with Owen Sutcliffe.

He held out his hand to Hawthorne, "Sam."

Hawthorne did not take it. He was thinking about the week he'd spent in a Nairobi cell. "You people down here definitely landed me in a heap of shit."

Owen shook his head, "That isn't fair, Sam. We were not to blame. We have to talk about it. Right now we have other work to do down here, don't we?"

They drove to the institute and gathered in Sutcliffe's house, where Wangai filled them in on everything they knew about the Enemies of Man. Kinyanjui got on the radio to his gatemen to check on which vehicles had entered the park that day. Nothing unusual was reported. Twenty vehicles had entered the park, and all but three had left already. The occupants of these vehicles were booked into the Lodge.

Kinyanjui said, "Look, I can organize a search of the park right away, but you have to tell me what we are looking for."

Everyone turned to Maya. "We do not know exactly. What the man said on the phone was that he would show us what could happen if that tape fell into the wrong hands. If they have any way of operating the equipment, if they know what they are doing . . ."

"Which would not be difficult," interrupted Sutcliffe.

She shot an angry look at him.

"Really . . ." complained Sutcliffe, holding up his hands.

Maya mellowed slightly. "It is true, the project has been widely publicized and several detailed articles have appeared. Anyway, if they set the gear up properly, it may attract several bull elephants."

"How many?" asked Kinyanjui.

"Three, four, a dozen, maybe even more, maybe none. I don't know. It depends how many bulls there are within a six-mile radius of the equipment."

"And they could do this," said Wangai, "to trap the elephants and harm them?"

Maya did not say anything, but the reply was in her eyes. She could not imagine anything worse.

Kinyanjui sighed. "Well, unless something is definitely happening out there, it is going to be pretty hard for us to find anything. We'll try, though." He stood up. So did Maya and Hawthorne.

"Mind if I come along as well?" asked Wangai.

Kinyanjui shrugged his assent. In the end they all drove back to the airstrip, where a twin-engined aircraft and a helicopter had landed. The Tsavo crew came equipped with night-vision goggles that helped them search the park for illegal movements after dark. Some after-dark game drives were permitted to operate under special license, provided they gave advance notice of their intended route to the authorities. That way, any night activity picked up by the pilots could be radioed back to the station for clarification, before they arranged an interception. Two rangers flew with each pilot. The doors had been taken off both machines to allow easier vision of the ground, so all the air crew wore woolen hats, scarves, and thick jackets. They flew at little more than a hundred feet above ground most of the time, but it was still cold.

Kinyanjui spread out a map of Tsavo East on the hood of his vehicle, while one of his men held up a powerful flashlight. He allocated transects to be flown by the pilots and then got on the radio to dispatch ground crew to strategic points in the park to await further instruction. He accomplished all of this with a speed and efficiency that impressed Wangai. The detective told the warden that the SFU would also be arriving soon and might be able to take over from some of the rangers. Kinyanjui was almost offended.

"I think we can handle this matter without outside interference," he said. Kinyanjui went off with his driver to join the search while the others returned to the institute. If anything was discovered, they would be called by radio. Sutcliffe had a car and driver ready to take Wangai, Hawthorne, and Maya anywhere they needed to go.

At Sutcliffe's house, Wangai settled down to rest in an easy chair. Hawthorne and Maya went outside to the veranda, and Sutcliffe followed, forcing his company on them. For a while, none of them said anything. They sat in silence, listening to the grunting of hippos, a sonorous bass to the shrill ring of the crickets. Then Sutcliffe sighed, looked at Maya, and said, "You don't like me much, do you?"

Maya looked away, embarrassed.

"Oh, I understand. It's my bad taste," said Sutcliffe. "I'm full of it. 'Adopt a   187

Hippo,' 'Giraffe Circuses.' I'm a whore. I have such an uncouth reputation for raising money, as your boyfriend here pointed out."

"Excuse me . . ." interrupted Maya.

"Boyfriend? No, did I say that? Must have been something I saw. You two have such a . . . packaged look. Anyway, I'll do anything to bring in the money to keep this place going. It costs a lot."

"What're you getting at?" said Hawthorne. "You know neither of us are much in the mood for this right now."

"All right, I'll get to the point. Maya, when are you going back to work?" She didn't answer.

"You are going back, aren't you?" Sutcliffe said, leaning towards her, his elbows resting on his knees.

Hawthorne watched her. She looked closed in, unresponsive. He said, "Give it a rest, Sutcliffe. She's been through a lot."

"Sam!" she said.

"What?"

"Don't speak for me."

"Okay, I'm sorry, answer the man. Are you going back?"

"I don't know," she snapped.

Sutcliffe sat back in his chair. His legs, covered with black hair, stretched out comfortably towards Hawthorne, one foot resting on top of the other. "Well, I can't blame you, but you know someone has to carry on. It is vitally important work. If we can't understand the modes of existence and communication between creatures on our own planet, how will we begin to understand what is happening when we encounter other life forms in outer space?"

Hawthorne laughed. "You're not serious."

"I am."

Hawthorne laughed again, and Maya smiled.

She said, "You mean, I am taking an extraterrestrial language course?" She laughed as well.

Hawthorne thought, Sutcliffe is a bear, but this is good for her. He's taking her mind off whatever is happening out there.

Sutcliffe wasn't daunted. "You can laugh. I don't mind. In fact it is a very sexy publicity angle. I've got a few more. How about elephant tapes? Totally soundless infrasonic elephant tapes. Get the tapes donated by one of the big record companies, sell them blank for twenty dollars apiece. Tell people they're buying a recording of the mating song of a female elephant."

Maya shook her head.

"No?" said Owen, "Okay I've got another one. The Zimbabweans claim they have thirty-five-thousand elephants too many. We raise the money to have the whole lot relocated to the Selous in Tanzania. You know that place has a quarter the elephants it once had. It's a chunk of prime pachyderm real estate going cheap."

"Ridiculous," said Hawthorne.

"Why?" protested Sutcliffe.

Sam said, "Even I know that relocating elephants is no picnic and costs a fortune. The Selous is hundreds of miles, maybe a thousand, from Zimbabwe."

Sutcliffe held out his hands, "Lay a figure on me Sam; let's go out and raise it. You never know what can be done until you've tried." He switched his attention back to Maya, studied her a moment. Shifting in his seat again, he looked around at the blackness hanging over the Galana and rubbed his chin. "Of course, if you go back to your project, Maya, we won't need gimmicks. Listen, I've got a serious proposal. You can use our entire fund-raising network in the States, any way you want, to raise whatever money you need to get that project started again. You can have total control."

Nobody said anything for a moment.

He went on, "You can use it anyway you want. Your words. Your appeal. No crass, uncouth slogans." He was smiling, almost embarrassed.

Maya said, "That is very generous."

"Isn't it?" said Owen.

Maya shook her head. "I don't understand. We oppose each other on so many things. Tell me, when the ivory vote comes up in Parliament, whose side will you be on?"

He looked at her, a hand covering his mouth, breathing out hard.   189

Shifting the hand to his arm, he said, "Look, all of these countries are poor. They need land and money. Tusks are a resource. Countries like Zimbabwe, and Kenya for that matter, have invested time and cash in protecting their elephants. They deserve to benefit from that as much as they can. They should not have to forego the opportunity because other places like Zaire or Sudan are too corrupt or too uninterested to tend their own resources."

Maya said, "You talk as if this was just business. It is not. Look, you think of a coffee farmer. He does not worry if his neighbor's crop gets destroyed. Maybe he is even glad, because this may raise the value of his own crop. Is it the same with ivory? Will the people in these efficient countries be rejoicing about the decline in elephant populations elsewhere because it will increase the value of their own 'crop'? I do not think so! I do not think that the money they obtain from these sales is worth the damage it does to elephants elsewhere. It is as Kariuki said. If you look at this issue from the point of view of a single country, of course it looks as if they should have the right to sell ivory. But when you look at the whole of Africa and the danger this poses to the survival of a species, you have to say no, it does not make sense to endanger them."

Sutcliffe sat back in his seat, grinning at Hawthorne. Gesturing towards Maya, he said, "She's great. Really great. Look at that." He leaned over and patted her hand. "You know what? I'd hate to see you or that project go under because of this business. You let me know just when you're ready to get back to work." He stood up and went back inside the house.

"He's quite something," said Hawthorne.

Maya was shaking her head. "It's so hard when . . ." she began.

"What?" asked Sam.

" . . . someone you are so . . . opposed to offers you something you really need," said Maya. Having enough money to start the project again was at least half the battle; she knew Sutcliffe could provide it. For the first time, returning to Amboseli did not seem impossible. She chewed her bottom lip.

"Can you do it?" asked Hawthorne.

190   "What?"

Sam leaned forward. "Blind yourself to his personality long enough to dig your hands into his very deep pockets?"

She looked Sam in the eye. He raised his eyebrows, questioning. She smiled, "You know, I just might do that."

"Knew you would," said Sam.

"Yes, I knew you knew I would."

"Hey!" shouted Sutcliffe, sticking his head around the door. "You wanna come in and see the big race?"

Maya and Hawthorne both stood up. The race had to be seen, in spite of everything that was going on. The race had been on the nation's mind all week. It was the Olympic final of the five-thousand meters. After their victory in the ten-thousand meters, the Kenyans were bidding again for all three medals. Hawthorne and Maya stood behind Sutcliffe's chair. Wangai woke himself up. The Olympic theme blared out.

"Let's see if these guys can really pull it off," Sutcliffe murmured.

CHAPTER TWENTY

LMOST EVERY TELEVISION set in the country was tuned in to the race. Those without their own sets crowded into smoky, public viewing rooms to watch the broadcast: children on the floor at the front, men occupying the seats, and women mostly standing at the back. The runners limbered up around the starting line, their dancing shadows etched black and sharp by the sun.

The three Kenyans owned the fastest qualifying times for the final. The oldest of them was twenty-eight, tall and thin, a hero already in his village of Londiani. He was called Kiprono. The other two were Waruru and Shete. Waruru was stocky and strong. Shete was the youngest, the best looking, and most muscular of the three. Several cereal manufacturers in the United States were already bidding for his endorsement of their products. The three men touched hands on the starting line. All over Kenya a roar went up. Never had there been such unity.

The ivory warehouse was on an industrial estate just outside Mombasa. Ordinarily it was guarded by seven armed men, four patrolling the compound and three located inside the building. There was also an alarm linking the complex to the police station. The warehouse itself had a steel frame and wooden walls, and had not been designed as a fortified structure. The Wildlife Service had assumed that a secure fence and the visible presence of armed guards was sufficient deterrent. At eight o'clock, however, none of the guards were in sight. They'd all gone into a small room west of the main warehouse, which was their communications base, to watch the race. One of them had brought in a crate of Tuskers beer. It was against the rules to have alcohol on the premises, but this was a special night. None of them expected trouble. Their weapons were stacked near the door.

The starting gun cracked. The race began and Waruru took the lead. Shete was third and Kiprono was fifth. Inside the warehouse guardroom, seven men shouted the runners on, as if a satellite were beaming their voices all the way to the stadium. It was no different in the rest of the country. People were involved. Some of them even wept. Everyone was united. The Kenyans would leave the rest of the world in the dust. Shete moved up into second place. Kiprono moved into fourth. The country roared. In anticipation of success, Tusker bottle caps flipped to the floor in all major towns.

The Wildlife Service had erected a steel gate at the entrance to the warehouse compound, and there was a chain link fence around the rest of the perimeter. It was ten feet tall, with two rolls of barbed wire twisted around the top. A dark figure packed explosives around the base of two wooden supports of the fence. It did not take much to dislodge them. The foundations were not deep, and the noise of the explosion was not much louder than the crack of a starting gun.

One of the security guards glanced out through the open door, but his attention was swiftly drawn back to the screen. Waruru had dropped into second, then third, then sixth position. Even Shete seemed to falter, and for the first time, a non-Kenyan had taken the lead. He was a wiry German, a solid, grim-faced athlete.

Three men ran over the fallen fence and, on the balls of their feet, sped silently across the compound, carrying their weapons shoulder high, heading straight for the communications base.

Kiprono had taken the lead. It was a magnificent run. He sprang from the rear like a cheetah trouncing a gazelle, eating the track with his feet. The country stood up, screaming victory. The camera gave a closeup of Kiprono's face: a mask of agony and ambition.

The intruders burst into the guard house, caught the men inside shouting at the glowing box, saw their delight, and then heard the shout of interruption. Gunfire erupted from the weapons, creating a frenzy of blood, noise, and men's dying cries. Afterwards, one of the attackers doused the place with kerosene, while another, a local brought in by Gerry Wong, got on the phone, calling the police, telling them that they were having some problems with the warehouse alarm and would see to it right after the race was over. The man hung up, glanced at the television, and shouted victory at his countrymen.

Inspired by Kiprono, Shete took off, chasing his compatriot's ten-meter lead. The two runners powered down the back straight, leaving the rest of the field gasping in their wake. Waruru was in fifth position, then fourth. The country sweated with him.

There was a loud explosion, and the door of the warehouse came flying out, crashing down in a mass of tangled metal. The trucks drove up, and the back ramps were lowered. Two forklift vehicles rumbled down the ramps and into the store. Each forklift carried a powerful beacon on its roof, which lit up the interior of the warehouse. The men gasped. Ivory was piled up four crates high, twenty crates deep all over the floor, acres of it, millions of dollars worth, far more than they could possibly handle. One of the forklifts carried a tank of gasoline with a long hose attached, which was deposited on top of a stack of ivory.

Shete was gaining on Kiprono. Kiprono seemed to miss his stride and stumble. The country gasped. He recovered, but Shete was there at his shoulder. Waruru was a head away from third place. The face of his German opponent was riddled with pain. The German dug into his soul and dragged out a final bid, but the break was weak, and Waruru stayed with him, hanging on the edge, pounding the track. The world was roaring.

Viewers wept on their knees. Shete pushed on, stride by stride, gaining inches on Kiprono, until the younger man was out front and winning. The tape was a quarter-lap away. Shete turned the last stretch. Kiprono came back at him, rising over his right shoulder like the morning sun that will not go away, breathing down his back, pushing his life to the limit. The pain was immense, air screamed in and out of their lungs, their hearts burst with blood. Shete ducked for the tape but Kiprono, the more experienced runner, pushed his chest forward a micro-inch further, taking the gold with a new world record.

Waruru also picked up his cross and ran. The German sensed it. Waruru grazed the air with the harshness of his breath, the ground pulled away under his feet as he gained equality with his opponent's shoulder, then surpassed it. Shete and Kiprono turned round to catch their brother coming in third. They hugged and wept. Their triumph was felt by millions. All over Kenya people shouted and embraced.

It took them twenty-five minutes to load the trucks. On the right of the store was a glass-fronted office. The hosepipe was hauled across and the stopcock turned on. Gasoline gushed out forcefully. The office window was smashed and the interior sprayed, the computers, desks, and filing cabinets. Then the hose was dragged down the aisles, fluid splashing over the ivory they had to leave behind. Carrying a can dribbling kerosene onto the ground, one of the men walked back to the place where the perimeter fence had been flattened. The others followed in the trucks, and once the vehicles had driven a safe distance, the man struck a match and tossed it onto the kerosene trail. He immediately turned and fled towards the trucks, diving to the ground as a shaft of pure fire lit the sky. The conflagration ripped the shell of the warehouse apart, engulfing surrounding buildings.

Jubilation seized the nation. They cried and shouted and danced and took the celebration out into the streets. The crowds thronged in villages, towns, and cities. Shete had grown up in Mombasa, and the people of his city ran out under the stars, jamming the streets with their vehicles, honking their horns, banging drums, and singing songs from the old days. People swarmed around every vehicle to give the news to the occupants, in case they had not heard.

The trucks stuffed with ivory were caught in this jam. A couple of kids even climbed onto the front bumpers, as if they were part of the furniture in an adventure playground. One kid crawled right up the hood and was

staring at them through the windshield, grinning a maniac kid's grin, small even white teeth in a black face. The men inside glowered back and muttered to each other.

There was an explosion, which made them all jump, even the kid, but it was only a firework, a rocket. Eventually, the kid slid off the hood, excited by the noise of a drummer, but the crowd was as thick as ever. Sounding the horn had no effect. People thought they were merely joining in the celebration.

It took an age, but gradually the trucks eased over to the side and escaped down a narrow street into the Chinese Quarter. Few people were out celebrating in that neighborhood, and the street outside Wong's juice factory was as quiet as death.

CHAPTER TWENTY ONE

AT THE END OF THE RACE, Owen Sutcliffe was on his knees, his fists raised to the roof in a victory salute. Wangai was on the floor beside him, his face close enough to see the individual lines of light creating the image of the three heroes staggering around on their lap of honor. The detective turned and looked at Maya, the only other Kenyan in the room. Their eyes met.

"It is great," she said, happily. "Just great."

Wangai nodded, sighing, climbing to his feet.

Sutcliffe leapt up too. "This calls for a celebration!" he shouted. He produced a bottle of scotch and pushed some on Hawthorne and Wangai. Maya refused. The glow of the athletes' success was already fading into the shadows.

She wandered back onto the veranda and stood leaning on the wooden rail, listening to the night.

Hawthorne followed. "You okay?" he asked.

She nodded.

"That was some race," he said.

She nodded again, smiling.

The hubbub of the night, all the frogs, crickets, myriad night flyers with their buzzing wings, whining mosquitoes, whirled around them, enveloping them. Maya said, "I keep thinking that I will hear something, or at least sense what is happening out there." She whispered, "It is so stupid."

Hawthorne said nothing.

"When I started at Amboseli, I never thought I would become so involved. I thought I would be there for a couple of years, then move on, perhaps go to the States or something. I did not know . . ."

"What?" he urged quietly.

"That it would become so . . . addictive. It's like a soap opera. I cannot switch off and go away, because I have to know what happens next. I have to see the next generation born, grow up, struggle, fight." She laughed.

Hawthorne coughed. "It's good to see you this way."

"What do you mean?" she said.

"Ready to pick it all up again. I mean, I thought you would, I just didn't know if it would happen so soon."

"Neither did I," she said. She looked into the night, then touched Sam's arm and pointed at a large, rounded shadow moving through the moonlight, its large head nodding over the grass. It was a hippo. At night, when it was cool, they came out of the Galana to graze.

At ten o'clock the news came on. They all heard the president's announcement of the national holiday that would be held in honor of the Kenyan runners. They also caught a brief report on the ivory warehouse fire. Seven men employed to guard the warehouse were missing and feared dead. The newscaster added that an estimated thirty tons of ivory had been stored in the warehouse, valued at fifteen to twenty million dollars. Fire investigators were already blaming arsonists.

Wangai slammed down his glass of scotch, leaping to his feet. He stared at Hawthorne. "It is them!"

"I would say so," said Hawthorne.

"It might not be," said Maya. "There are plenty of people who wanted that ivory destroyed, including me."

"But you wouldn't risk the lives of seven guys to do it," said Hawthorne.

"Maybe they ran away," said Maya. "What would you do if you were supposed to be looking after twenty million dollars worth of stuff that went up in flames?"

"This was arson, Maya," said Hawthorne, "not an accident. This is them all right."

"They knew that we would be in Tsavo," said Wangai, "crawling around the bush looking for them . . ."

"While they got busy somewhere else," Hawthorne finished off.

Wangai looked at him, eyes opening wide, a surge of heat flushing his face. All along the terrorists had been leading them by the nose. They dropped a clue here, a piece of evidence there, but if the police showed any sign of coming too close, the trail was wiped clean. Like that house in Langata. Wangai felt worse because he'd let himself be sidetracked. He remembered days ago thinking about the ivory. He should have seen this coming.

"Look," said Wangai, "Kinyanjui seems to have everything under control here. I might be wrong but . . ."

"You're going to Mombasa," said Hawthorne and straight away knew that he had to go, too. He looked at Maya, nodded towards the veranda, and she followed him outside.

"You are going with Wangai," she said, before Hawthorne could speak.

"Look, I know you have to stay here, and the idea drives me crazy, in case we are wrong and that gang of lunatics is really out there somewhere."

"It is okay," she said.

"It isn't." He looked at her, turned away, came back again, then stretched out a hand, held her arm, pulled her close.

It was so easy. She fell against him, held him, took the full force of the embrace, drew it out of him, built on it until his mouth, hunting from her shoulder, up her neck, around her ear, finally found her lips. The kiss went deep inside, turning the darkness behind her closed eyelids inside out so that every part of her body opened up, yearning for him. It had to stop. They both pulled away.

His mouth buried next to her neck, he said, "Great timing."

Her shoulders shook.

He pulled back, looking at her eyes. She smiled, the smile he loved. It was right out of her soul. He kissed her again, lightly.

"I don't like it," he said. "I'm going to have Sutcliffe call Kinyanjui and get one of his planes to fly you out."

She pulled away from him, protesting.

"What?" he said.

"What are you talking about? Stop taking charge. It isn't your decision."

"I . . . only . . ."

"I am sorry you feel bad about leaving me here. I feel bad about you going to Mombasa, but you cannot stop me staying and I cannot stop you going."

"I love you," he said.

"You think you can just order things around to suit yourself. I have not been myself lately, this is true, I have not been strong, but it was not a permanent personality change . . ."

"Did you hear me?" he said.

"Yes, I heard," she snapped, "and it is very typical of you to deflect the argument like that."

"It's true, though," he said quietly. "Besides, it explains the argument."

Maya caught the air in her mouth, about to retort. She couldn't, though. Couldn't say a word. Couldn't break the moment. She wanted to say that she loved him, too, but the words wouldn't come out. They seemed wholly inadequate to describe the sensation.

He kissed her again. "I'll see you," he said, turning away. "I'll call you."

He was already at the end of the veranda when she shouted, "Sam!"

He stopped. Turned around, grinning. "Isn't this where you run into my arms?" he shouted, holding his arms wide open, but before she could reply or do anything, he waved and disappeared round the corner of the building.

She ran then, caught him climbing into the front seat of one of Sutcliffe's land cruisers. The driver had turned on the engine. Wangai was leaning out of the back window. It was too public.

"Yes?" Hawthorne said, sitting down in the cab.

"Take care," she said, backing away, awkward.

"Uh-huh," he said. "Sure. And you."

He slammed the door, and the cruiser moved off, disappearing down the trail in a halo of light.

Hawthorne and Wangai got to Mombasa a little after one. The city was still alight with the all-night street party celebrating the race, but Sutcliffe's driver made his way through to the burned-out warehouse. The scene was crawling with cops and fire officers. Several strong generator-powered floodlights helped give it a macabre, theatrical atmosphere. The walls and roof of the building were gone; a tangle of twisted metal beams creaked eerily in the night breeze. The whole place smelt acrid, pungent, and here and there the ashes still smoldered around hollowed tusks that were only partially destroyed. It was already certain that several of the warehouse guards had been killed, but at that moment it was hard to tell how many. A couple of policemen were scouring the ashes, picking up pieces of human flesh with tweezers, and slipping them into plastic envelopes.

The inspector leading the investigation was a Moslem called Ali, an overweight man with bulbous cheeks and bloodshot eyes tearing from the effects of smoke. Wangai remembered him from the corruption investigation he'd led years before. Ali had been a junior detective then, and his boss had been one of those who'd lost his job, pension, house—everything—because of the payoffs he'd taken from a prostitution and drugs racket. Maybe Ali had got a promotion quicker because of the scandal, but Wangai still couldn't be sure of the inspector's support.

Over the years, the detective had received plenty of criticism over the way the findings of that investigation had been handled. People inside the department thought the dismissals could have been dealt with more tact, in a way less likely to damage police morale or public faith. Wangai had known, though, that unless he'd made a real public stink about the Mombasa case, the point would have been lost, and half the guilty cops would have got off with reprimands.

Wangai approached Ali cautiously, making sure that the inspector understood his credentials and the reasons for his interest in the warehouse arson. He noticed Ali flashing worried looks in Hawthorne's direction.

"What is wrong, Inspector?" Wangai inquired.

The inspector pursed his lips, breathing in through his nose so hard that his nostrils were sucked right in. He let out the air with a sigh. "It is just this *mzungu*. What is he doing here?" Ali hissed. Before Wangai could say anything, Ali went on, "Publicity is not good, Wangai. He's a journalist, no? What do we want with that? Him going about criticizing our methods."

Wangai nodded. "You are right," he said. "But you know, every time I try to push Mr. Hawthorne out of this case, he comes bouncing right back into it." The detective shrugged. "I cannot do a thing about it. He is being used. I do not know why, but I do think that if I keep him close by I have a better chance of finding out." Wangai drew a little closer to Ali. "He is my bait," the detective whispered.

Ali stepped back, nodding knowingly.

Wangai and Hawthorne went across to the wrecked warehouse, followed by Ali mopping his copiously weeping eyes with a large handkerchief. Hawthorne leaned over and picked up the end of a burned tusk, which crumbled in his palm. Ali called over a suited man who was crawling over what had once been the office, introducing him as Geoffrey Mitui, Director of the local Wildlife Services, Coast Division.

"What can you tell me?" asked Wangai.

Mitui laughed bitterly, holding out his palms. "This is a disaster. A disaster. We have lost everything."

It was getting towards two-thirty in the morning when Hawthorne and Wangai woke their driver, who had been curled up on the front seat of the car. He steered carefully between the ranks of police vehicles and fire trucks still cluttering the roads of the industrial park, and then pulled to a stop at the main road. On the right the ground fell away sharply into a ravine, and Wangai could see the glimmer of reflected lights in a calm finger of water below. The channel gave off a chemical odor caused by pollutants from the industrial estate, which the surging tide never quite managed to flush out. Next to the water, Wangai also noticed a flicker of real light.

The gears of the vehicle crunched, and the car lurched forward, but Wangai flung open the side door and dived out. The driver sharply applied the brakes, flinging Hawthorne, who was half way to following the detective, off balance.

"Just hold it," breathed Hawthorne.

He chased after Wangai, slipping and sliding down the bank, hating the stink of the place. Lights from the road above picked out the bloated bodies of birds and fish floating dead in the water. At the bottom of the slope there was a muddy path, not two feet wide, and up ahead was a squatter's shack.

The door was a piece of tin lifted to the side. A skin-and-bones dog lay next to it, the ugly shadows of its haunches picked out by the flicker of candlelight coming from inside the shack. The occupant was a big man with rotten teeth and mad eyes, leaning over a table.

Wangai shouted, "*Hodi!*" which was a polite way of announcing oneself.

The man was startled. The shock was so great he upset his table, scattering everything across the floor. Then he cried out, so loudly and suddenly that Wangai stepped back, bumping into Hawthorne, fearing that the man would turn violent. The wail turned into that of a vexed child. The tramp sat on the floor, sobbing, surrounded by the mess of his work: flutters of silver paper, lumps of foil, decorated packages, bottle tops, and plastic canisters. Wangai had seen it before, understood. These were the man's possessions, his treasures; he would admire, sort, and gloat over them. Casting his eyes around the dim hovel, Wangai made out a fat bank of plastic bags, all of them probably stashed with the tramp's "valuables." Some packages, Wangai noticed, had been ripped apart, and the pictures stuck on the wall, probably with cow dung for glue. There was a gallery's worth of garbage art on his walls: the geometric designs of Kimbo cartons and Blue Band margarine packets juxtaposed with rows of Omo packages showing the schoolgirls with whiter-than-white shirts.

Wangai crouched down beside the man and lifted a piece of silver paper. He saw the anxious flicker in the squatter's eyes, the restlessness of his desperate fingers. The detective held out the silver shred, and the man snatched it out of Wangai's palm. Wangai stood up, set the table back on its legs, and started putting the man's possessions back onto it, organizing the pieces into their proper piles as he did so. The collecter stood up as well, grinned, laughed in a gutteral voice, and began working with the detective, casting the occasional worried glance at Hawthorne, who had hung back by the door.

"You saw the fire?" asked Wangai in Kiswahili.

The man laughed deep in his chest, nodding his head. "Big, big fire." He suddenly looked worried. "Not me! I not make fire. Big noise. Boom! Boom! Like sky breaking. I go up. Look see." He laughed again. "Fire good for belongings." His face fell again. "But everything finished. Nothing there."

He glanced at Wangai, leering shiftily. Then, casting his eyes across the table, he lunged suddenly for a lump of green glass. He lifted it close to his eye, looking through at the dull-green world beyond. The piece had probably been in the water for a while, for the edges were as smooth as a stone.

"You didn't see no people then," Wangai said.

The man laughed, swinging the green glass around so that he was looking through it at the detective.

"They are saying that people made that fire," said Wangai. "Everyone will want to speak to you."

The man lowered the glass. His face was stricken. He glanced around the hovel as if seeking some place to hide.

"You set that fire, old man?" asked Wangai.

The man stood back, squealing, yelling, then, lifting the table up, he threw it across the hut towards Hawthorne, his possessions flying out like a garbage rain.

"Jesus, Wangai," muttered the journalist.

The man retreated to the bank of plastic sacks and lay down on top of them, gazing sullenly up at the roof. Wangai knelt beside him.

"*Mzee*," he whispered, using the polite term for a respected man, "I know you did not set that fire. You are not a bad man. Did you see anybody up there, though? Was there anyone else?"

The others lips pursed sulkily. "I see no men. No men. Only trucks."

"Trucks?" Wangai repeated, interested.

"I know trucks, all of them from all the factories, not those trucks. Never come before," the man said, whining childishly. "I like trucks. Sometimes get good . . ."

He broke off and leapt up off the bed of garbage, almost knocking Wangai over, and started rummaging through the plastic bags. From the bottom of one stack he produced a number plate wrapped in newspaper several years old. He displayed it for Wangai, grinning proudly, showing his blackened teeth.

His expression changed abruptly when Wangai tried to take it from him. He snatched the number plate behind his back and, turning around, jealously re-wrapped the metal board.

Hawthorne hissed, "They stole some of the ivory before burning it."

Wangai held up his hand to silence the journalist. "Did you see the number on any of the trucks tonight?"

The big man looked at him, shocked, then he laughed, shaking his head, stopped, looked at Wangai and Hawthorne, then laughed again.

"It's no good," said Hawthorne to Wangai. "You're not going to get anything out of him."

"Be quiet." Wangai looked around the hut, at all the garbage art stuck on the walls. "*Mzee*," he said, "did the trucks have a picture?"

The man grunted, looking surprised, then nodded, giggled. He turned to the pile of plastic bags and started pulling them apart, pulling out their guts, filling the place with garbage and its old, sweet, rich stink. Finally he held it up, like a trophy won in a stadium before a roaring crowd. It was part of an old cardboard carton that had once held pasta. At the bottom was a symbol of a trident entwined with several strands of ivy. The big man grunted forcefully, looking at the image.

Wangai took out his wallet and offered five shillings for the old carton. For a man like that this was a fortune, but he looked horrified, stepped back, banging into the wall of the hut with the scrap of carton hidden behind his back.

Wangai put away his money. "Pick up the table," he told Hawthorne. The journalist breathed out a sigh, lifting the shaky table.

The detective felt through his pockets and started emptying them onto it. "Come on, Mr. Hawthorne, help me out."

Hawthorne shook his head, smiling, and complied. "What do you think you are going to get out of this?" he asked.

Wangai shot an enigmatic look at the journalist, then turned to the man, gesturing that the belongings on the table were all his. The big man's eyes opened as wide as a couple of *sufurias*. There were plane ticket stubs, paper clips, coins, empty film canisters, chocolate wrappings, a pencil, a pen. Mesmerized, he stepped forward to the table, letting the carton scrap drop from his hands. Wangai whisked it up off the floor, and in seconds he and Hawthorne were outside the door.

They went back to Inspector Ali and asked him to check whether the amount of destroyed ivory corresponded to the full warehouse load of thirty tons, also asking him to get the trident and ivy logo identified. Ali was obliging, though skeptical about the value of the information, once he learned its source. Afterwards they drove into town, and Hawthorne booked them into the only air-conditioned room available at the Castle Hotel. It was freezing, the blankets were inadequate, and the infernal racket of the air-conditioner, combined with Wangai's snoring, made sleeping difficult. When Hawthorne got up the next morning, he felt worse than when he'd gone to bed. They had breakfast on the terrace, coffee and rolls, which they ate and drank in silence. Hawthorne signed the bill and went to buy a newspaper, which was covered with the triumph of the Kenyan runners. On page three he read an account of the warehouse fire, which was presumed to have been set by environmental extremists, probably the Enemies of Man, though no one had yet claimed responsibility. He scanned the article for reference to the amount of ivory lost in the blaze, but the newspaper gave the same information as the television broadcast of the previous evening. The editorial section was a pro-ivory trade piece that complained about foreigners depriving Kenyans of income from what was a valuable national resource, the country's elephants.

Hawthorne put a call through to the Sutcliffe Institute and was relieved to hear Maya's voice.

"They have found nothing yet, which is very good, I think. We are going out in the helicopter to join the search soon."

Hawthorne had to stop himself from telling her that he didn't want her to go. He knew it was pointless. "Just be careful," he said. "You know those people are capable of anything."

"Don't worry, I'll be fine," she replied.

CHAPTER TWENTY TWO

THE HELICOPTER CUT paths across Tsavo East, pulling high so that they saw across miles of wilderness and could pick out herds of cape buffalo, giraffe wandering sedately across the plains, baboon troops scampering over the ground, and zebra quietly grazing alongside gazelle, waiting for a big cat to strike. They saw elephant too, whole families in rivers or stripping bark from acacias. They ignored these, only diving low to ground when they caught sight of a lone bull or group of bulls. Then they circled around the group, looking for signs of wreckage. Before they set off on the flight, Maya had told Sutcliffe that if the equipment had been properly set up they would most likely find it in pieces, torn apart by an angry bull searching for a mate. On the other hand, if the gear had not been tampered with and was still running, they should look for signs of bulls moving in a particular direction, especially bulls in musth.

She hung out of one side of the helicopter while Sutcliffe searched from the other. They used binoculars to scour the ground below. The wind whipped their faces. Sutcliffe had tied a bandana around his forehead to stop his hair from stinging his face. After a while he shouted and pulled Maya over to his side of the craft. He pointed out a lone bull elephant heading north steadily. They circled the animal, and a hundred yards off, directly in the bull's path, was a glint of light reflected from something metallic.

"It could be the solar panels," yelled Maya. "Let's get a closer look."

Sutcliffe nodded, tapped the pilot on the shoulder, and pointed in the direction they wanted to go. The reflection disappeared and they lost its source for a moment, but by following the line pursued by the bull they managed to locate it again.

"There it is!" yelled Maya, looking down on the speakers, the infrasonic recorder, and other gear, all of it apparently undamaged. "It's okay!" She thought how wonderful it was that she at least had some gear to get back to work with.

Sutcliffe patted her on the arm. He pointed at the bull. "He's heading right for it," he bellowed. "He'll get there before we do, there's nowhere to land. We have to try and head him off."

She laughed, shouting, "Owen, have you ever tried to change an elephant's mind when he's intent on something?"

Sutcliffe held up his hands helplessly.

Maya yelled, "Let's try anyway. See if there are any vehicles close by who can help."

Sutcliffe leaned forward. The pilot lifted his headphones and Sutcliffe shouted straight into his ear. Though she was only a couple of feet away, Maya could not hear a word Owen said. Almost immediately, though, the helicopter came around and descended close to the ground. The tops of the acacias looked almost close enough to touch. The ground shot past underneath them at an incredible rate, while the power of the blades whipped the dry earth into a frenzy of dust and flying vegetation. Maya switched position, so that she was looking over the pilot's shoulder. He was heading straight for the bull.

Maya leaned forward, shouted in the pilot's ear. "Stay well clear of the instruments down there." The pilot nodded, pulled up again, and swung the helicopter around, so that he was approaching the elephant from the side. He hovered next to the elephant's path, trying to ease the beast away from it. The elephant whirled around, throwing his trunk about, bellowing, though none of them could hear it. He tried to continue forward but the helicopter bugged the path all the way. The elephant was a wise old beast, though. Pretty soon he realized that the helicopter could not bother him so easily if he tucked himself under a large acacia. He was only about thirty yards from the place where the equipment was set up.

"We have to try and get that thing switched off," yelled Sutcliffe. "If we hold the elephant here, maybe one of the ground crew can deal with it."

Maya nodded. At that moment, the elephant came out from under his tree, and headed east, away from the transmitter.

"What's going on?" yelled Sutcliffe.

"I don't know. Maybe someone else is singing a better song!"

"Let's get this baby on the ground," Sutcliffe said.

There weren't that many trees in the area, but there were just enough to make landing a helicopter a risky business. Eventually, the pilot came down an all-weather track a quarter mile away. They radioed the coordinates to Kinyanjui.

"You just wait for me," Kinyanjui insisted. "You do not go near to that equipment until I am there."

It was close to noon, and the bush was as silent as it ever got. Maya and Sutcliffe, like most other creatures, sought shelter from the blazing heat of the sun. Maya's back was damp with perspiration, but she felt more relaxed than she had in days. At least the elephants attracted by the magnetic call of the tape did not appear to have been harmed. She took a water bottle out of her small back pack and drank most of it in one go. Sutcliffe smiled at her.

"Course, you're not really used to anything as rough as this," he said.

She laughed.

"It must be nice to live in a park," he added, still smiling. "That is all Amboseli ever will be. This is different. This is real wilderness." He threw his arm out in a magnificent gesture that was supposed to absorb all of Tsavo's eight-thousand square miles. He was teasing her.

"Is that what you think about when you are sitting in a jacuzzi in Hollywood with all those beautiful women?" she asked, watching him from the corner of her eye.

It was his turn to laugh.

"I have read those stories about your fund-raising campaigns," she went on. 211

"Oh really?" commented Sutcliffe.

"Yes, I have, and . . ."

"What are you then . . ." he interrupted, "jealous or something? Believe me, when you go across to run your campaign, I can let you have some very interesting addresses."

"Not at all," she laughed. "You know, some of us do have the stamina to take this kind of life year-round. Others go bush-crazy if they do not get out to America every six months. I can understand that at your age this lifestyle must be an effort."

He laughed out loud.

"Though of course," she continued, smiling at him directly, "you do have a very comfortable life up there at your institute. Some researchers do still live in tents, you know."

"Oh, I think I prefer mud walls and a good solid dung floor," he retorted.

"Tastefully done?"

"Oh naturally," he replied. "That's given me an idea. Maybe I'll suggest it to an interior design magazine."

"What!"

"Dung floors; hygienic, recyclable, enviro-friendly dung floors. Maybe they would want to illustrate the piece with a few shots of the institute." He winked at Maya. "It'll cost them, of course."

When Kinyanjui picked them up, they took a circuitous approach to the machine, eventually pulling up in a glade, facing the recorder with its silently flickering dials and sun-powered machinery. Kinyanjui and a couple of his men fanned out, their weapons held in readiness while they scanned the bush for signs of human life. Sutcliffe and Maya climbed out of the vehicle and walked towards the recorder. In line with the banter that had been going on between them, Owen requested the honor of switching off the machine. Maya agreed, hung back, smiling, watching him.

She shouted, "Are you sure you know how it is done?"

He waved his hand in the air.

"I know you are only an armchair zoologist," she shouted again, "the technicalities might defeat you."

He turned around within arms-reach of the machine, grinning, and, with a flourish befitting the wildlife showman he was, Owen Sutcliffe stretched a hand towards the central console.

Maya realized something was wrong. She saw wires that should not have been there. She yelled at the same time as Sutcliffe flicked the switch. There was silence for a moment, then an explosion ripped through the glade and sent Maya flying to the ground. When she looked up, Sutcliffe was lying motionless. She half stumbled, half ran to him, Kinyanjui right beside her.

"Owen!" she yelled.

Sutcliffe's eyes flickered. He tried to open his mouth, tried to speak, nothing came out. Blood was pouring out of the base of his arm, where his wrist ended, where his hand should have been.

"Oh, my God!" yelled Maya. "Look what they have done! Look!"

"Be quiet," said Kinyanjui, softly, firmly.

Maya silenced herself. She watched Kinyanjui kneel down beside Sutcliffe, pull a whistle cord out of his jacket, lift the damaged arm. The wounded man gasped, fainted. Maya caught her breath, put out a shaking hand towards Sutcliffe's head, touched his forehead lightly. The warden tied a tourniquet tightly above the elbow. He yelled at the driver, who brought the vehicle across, and together they bundled Sutcliffe inside.

Maya sat beside him, trying to hold his body still while the vehicle thumped over the uneven ground to the helicopter. Kinyanjui was on the radio issuing instructions and orders. He glanced back at the wounded man, at Maya. She'd wrapped a cotton scarf around the end of his arm. The scarf had been pale lemon. It was now soaked with blood, which still continued to flow.

Kinyanjui leaned over, lifted the damaged arm. "Hold it up like that," he said.

Maya took the arm, felt the dead weight of it. Sutcliffe began to shiver, his lips quivering, cheeks sunken. Still holding up the arm, she reached into the back of the vehicle and grabbed a blanket, pulled it across Owen's body. It was better doing something practical to help calm herself.

They transferred the limp body to the helicopter. Kinyanjui and Maya went too, the roaring drone of the engine knocking against their anguish. 213

Maya was shaking, knew it could have been her, should have been her. She didn't move her eyes from Sutcliffe's face, pale despite his tan, the lips and eyelids covered with thin blue lines. A prayer for his life murmured along inside her, a perpetual silent chanting. Tears rolled down her cheeks.

Everything was so fragile, so easily spoiled, destroyed in a moment. A bad decision, a careless thought, something as small as that. Hadn't they known it was dangerous? Hadn't Kinyanjui reminded them himself? How could she have forgotten so easily? She'd been taken in by the belief that because the elephants were safe and the sun was in its heaven or something . . . everything had to be fine. Just a second more, a little more care, and they would have seen it all. The scene ran over and over in her mind as if by thinking about it, she could change it, but the result was always the same. She came back to him, lying there, unconscious, bleeding.

The helicopter landed at an airstrip in Tsavo West, where Kinyanjui had arranged for a plane to fly them to Nairobi. A local medic attended to Sutcliffe, who was soon settled on board, Maya sitting beside him. She saw that everything possible was being done for the injured man. Kinyanjui had worked wonders. She looked at the warden, gratefully, murmuring thanks.

Kinyanjui looked almost ashamed. "I will try and reach Detective Wangai and tell him what has happened."

Then he slammed the door of the aircraft, and soon they were climbing into the sky.

CHAPTER TWENTY THREE

T

HE STREETS OF MOMBASA were deserted. Most people had followed the president's advice and taken the day off. They lay in bed, recovering from the excesses of the previous night, sweating through the heat of the morning and into the high hot time of siesta. Since Sutcliffe's driver had returned to the institute, Wangai and Hawthorne took a taxi through the empty city streets, heading for the wholesale business that used the logo of the trident and ivy. When they reached the place, they found a rotund man standing at the base of a ladder, shouting instructions to an Indian youth, who was attempting to fix a new business sign to the premises.

Wangai leaned out of the taxi window. "Mr. Krishna Lal?" he enquired.

The man on the ground turned around. His black hair was plastered to his head with sweat. "That is me," he replied, looking curious, suspicious.

While Hawthorne paid off the cab driver, Wangai went across to Lal and introduced himself. The Indian invited them inside, leaving them to sit in a cluttered, air-conditioned room, the walls of which were covered with brightly colored portraits of Hindu deities. An old woman wearing a tired, faded sari and bedroom slippers brought them hot, sweet tea laced with cardamon. Lal appeared in the doorway behind her, his hair freshly combed back off his fleshy face. He introduced the shy old lady as his mother, putting his arm around her, pulling her into his armpit. The old woman looked embarrassed, extricated herself, and departed.

Almost immediately, Krishna Lal launched into a speech that focused entirely upon his role as a model citizen.

"Goodness, I am a member of umpteen social causes, including the Jaycees, Lions, and Rotary. I am bending over backwards to be of service." His face had a jolly expression that also contained just a hint of fear. "What is it that I can be doing for you, gentlemen?" the businessman asked, his eyes darting between one and the other.

Wangai told Lal that his trucks had been seen in the vicinity of the ivory warehouse the night before, around the time of the fire. "We have established that several tons of ivory were stolen from the warehouse before the fire was set," Wangai told him, passing on the news, which they'd only just received themselves from Inspector Ali. Then the detective pulled out a drawing of the ivy-entwined trident and set it on the desk. He watched a cloud pass over Lal's face.

The Indian sat down behind his untidy desk, found the phone, and prodded the numbers angrily with a pen. When someone answered, Lal spoke loudly in Gujurati, his tone harsh and aggressive, completely different from his manner with the two visitors. While on the phone, he was in perpetual motion; tapping his pen on the table, noisily slurping his tea, or playing with a set of worry beads. Eventually though, after scribbling some notes onto a pad, Krishna Lal set down the receiver, beaming as broadly as his godly namesake.

"Well, there is a most simple explanation about these trucks. Allow me to show you something." He opened a closet, and out of its untidy interior he pulled a large square of cardboard. Turning the card around he pulled up the cover paper and revealed a drawing of the trident, this time with two snakes coiled around it.

"Very good, no?" Lal said.

Wangai smiled, though without much warmth.

Lal explained that this design was his new logo. It was on everything, including his new trucks.

"Business is very, very good, you see," he said, "and for that I give thanks to God nightly." The vehicles Wangai had asked about had been sold months ago.

"But you seemed so disturbed," commented Wangai.

"Hah," said Lal. "Indeed it is true, because transporting is not my side of this business. That is my cousin, and he just now informed me that the sale went through a long time ago, and he has also given me the name of the new owner. You see? I am always most anxious to be of help to all the authorities."

Lal handed over the name and address of the truck owner. It was a Mr. Wong, who ran a juice factory in the Chinese district.

The same morning Silvia awoke in that damp, steaming room and knew she had deluded herself. Waves of self-pity erupted in her gut, filling her head with pain. It was the first time in years that she'd cried. During the night, she'd dreamt of tentacles spreading over the city, pushing along the roads she'd traveled in her escape. She saw the truth behind that image. She was still connected to Zhu, could not escape him; indeed there could be no escape except through him.

Pulling the threads of herself together, she arose, bathed her face, dressed herself, cleaned up the room and went outside to a phone booth. She dialed the Wongs' number. Mrs. Wong answered, and Silvia asked for Zhu.

Mrs. Wong recognized her voice. "Why should I let you speak to him?" she hissed.

Silvia did not answer. She heard Mrs. Wong breathe down the phone, then the clatter as she set the receiver on the table, and her footsteps crossing the linoleum. She heard the voice shouting for Zhu. There was a delay and then some murmuring. Suddenly he was there.

"Babe." A statement. As if he'd known she would have to come back.

"Hello, Zhu."

"Why did you do it? You should have come to me."

"It's best this way," she said. "I know you've got other things on your mind."

He sighed down the phone. "Babe, you are the one thing, you know? I can't tell you how bad I feel. I can't tell you how ashamed I was. Did you   217 think about Gerry Wong? What was I to say to him? He lets us sleep in his house, and then you steal from his wife. You made me look very bad."

"I'm sorry, Zhu."

"You're sorry?"

"Sure."

"Okay, so you come back here now. You must have got yourself a disguise. I found your hair all over the floor. You'll be safe. You come back here and we'll sort something out."

She hesitated. "What kind of something?"

He barked a laugh. "Don't worry. Everything will be fine. Get back here."

"I can't do that, Zhu."

Silence. His tone shifted, getting harder. "I'm sorry to hear that."

"Look, Zhu, I guess I'll see you at the ship."

Silence. "The ship?"

She'd heard already about the success of the ivory raid. She knew that the tusks would be at Wong's place, getting packed into juice crates. The consignment was supposed to go across to the port around three that afternoon, when Wong's men went on duty in the customs shed. She said, "I was thinking that maybe I would go along there in about an hour. You could meet me, couldn't you? Then you could talk to the captain so that it would be all right for me to go aboard."

He sighed again. "I dunno, babe, we got a lot of stuff to deal with here. Maybe I should see you later, when we're ready to bring it over."

She sucked breath into her lungs. "I don't think that will work."

"Why not?"

"You know . . . well, maybe something will happen and you'll leave early or something."

"So you give me your number, and I call you."

Her lips quivered at the phone. "I can't do that, Zhu. No, you know, I'm feeling very bad out here. I want to get somewhere safe."

"I wouldn't leave you behind, babe."

"Yeah, I know I'm paranoid, but I want to move right away. I can give you an hour . . ."

"Then what, babe?" He was aggressive now. "Are you threatening me?"

"No, Zhu, but, you know, who knows what could happen?" She paused. "Umm, there's police everywhere. Maybe I will get picked up, and then they might make me tell them stuff. I don't want to tell them anything, Zhu, but you've got to help me."

Silence.

"Okay, I'll meet you. Where do you want it to be?"

The first day in Mombasa she and Zhu had gone over to the port. "You remember that place we saw by the docks? You know, it was called J. Kariuki and Sons, just like him. Remember you pointed that out?" She could almost hear him sneer down the line. "Do you remember it?"

He sighed, then snapped, "Yeah, sure I remember."

"Okay, I'll meet you there. About twelve-thirty, okay?"

Wangai's Sunday suit was in a worse condition than the one he wore every day. He hadn't washed that morning and smelt like it. The temperature was in the nineties. The detective took out a large handkerchief, wiped his forehead and neck with it. Stuffing it back in his trousers pocket, he looked around at the sun-baked streets. The houses were ordinary enough, with wooden doors and shuttered windows colored pale, pastel shades, the paint flaking and blistered.

It was around noon. Hawthorne and Wangai were standing outside a small Chinese grocer's shop, open despite the holiday, drinking warm colas. A couple of kids came along, begging the strangers for coins. They were beautiful looking, Afro-Chinese, wearing rags and no shoes, with greedy glints flashing in their eyes. Wangai dug in his pocket to give each of them a shilling. It was nothing, but the kids looked happy, like they'd scored off an old fool. They ran off down the street, giggling and shoving each other with delight over the booty.

"That is it, then," said Wangai, looking over at the small factory. It was diagonally opposite, across a minor road junction.

"What're you going to do?" asked Hawthorne. "Go over and knock on the door?"

"I am no hero," murmured Wangai, downing the dregs of his cola. "I would say it was time to call in the cavalry."

"Fine," said Hawthorne.

"You stand watch while I make the call."

Hawthorne swallowed audibly. "You don't have a radio or a phone with you?"

"No, I don't have a phone."

Hawthorne shot a look at him. "Do you think this is really it? D'you think it's really them in there?"

Wangai shrugged. "I don't know, but we have to find out. Just watch, okay? Even if someone comes out, don't do anything."

"Right," replied Hawthorne uncertainly.

Wangai walked away up the street to a phone booth.

Hawthorne dumped his can in the trash and stepped back inside the shop to buy another newspaper. Then he crossed the road and slipped into a dirt alley opposite the factory, positioning himself in shadow, though with a complete view of the double-doors of Wong's place. He felt vaguely stupid, though keyed up and frightened at the same time. He shook the paper open to the center page.

A while later a door slammed halfway up the street, and he looked up. Hawthorne saw an athletic-looking man, fortyish, Chinese, wearing training pants and vest, a satchel slung from his shoulder, walk along the opposite sidewalk towards a Toyota saloon. The man looked around, inquisitive. Hawthorne pulled back, burying his head in the newspaper. He heard a car door slam, looked up again as the Toyota drove off, and then wrote down its number.

After hanging up the phone, Silvia left immediately for the port. She wore the nylon blouse and flowery skirt, and carried the rest of her stuff in the plastic bag, though the loaded gun was in a hip pocket and she'd put most of the money into her underpants. It was hard to find a taxi. She walked a long way, passing shop windows and catching glimpses of her shabby reflection, the ugly clothes, the round shoulders, the mouth sunken at the corners, her hair matted and sticking out from her head. Despite what she'd said to Zhu about being unsafe, she felt very anonymous. There were a few people around, but nobody looked at her. She was used to men shouting at her body, as if it were separate from her, a thing she carried around and displayed, but in this disguise no one saw her figure; it was no more than the shell that contained her spirit.

Eventually, she found a taxi and asked the driver to take her to the port. She thought the gods must be with her, because five minutes later he pulled off the main road onto a narrow sidestreet.

"Where're you going?" she asked him.

"There are too many roadblocks this morning. I know a short cut."

She arrived at the port about fifty minutes before the meeting with Zhu was due to take place. Even so, she stepped out of the cab warily, in case he was already there. It was also possible that he'd sent Sen down with a high-powered rifle, and that she was at this moment being lined up in his sights. But it was unlikely. She knew Zhu would want to handle her himself. A matter of saving face.

She stood on the sidewalk, noting how quiet the place was. The wide road swept through the massive dock gates like a mighty river flowing to the sea. The gates were open, and she saw a few men beyond, sitting in the shade against a wall of containers, playing cards. Cranes loomed over the wharf like the necks of great petrified dinosaurs.

She walked away from the dock entrance towards the two large wooden warehouses, standing one behind the other, that belonged J. Kariuki and Sons. The owner's name was written in faded blood-red letters, two feet tall, along the top of the front building. Zhu had pointed it out to her and laughed at it. Silvia slipped through the open gate, into the yard, and stood on a wide empty apron that on a working day would be used for trucks loading and unloading at the warehouses. On her left, a tall, wire-mesh fence ran along for a hundred feet before turning left to enclose the neighboring property. On her right were the Kariuki buildings, with a narrow lane passing between them. Straight ahead, beyond the warehouses, was a railyard with some old wagons and several abandoned passenger carriages.

She knew the range of the small pistol she'd taken from Mrs. Wong   221 would not be great. She didn't trust her aim, either, so she rejected the lane between the two warehouses as a place to mount the ambush because there was no room for retreat. The closest secondary cover was at the far end of the buildings, perhaps a hundred and fifty feet away. If she had to make a run for it, she'd lose. Instead, she walked up towards the railyard.

The heat of midday beat through the nylon blouse, scorching her back. She ignored it, studying the layout of the railyard ahead. As she drew closer she could see the layout of lines more clearly, fanning out over the dry Mombasa dust like the skeleton of a massive hand, the rails gleaming like bones in the sunlight. Tufts of hardy grass grew up among the sleepers, and there were a few goats grazing among the garbage. Far away on the other side of the yard, close to the wharf, a couple of African men strolled away along a black tar road.

The ground was hot and rough; sharp stones dug into her feet through her sandals. As she got closer, the passenger carriages that occupied the nearest rail loomed over her, looking huge. There were five or six carriages on that rail, all linked together and marked with the old logo of the East African Railway. The last two curved away out of sight, around the back of the Kariuki warehouse. She climbed up and tried a door; it was stiff, but it opened.

The train was a wreck. Glass from the windows and compartment doors lay along the corridors. Seats had been slashed or removed altogether, and all the fittings, basins, lights, blinds, toilets—everything—had been ripped out. Birds had been nesting in there on top of luggage racks, and there was plenty of insect life; probably rats as well, though she didn't see any. She walked along the train, discovering dead fires abandoned by kids or vagrants, stepping over holes in the floor, walking through dust and debris, looking up at the blue sky through the broken ceilings. She realized that this place might be her sanctuary or her grave.

The loss of seven Mombasa men was too important for the local police to take a day off. Not only was Inspector Ali's force on duty that day, the Special Forces Unit was on hand as well. Kinyanjui had sent them on from Tsavo. After receiving the call from Wangai, Inspector Ali ordered his men to cordon off the Chinese Quarter. They set up road blocks, using hefty planks of wood, viciously spiked, which forced all traffic into single, staggering file. The SFU troops were assigned to block the rear of the building, and three police vehicles were positioned out of sight at both ends of the street. When everything was in place, Wangai and Ali took an indirect route along two or three back lanes until they were coming up the path behind Hawthorne.

"Anything new?" murmured the detective.

Hawthorne shook his head. "Quiet as a church. One man came out of a house down there. He got into a car. Here's the number." Hawthorne tore off a piece of his newspaper and handed it to Wangai.

"What did he look like? Was there anything unusual about him?" Wangai asked.

Hawthorne shrugged and described the man.

Inspector Ali took the number and used his phone to get it on the search list. Afterwards, he said, "We have been wondering about this man for a while." He indicated Wong's factory.

"Why?" asked Wangai.

"He's too friendly with the customs division. Why does a juice maker have to be friendly with the customs division?"

Wangai smirked.

Ali shrugged. "What do you want to do now, Wangai?"

There was a pause.

"Well, I think I am going to call the factory. I am going to tell them that the police will be around soon with a warrant to search the premises."

Hawthorne sniggered. "Nobody calls up to say they have a warrant."

"No," said Wangai. "But they may think that African cops are stupid enough to do it. Whoever answers the phone might be shocked into revealing something. It might make them move out anything they shouldn't have in there. It would be a good idea to get them to open those gates. They look very solid. Besides, if they tell us that we are welcome to stop by anytime, we know we are wasting effort."

Ali handed over his phone and Wangai made the call. When a man answered the detective said, "Mr. Wong?"

"Ah, no, no, just a minute, who is this?"

"This is the police," said Wangai.

"Hunnh, ah, you . . . you want to speak with Mr. Wong?" stammered the voice.

"If possible. Is he at the factory today?"

"Ah, yeah, I mean no, I . . . er . . . don't know. What is it about?"

Wangai paused for effect. He could feel the other man's anxiety. "Perhaps you would get a message to him?"

"Ah, yeah, okay," said the voice.

"Tell Mr. Wong we have to come over and search his premises. It's a routine matter, but we have a warrant anyway."

"I . . . what for? What . . ."

"Just pass on the message, please?"

"Yeah," snapped the man as he slammed down the receiver.

Wangai said nothing for a moment. Then he looked at Ali, his face somber. "You better warn everyone to stand by."

CHAPTER TWENTY FOUR

SILVIA MARKED THE LINE of sight from various coaches and found the best angle in a compartment from which she could see all the way down to the gate. From there, she would be able to watch Zhu as long as he came straight towards her, and, if he got within ten or fifteen feet of the train, she could take him. It seemed very easy, but she knew it wouldn't be that way. It never was. For one thing, Zhu would have had his pick from Gerry Wong's arsenal, while her gun was practically worthless. Her best weapon, she knew, was her knowledge of him. Zhu possessed such a high opinion of himself that he would not really imagine her to be a threat, and because of this he might make mistakes.

She heard a car drive up and a door slam. A practiced assassin would get out of the car a hundred yards away and approach silently on foot, but Zhu would be feeling confident, and he would also be hurrying. He'd think of this as something he had to tie up fast before he got on with the rest of his life. She hung back in the shadows of the compartment and saw him come in through the gate. He hovered there, uncertain where to go. Then suddenly he looked straight towards her. It wasn't possible for him actually to see her, not from that distance, and yet it was as if he knew exactly where she was. She was so shocked, she pulled back from the window, out of sight, and leaned back against the dusty wall of the carriage, her breathing short and sharp, her eyes focusing on the sign that read, "In Case Of Emergency Pull Cord."

It was a mistake, though, to have pulled back from the window, because, when she slipped one eye around the frame again, she saw that the apron beside the warehouses was empty, and Zhu was gone. She didn't know where, and she still had not seen what weapons he was carrying. She didn't move for a moment; not trusting herself, because, if he was hiding some-place, watching the carriages, the slightest movement might give her away.

She tried to think. Maybe he'd gone back out of the gate. Maybe he'd gone down the lane between the two warehouses. She heard something, a shuffling. Maybe it was only a cat, or maybe it wasn't, but she couldn't stay where she was. That compartment was a trap.

Slowly she eased away from the window, edged along the wall, and slipped into the corridor, clutching the gun in her palm. She set off quietly down the length of the train, silently stepping over the dusty floor, slipping through the broken carriages, looking out of the windows, searching for him.

"Hey, babe!" The train shook. He was on the train. He must have gone down the gap between the buildings and got on at the other end. He laughed. He was still some way off, maybe two carriages down. "Babe, shall we do it here?" he shouted, laughing again.

She waited, standing still, listening, aware of him threading through the train, occupying the carriages, taking them over, space by space. Sweat trickled down her face and between her breasts. She jumped when he spoke next because he seemed to be so much closer.

"Why are you afraid of me, babe?"

Her stomach rolled. She gritted her teeth.

"Speak to me!"

Silence.

He sighed. The carriage shook slightly, and she imagined he must have slumped against the wall. "I got a story to tell you. It's about that Macao job. That is what's bothering you, isn't it, babe? I don't know why, but ever since then you been acting strange."

There was a pause. She wanted to yell that she knew Zhu had sent her to deal with Joey Han's partner in Macao, and then he'd told Han where she was. She wanted to demand why. What kind of offer could Han have possibly made him? Had it been for money? How much was she worth?

"Babe, you know, you and me, we shall be laughing over this some day," Zhu said, his tone almost sounding relaxed. "You know that Joey Han? He came to me and said he'd seen my woman in Macao. He'd had you followed to your hotel. He'd sent his men to investigate and found out you were registered under a false name. He figured that you must be fooling around with some other man." He laughed. "Man, I thought that was funny. There you were, doing a job on his partner, and Han is trying to sell me the proof of your infidelity."

There was another silence. She knew he was waiting for a reply. She bit her lip to stop the words coming out. He had to be lying, and yet his words were already worming their way to her heart.

"Babe, I've always loved you, you know that. You pissed me off in Amboseli. Okay? That's all. I just can't stand that kind of disruption. Jesus. Pulling a gun on your own brother in the middle of a job. What were you thinking?"

"How come you never told me about Han before?" She blurted it out before she could stop herself. It was too late now. She'd given herself away. "How come you looked so surprised to see me when I got back from Macao?"

She could tell he was smiling as he replied. "You are one suspicious woman." He laughed. "I remember when you came back. You looked fucking amazing. I never saw you looking so beautiful . . ."

"Zhu!" she shouted. "You are lying."

"Babe, I never said anything to you about Han, but we had other things to discuss. He was strictly past tense. As far as I know, he is feeding the fishes."

"You . . ."

"Did you think I was going to let him go around saying that shit about my woman?"

She couldn't say anything. She felt defeated, confused. Maybe he was right, and all the time she'd been wrong. She'd put herself through all that for nothing. She'd imagined things.

"Babe, I love you. I need you."

She gasped. Tears pricked the corners of her eyes. Everything that had happened in the last few days turned upside down. Had she been that wrong? She flashed back through events in Macao, the shooting of Han's partner, her shock on finding his men back at her hotel, asking for her, using her alias. The escape, her panic. She'd allowed it to color everything.

She heard Zhu sigh. "We've got so much to look forward to, babe."

His voice had the tone of the old days, when everything had been good between them. She longed for that time and, the more she wanted it, the more possible it seemed to reach out to him. They just had to get out of Kenya and make a fresh start. "Zhu," she whispered, "I don't want to do any more jobs like this, okay?"

He chuckled softly. "Sure, babe, we are rich. We can all retire."

"I'm so sorry, Zhu."

He sighed. "Yeah, me too. I know you were meaning to use that gun on me, but it's okay, babe, I forgive you."

"What?"

"I said I forgive you."

She froze. Her fingers, which had relaxed their grip on the gun, were once again wrapped tightly around the handle. It burned against her palm. Those words were all wrong. She closed her eyes, fighting down the surge of adrenaline, fighting against the swirl of conflicting emotions. It might be true, what he said about Han, but that did not matter now. He knew that she had been intending to kill him. There could never be any forgiveness for that, not from Zhu. He never forgave anyone. It was a trap. He was trying to lure her into the open.

She gulped breath, turned, and plunged into headlong flight, tearing along corridors, flying through the connecting doors, past broken walls and windows and pipes that stuck out of the woodwork, now connected to nothing. She imagined he was right behind her, could almost feel his breath on her hair, and hear his feet crunching the debris. She tried a door to get off the train, but it was stiff and wouldn't move. Panic overwhelmed her. It was a nightmare. She should never have spoken, never have let him know where she was. She should have kept calm, waited, then taken him by surprise.

The thought calmed her a little. She moved on silently to the next carriage and tucked herself behind a connecting door, listening, trying to think. She could hear him. He was taking his time, moving up the train, checking every compartment. There was a chance that she could get off the train without him seeing her.

Then she heard his portable phone ringing. His voice murmured into it, and then he shouted, "How the fuck . . . !" He paused, listening to a protest it seemed. Then he shouted again, "Just get the fuck out of there. Now! Bring the trucks out. You hear me? Sen! Sen!"

Sen must have cut him off.

"You shouldn't have done that!" she heard him yell, and realized that the words were directed at her. "You betrayed me!" he screamed. She heard his feet stamping along the train towards her. She couldn't understand what had happened, only that he seemed to blame her for it. She heard a shot and was surprised, realizing that it had come from a hand gun with a silencer. Zhu wasn't using one of Wong's bigger weapons, and suddenly she understood why. They were too near the port. Zhu would not want a fleet of police cars descending on the area, not when he was intending to bring the ivory through there. He needed to kill her quietly.

The gates of Wong's juice factory slowly opened. Wangai watched the gap of darkness behind widen until he could see the trucks inside. The engines started up, purple exhaust billowing into the street. The trucks were going in reverse, and a young man stepped through the opening gates to direct them. Wangai, Hawthorne, and Ali shrank back into shadow, Wangai praying that the cop cars at either end of the street were well out of sight.

There were two trucks inside. He could see them clearly, as well as two men beyond, holding submachine guns.

Wangai's radio crackled. "What?" he demanded.

"We have a pedestrian." The caller was an officer stationed further along the street.

Wangai couldn't see that far and did not dare to stick his neck out.

"Who?"

"A woman," the voice said down the radio. "Exiting a house about half way along. There . . . wait a minute, yes, there is a man with her."

"Okay," said Wangai. "Grab them as soon as we start moving. Nobody leaves this neighborhood."

The truck edged out, its engines roaring, exhaust fumes penetrating the narrow lane where the three men stood and making their throats taste of machines. Wangai waited until the first truck was fully blocking the gates and then issued the code word for the operation, "Ivory."

Sirens screamed and engines roared as the police cars tore along the street, screeching to a stop each side of the truck. The man who had been directing the exit of the vehicle ran back inside the factory, where there was total confusion. Wangai saw men shouting and running, most of them going to the upper floor by an outside stairway. The truck driver was trapped, at least that was what the detective thought until the Kalashnikov appeared in his hands.

Wangai dragged Hawthorne down to the ground. He heard the zip of fire from the weapon hitting glass and metal as it raked the police cars. They heard the screams of the men inside. The detective pulled out his own weapon. It was no match for an assault rifle. If he missed, then the Kalashnikov would be turned on the alley. Wangai tugged on Hawthorne's collar, trying to push him back into cover, but the journalist would not budge. His camera was glued to his eyeball. Meanwhile the driver was climbing down from his cab, still firing at the police cars. Wangai raised his gun, noticing, as he lined the man up, the peculiarly flat contours of his adversary's face. He squeezed the trigger and hit the driver in the shoulder. The man staggered, turned towards Wangai, bullets from his assault rifle spraying the buildings. Wangai fired again, hitting the man's stomach, then again and again. Bullets from the Kalashnikov blasted a line along the pavement towards the alley, but they stopped short. The driver collapsed.

"Shit!" It was Hawthorne.

Wangai reloaded his weapon, taking bullets from the pockets of his
Sunday suit. His eyes scanned the scene, taking in the two policemen,

probably dead, in the car nearest him and the injured officer crawling out of the car behind. He scanned the interior of the factory for signs of movement and saw none. He told Ali, "You deal with the injured. I will go inside."

"You need the army," said Hawthorne.

"I have the army. Can't you hear them?" Automatic fire came in bursts from the other side of the building. "Help the inspector, Mr. Hawthorne."

Wangai used the truck as cover, crossing to the police cars on the other side. The officers were out of their vehicles and crouched behind the doors. They were armed like Wangai and had even less experience than he in using a gun.

The detective got the head of the SFU unit on the radio. Over gunfire he heard the man say, "They're all over the place. We were watching the warehouse, but they've been trying to get out of the houses all the way along here. We might even have lost some of them."

"How many are there?"

"Left? I think only one or two maybe, on the upper floor. I'd say three are dead or injured, but we can't be sure. Listen, that warehouse has to be linked to at least four or five houses down the street."

Wangai thought of the man and woman who had tried to leave just before the raid began. He called the officer who had alerted him to the pedestrians.

"The man ran back inside his house, but I have the woman."

"How far along the street was the house she came out of?" asked Wangai.

"Oh . . . about the fifth or sixth from where you are."

"Okay," said Wangai, anticipation filling his head because he'd just got the idea that the woman must be Lee-Soto. "You did very well. Do this. Search her. Take her in right now and lock her up."

He turned to the officers beside him. "We're going inside. There are two men in there, maybe more, all heavily armed. Three of you will go along the bottom floor. The rest of you come with me."

Wangai ran to the warehouse wall, the others followed and they edged their way inside. The detective led his men up the outside stairway, which had been used earlier by the fleeing men. They crossed an office and passed into the first house, moving stealthily along the dusty corridors, searching 231 every room methodically, passing stairwells, turning this way and that, sweeping the warren with their eyes and weapons. They heard doors crashing below, kicked off their hinges by the other search team. Wangai's men also smashed into rooms, where they discovered crates of weaponry; an unbelievable haul.

The shooting had stopped. Wangai called the SFU captain, who said his men were entering the ground floor of the building now. "Be careful, though, I'm sure they must be somewhere upstairs. We will follow you."

Wangai and his men ducked around corners, following all the rules of the book whenever they broke into a room, two officers on each side while a third kicked his boot just below the handle, then dived out of the way. Eventually, though, they ran into a brick wall that closed off the corridor. Wangai called the captain again. "There's nothing here."

"They must be . . ."

"There's nothing. It's a dead end."

He heard the captain swear into the radio.

"Sir?" said one of Wangai's officers. "Look at this."

It was a ledge in the wall, a smooth, fine, straight ledge not more than a few millimeters thick. It ran up from the floor and along to the side. It was the edge of a door that had not been properly closed. Wangai touched the line of the ledge, felt around the wall for anything that might release the door. The young men with him did the same. Then one of them yelled, "Sir! I've got it."

"Don't . . ." began Wangai. No one was in position. Two officers were completely exposed, standing right in front of the door, but before he could stop it, the recessed button was pressed and the door flew open.

Silvia's brother, Jimmy Chi, was inside, sitting on Gerry Wong's dragon-embroidered bedcover, cradling an MP-5.

Wangai was already moving, diving towards the exposed men, shoving them aside when Jimmy unleashed the full power of the weapon. Wangai felt pain cutting his shoulder in two. He rolled to the side, out of the line of fire, but he was too late for the officers.

He heard the yells of his other men and the pounding feet of the SFU troops as they charged along the corridor towards him. Blood poured from his shoulder wound as he watched one of the soldiers toss a tear gas canister into the bedroom. Wangai heard the man inside coughing and choking, then three SFU men went in and wasted the room with their weapons.

Silvia found an outside door which opened easily. It was on the railyard side and on the next line, barely ten feet away, was another set of carriages. She knew she would be better off if Zhu had less idea of her location. There was a chance that over there she might have greater opportunity to surprise him, if she could only get off this train without him knowing.

Slowly, she eased the door open and lowered one foot onto the wooden step, but as she put her weight onto it, the step gave way and she fell heavily, the shock vibrating right through her ankles. The moment she hit the earth she knew he must have heard it. She dived for the next train, yet even as she ran, she caught a glimpse of him leaning out of a window. Her knees rose one after the other, driving her toes into the ground, pushing off. Then she was actually in the air, flying onto her belly, while a bullet skimmed over her head and struck the body of the train. She hit the ground, belly-flopping, dragged with her elbows, and, working her legs like a frog, she scrambled for the lee of the train. She crawled in between its great grey metal wheels, under its fat underbelly, and lay there panting for a moment among the dark sleepers. Then she dragged herself through and out of the far side of the train.

Finding an open door almost immediately, she climbed aboard, ran across the train, and caught sight of Zhu running across the gap. It was too much, the excitement of seeing him there, exposed, in the open. She fired. Bullets hit woodwork, a window, and one flew into the sky. She had no control, lousy aim, missed him by miles. She fled along the corridor cursing herself. She had only two bullets left.

But this train was shorter than the other. She slammed into the end. The panic was immense. She imagined bullets hitting her in the back and tore around, leaned against the last exit, panting, forcing the pounding blood in her veins to calm down so that she could listen for him. Slowly, she retraced her steps and found her niche, the place where she could mount the last attack, where she would live or die. Once she'd made that choice, she lost all fear. Nothing mattered anymore.

She was standing against a concertina wall beside the connecting door of the last two carriages. The wall was made of heavy black canvas and had been designed to aid the flexibility of the old train when it shunted and bumped over the rails. She noticed that the old canvas of the wall had been perforated, and through the narrow slit she could see a similar canvas wall at the end of the adjoining carriage. This was in better condition, but there was one small hole in the fabric, around waist height.

She listened, sensing rather than hearing Zhu's feet as he came closer, feeling them almost, as if this train were her body and he were trampling across it. She heard him pass through the connecting door into that adjoining carriage, then he was silent because she knew he'd sensed *her* silence and that he also realized that finally the time had come.

The gun sat in her palm, an extension of her body, of her hate. There was no sanity; no peace. There was only the soft fall of his foot. She tried to diminish her own presence, to become part of the wall, the floor, to lose the very feeling of life, which she knew could be transmitted in the same way that a dog sensed fear.

She studied the chink in the concertina wall opposite and saw the light shift. His shadow stroked it. She smiled, because she knew he would become impatient. She heard his foot scrape the floor. The wall shifted slightly. He was leaning against it. She was sure of it. Slowly she raised the gun. She knew his height, guessed his position, prayed, and said goodbye to herself, because if she failed there was no hope at all. She squeezed the trigger and fired straight through the canvas fabric into his spine.

Wangai insisted on seeing the captured woman for himself before going to the hospital. He had to be sure. The Enemies of Man had done far too much damage. Four policeman had been killed at Wong's, and many more had suffered injury. His shoulder hurt, but not as badly as his heart. The woman was his only prisoner. There had been one other, a man later identified as Gerry Wong, but before Wangai could get to him, Wong had been killed by a police bullet. The detective was more annoyed than distressed. He understood the anger of his men, but he couldn't interview a corpse. He wanted to be sure that nothing of the sort could happen to the woman.

The police station was in a new two story building, with a facade of mirror glass that reflected its view of the channel surrounding Mombasa Island. Wangai walked along the path to the main door, oblivious of the vision the mirror wall threw back of himself: the jacket bloody from his right shoulder to his elbow; his arm held against his chest in a sling improvised from a torn shirt. Pain was written in every step he took, but his thoughts were all of Lee-Soto, for he could not conceive of the prisoner being anyone else. Only rarely did he get this obsessed about the capture of a criminal, but Lee-Soto, or whoever she really was, had hurt too many good people. It was very personal.

They'd put the woman in one of the basement cells. The lighting down there was harsh and bright. Wangai walked the length of the steel-grey corridor, his shuffling footsteps echoing to the ceiling. They'd put her in the final cell, which had floor-to-ceiling bars. He slowed as he approached, treading silently. When he first saw her, she was sitting on a bench, turned away from him, her body slumped over. He looked at her for a moment, his good left hand holding the bars.

"What's your real name?" he asked.

The woman turned around. He saw the plain round face, the thin lips, the narrow eyes.

It wasn't her.

His mouth gaped, and he couldn't shut the rage inside. "Where is she?" he yelled. With that single cry, all the energy he possessed seemed to vacate his body. He could hardly see. He was practically fainting. He felt the metal bars of the cell pressing into his forehead. His shoulder felt like a hundred shattered pieces, falling apart like himself.

"Who are you?" he whispered.

"Su Wong," she replied. "My husband Gerry . . ."

Wangai said with closed eyes, "He is dead."

The woman cried.

Wangai didn't say anything for a while. Scenes replayed themselves. He remembered the eyes of the young men killed because a door opened suddenly when no one was ready. It was an effort to drag himself back to the present, but he realized that Mrs. Wong was all he had. He straightened up. "Tell me, Mrs. Wong, do you want to be convicted as an accessory to murder, or will you talk? You decide right now. There's no time but, if you help me, I will help you."

"But I have not done anything . . ."

He studied her. "Mrs. Wong, we found ivory in your trucks. We found enough guns in your factory to start a small war. Four policemen were killed today. The Enemies of Man have been responsible for the deaths of twelve others, including the men at the ivory store. I think I can charge you with almost anything I want to."

"I am not involved with this Enemies of Man."

"But you know who they are, don't you?"

She said nothing.

"Mrs. Wong, one of those people at least may escape while you go to prison. I want to get that woman." He saw a flicker in the prisoner's eyes. "You know about her, don't you?" Wangai demanded.

The interrogation room had dull-lemon walls and the usual battered furniture, though the small barred window overlooked the glittering channel. It was late afternoon and the shadow of the window bars lay across the floor. Mrs. Wong was brought in and sat on a wooden chair, facing the window. The shadow bars licked her feet. Wangai sat against the wall next to a small table and was about to begin when the doctor arrived. He was a thin man with a sallow complexion. His twenty-five years on the force showed in every deep wrinkle of his tired face.

Wangai indicated his shoulder. "I need you to do something about this."

The doctor raised his eyebrows. "Now?" He glanced at the prisoner.

"Yes, here. Now."

The doctor smirked.

"Just do it," said Wangai, "please."

The doctor sighed and began to examine the wound. While this was going on, the detective kept his eyes on Mrs. Wong. Her hands lay on her lap, one clenched in a ball that rolled from side to side while the other lay across it. Her eyes were cast downwards but flickered in frequent brief glances around the room, and her feet shuffled on the floor. Wangai gasped when his arm was rotated. The doctor stood back.

"You need to go to the hospital."

Wangai looked up. All the desires of his life were wrapped up in his expression. Nothing was going to stop him. "I will go to the hospital later," he said forcefully.

The doctor breathed in deeply and let out a long sigh. He shook his head, but he finally submitted, giving Wangai painkillers, cutting his Sunday jacket into shreds and doing the same to his shirt. The shoulder had been hit in two places. It had stopped bleeding but started again as the doctor cleaned up the wounds. While the doctor did his job, Wangai began asking questions. The room was bugged, and everything recorded, but a woman police officer took notes as well.

"What is your full name?" he asked.

Su Wong flashed him a glance. "I don't know anything about my husband's work," she protested. "I was only in the house. I never went to the factory."

"I asked your name," repeated Wangai.

The interview went badly. She would not answer personal questions. She denied everything. She knew nothing about the hidden door leading from her bedroom to the armory. "Really? Where would that be?" she asked.

Wangai fumed. He asked her about the people her husband did business with.

"I never met any of Gerry's colleagues."

"Colleagues!" yelled Wangai, almost jumping to his feet. Pain shot through his shoulder into the base of his neck. His eyes shut tight to close in the agony.

"I can't do this at all if you don't keep still," muttered the doctor.

The detective sighed, wiped his good hand over his face, and looked back at Mrs. Wong. Her thin black hair, cut straight at the chin, clung to her head like a cap. She'd sunk down into the chair like a cowering animal. She wasn't so strong; Wangai could see it. It was only that he was in too much pain, had lost too much blood. He wasn't running the interview efficiently. It was important to find out about Wong's illegal arms deals, but he really needed to concentrate on Lee-Soto. He turned to the policewoman. "Show her the photograph," he said.

The policewoman slipped a large portrait of Lee-Soto out of her file and placed it in Mrs. Wong's hands.

"Tell me about that woman," Wangai said softly. "You know who she is, don't you?"

The prisoner gripped the photograph so that the sides of it curled up.

"You know," Wangai lied, "it is because of her that we found out about your husband."

Mrs. Wong lifted her head for the first time, her small, blazing eyes staring at him.

"If it had not been for her you would not be sitting here now, and your husband would still be alive. It is very likely, unless you help us, that she will get away."

Mrs. Wong's eyes fell back to her lap.

Wangai nodded again at the policewoman, who stood up, poured a glass of ice water, and put it into the prisoner's hand. Mrs. Wong accepted it and took a small sip.

Wangai said, "Tell me about her. I think we only have aliases for her. Do you know her real name?"

"Silvia," whispered Mrs. Wong. "Silvia Chi."

Wangai sat back, sighing inside. "Where is she?"

"I don't know." Mrs. Wong looked up from the photograph. "You have to believe me. I don't know where she is. She called this morning, and Zhu went to meet her. He took the car."

"Who is Zhu? What car? What time was this?"

Minutes later Wangai wrenched himself away from the doctor. He stormed out of the room, along the corridor into the operations area. There were maybe forty people in there, including Inspector Ali, and it seemed as if every one of them turned to stare at Wangai. The detective became aware of himself. He was shirtless. The bandage around his shoulder showed spots of blood oozing from the wound. The loose end of the bandage trailed down his back. He halted, leaned against the wall, feeling slightly faint, and watched as Ali crossed over to him.

"What is it?" Ali asked. "You don't look good. I'll get a car to take you to . . ."

"The Toyota," breathed Wangai. "Find out if there has been any report on the car Hawthorne told us about. Remember?"

Ali went across to one of the desks, leaned over a console, issued instructions, spoke into a phone. Wangai waited and watched, then Ali spun around. He shouted, "Someone give this man a shirt!"

Half an hour later they were standing over the body of a Chinese male in a railway carriage. He'd taken one bullet at the base of his spine and another through the back of his head.

CHAPTER
TWENTY FIVE

AWTHORNE HAD GONE inside Wong's warehouse once it was secured. He'd followed the dingy corridors, looked into the drab rooms, seen the caches of weapons, and the bodies of the dead, lying in front of a door that led to a red room. Inside the room he'd seen the bullet-riddled corpse of the man on the bed, and the journalist had had enough. He just wanted to get out of the place and back to Maya.

Hawthorne went back to the Castle Hotel, put a call through to the Sutcliffe Institute, and was thrown into shock again because the institute was in total chaos. Finally he learned about Sutcliffe's injury, and that Maya had gone with him to Nairobi. He dived in the shower, caught a cab to the airport, and a couple of hours later he was on a flight to the capital.

He went straight to his house in Karen, half-expecting to find her there, and it wasn't until he opened the door to the empty living room that he realized she wouldn't come here, not yet. He called the hospital and picked up the latest news on Sutcliffe, whose condition was stable. He called Jackman and gave a rundown on events in Mombasa, and then tried calling Maya at her parents' place.

"Hello," she said, lightly.

"You okay?"

"Fine, yourself?"

"No problem. We got the ivory back." He told her the story. "Look, I have to see you."

"I know. I had to come here."

"Can you get away?"

"I will try, okay?"

"I'm waiting."

She arrived around nine that evening and found him sitting at a square wooden table on the screened porch at the back of the house, working on his story. He glanced up as she entered the screen door.

"Hold on a second," he said, tapping the laptop keys.

She sat on a wicker settee, watching his frowning forehead, his intense eyes gazing at the screen, the glow of the screen making his face shine. He completed his work, then sat back in the chair, looking at her.

"I think we have a situation here," he said.

"What kind of situation?" she asked.

He laughed. "Looks like one of those man-woman things to me."

"Is that all?" she asked.

He shook his head, murmuring, "No."

"What then?" she asked.

He sighed. "Could be one of those bonding issues."

She laughed. "Bonding!"

He switched off the laptop and lifted the machine. "Would you like to come inside?" he asked with exaggerated etiquette.

She followed. He set the computer down. Standing right behind him, she ran her fingers down his back, pulling his shirt out, slipping her hands inside, pushing them over his flesh.

"I could get used to this," he said.

She pulled his shirt right up and off his head and started nibbling his back.

"Say," he said, "d'you need some champagne to loosen up? I mean, I put some in the refrigerator."

She mumbled against his back.

"What's that?"

She turned him around. "I said, afterwards." She kissed him, her tongue right inside his mouth. His hands were holding her neck. They slipped down over her shoulders, under her arms, over her hips. She pulled away

242

from him to lift her shirt off over her head. He took her hand, led her into the bedroom, and undressed the rest of her. He watched her lying there as he stripped off his shorts, then lay down right on top of her.

He kissed her lightly. "You know, I really want this to last, but I don't think I can stand it," he said.

She guided him, rising to meet him. He groaned, pushing back, harder, stronger, until they were lost without boundaries, without sorrow or pain or even joy, without anything but this one driving need for the other. She cried out. He murmured something to the Creator. She pulled his hips against her, rising every time. Sensation erupted, flooding her limbs, her mind; he cried back at her and she felt him grow even larger and harder inside, until the release came and he lay down heavily, gasping and still.

They lay, arms and legs entwined, braided shades of sand and brown. He kissed the side of her head. She turned to look in his eyes.

"How was it for you?" he laughed.

She smiled, lay down again, resting her head on his chest.

"How are we going to work this?" He looked for a way to begin.

She didn't move. "Work what?" she asked, a fear still lingering inside that he would want to go back to the old relationship. She didn't want that, not after all that had happened. Things were different. She needed certainty, clear cut lines.

"This," he said.

"I don't know," she replied, holding back. "I suppose it will be okay."

He moved slightly, making her look at him again. "You know, I was thinking of . . ." His voice trailed off.

She kissed his chin, encouragingly. "What?" His eyes had a mellow look. There was nothing deceptive there.

"Marriage, actually," he said, wincing a little.

She raised her eyebrows, genuinely surprised.

"Is that a bad idea?" he asked.

"Well . . ." She'd never expected this of him.

"I thought it was quite a good idea, don't you?"

She smiled. "What . . . kind of marriage?" she asked, tapping her fingers 243 on his chest, feeling the sense of relief inside him. He meant it.

"Okay . . ." he said, "down to the details. That's okay. I've only been thinking about this for about . . . oh, three or four hours, haven't had much time to get a polished presentation together, but I'm ready to wing it."

She laughed. This was Sam, the old Sam.

He coughed. "In fact, I was thinking more or less of the usual kind, but with a few adaptations."

"Adaptations," she repeated, trying to be serious, trying to keep the lid on the climbing, soaring excess.

"You're really making me work hard at this," he said.

"No," she murmured. "I just want to be sure I know what you mean."

He breathed in. "Okay . . . flexible. Let's try flexible marriage. I'm here for you. You're here for me, but exactly where 'here' is . . . well, that could be debatable."

"It is a matter of geography, then," she said, joking.

"Geography?" he repeated, seriously, like an academic. "Yeah, that's part of it."

"What is the rest then?" Could there be more?

He screwed up his face, pushed a hand through his hair. She took the hand, pulled it down. "That's displacement activity. Tell me straight."

"Okay," he said. Suddenly he burst out laughing. "Genetics!" he yelled, pushing her over, rolling on top of her. "Genetics," he murmured again.

She smiled. "You mean a baby? A baby!"

"Uh-huh," he said. "I'm going to kiss you now because I really have to displace." The kiss was warm, deep. The urging stirred again, but he broke off. "I've got you figured, Saito, admit it, or else I'll stop right here."

She breathed in deeply. "Okay," she said.

CHAPTER TWENTY SIX

A VOICE ON DECK CALLED out in Arabic, dragging Silvia out of sleep; a shudder vibrating through the thin foam mattress brought her to the surface. She became aware of the manic cries of seabirds, the rolling swell of the sea, and, above all, the noisy droning of the engines. It was hot and the cabin was stuffy. She rose from the narrow bunk and moved to the porthole, unfastening the catch. The air outside was moderately cooler and carried the faint odor of diesel. She looked out across the endless blue seascape and smiled. A new life was beginning. She had a new identity, because she'd found the papers in Zhu's satchel as well as thirty thousand U.S. dollars. She'd used some of the money to pay for her passage on *The Pearl of Sidon*, and the captain had demanded more once he realized that the ivory consignment wasn't going to materialize. What she had left did not amount to a fortune, but it was a start.

She showered in a tiny mildew-streaked bathroom in water that was lukewarm and brownish. She combed her hair straight back off her face, dressed in her own clothes, and applied her make-up. One of the crew brought a breakfast tray to her cabin; a stale roll and tepid coffee, but she consumed everything. She felt as if she hadn't eaten in days.

Afterwards, standing among rope coils and chains on the metal deck, leaning against the rail, she was struck by the startling beauty of the day: the warm breeze whipping the waves, the few cotton ball clouds in the sky, the sea birds swooping and cawing over the wake of the ship. She looked down at the water churning against the side and felt an extraordinary peace.

By killing Zhu, she'd shed everything that was bad in her life. The possibilities for the future seemed boundless, and she felt capable of almost anything. She felt saved. It was almost a religious awakening, except she did not see it in terms of a god. She had seized control of her life and because of this, because she'd lost it and regained it, she was stronger than most people could ever be. She felt she could never be subjugated by anyone again.

She scanned the sea, enjoying the vast emptiness of it, and noticed what appeared as a disturbance on the horizon, a glitch in the line between water and sky. It gradually grew into a small boat. At first, she thought it must be a fishing boat, but it was traveling too fast for that. Perhaps it was a luxury cruiser. She fantasized briefly, imagining this vessel pulling up alongside. A wealthy, handsome man invites her on board. They sail away. She smiled, seeing the fast boat heading straight towards them, and only gradually did apprehension begin to grow. It was the insistence of it, the way it drove through the sea, flying over the waves, making no concessions, as if it possessed an agenda, a reason for needing to reach the freighter. Perhaps this was to be a liason among criminals. Perhaps the captain of *The Pearl* was dealing in drugs, and an exchange was going to take place. She let herself believe this for a moment, but panic began to seep through the facade.

She watched the approaching vessel, saw its emblems of authority, the badges and flags, the uniforms of the men on board, their peaked hats, and finally their epaulets and medals and their brown arms against the short white turned-up sleeves of their shirts. An African male sat in the rear, one shirt sleeve tied in a knot, so that he appeared to have only one arm. He was looking straight at her as they drew alongside and measured their pace to that of *The Pearl*.

Wangai noticed that she looked not much more than a girl, but he had no doubts. Her television image was seared into his brain. He'd got Lee-Soto. Mrs. Wong had taken her time remembering *The Pearl of Sidon*, and for a while he'd been worried that they would never catch up. Once the situation was explained to the coast guard, however, the pursuit had become a matter of honor.

Wangai hauled himself up and staggered into the cabin. The freighter captain was already on the radio, protesting that they had no right to impede the passage of *The Pearl*. Wangai grabbed the receiver.

"The woman on board your ship is a known murderer. If you want to continue using the port of Mombasa, I suggest you hand her over."

Almost immediately, the detective felt the pace of the coast guard vessel slow and he went back outside.

Up on *The Pearl*, a sailor came down from the bridge and tossed a ladder over the side. The girl watched. Wangai thought she must understand what was happening, and yet she didn't seem to have any anger. He'd seen men explode with rage over being caught for crimes far less serious than hers. Then he saw her turn away from the rail and disappear from view.

He called one of the young coastguard officers. "Quick, get up there. Bring her down. I don't want to lose her now."

She entered the cabin, almost floating, because nothing seemed very real. She could almost be dreaming. Perhaps she still slept. Perhaps she would awaken and find herself on the bunk again, moving to the porthole, and unlatching it to gaze at the sea and wonder at the peace. Perhaps this moment would revolve time and again, bringing her to the brink of escape, then gently pulling her back, like a whisper, because she didn't feel anything much.

She picked up the satchel, removed the pistol which she'd taken from Zhu, and moved across to the porthole. She would not leave the money for the captain or anyone else. The latch clicked open, and she dropped the bag overboard. As it fell, money fluttered out over the waves, and she heard crew members shouting and crying over it. Still looking out at the sea, she raised the gun, and put it against her head. She breathed deeply, feeling her lungs expand and contract, sensing the beating of her heart, the blood in her veins, the tensing of muscles, the sensation of touch and smell, and the sound of the birds that swooped all around the ship now that it was practically stationary. She heard, also, the door flying open behind her. She   247 turned, startled because somehow she had forgotten that they really wanted her. He moved fast, seemed to fly across the cabin, and pushed her hard so that her head cracked against the porthole rim. The gun fell from her hand and he kicked it aside. It slid across the metal floor, banging into a wall.

A gate had been opened in the railing to give easier access to the ladder. She allowed the young officer who had "saved" her life to guide her. She smiled at the thought because, in fact, she felt dead and took comfort from it. Only the shell of her body was making that awkward descent into the coastguard vessel. Her spirit had already flown. They could never possess that. If they wanted her body so badly she would allow them to have it. She surrendered nothing.

EPILOGUE

AWTHORNE WAS WORKING on a book about environmental politics when Maya called him on the radio. Her voice was hushed. "It's happening, right now. Right now."

"Am I too late?"

"I don't think so. But you have to be careful. We're southeast of Longinye. You'll have to approach from the west because of the wind. Call me again when you get close."

He shut down the laptop and stepped out of the tent, which he used as a study. Next door was the large tent he and Maya shared, which was now equipped with a double bed. A few months from now there would be a crib in there as well. How on earth they were going to manage was a never-ending conversational topic.

Hawthorne got into a small Suzuki and was soon heading down to the swamp. He'd learned to love this home, to see it with her eyes, her understanding. He'd moved in just after Maya returned from her successful fund-raising tour of the States. The research project was soon back on track, but the ivory trade in southern Africa was still in full swing. With the market for tusks flourishing in the Far East, poaching was on the increase all over. Even in Tsavo, the creatures weren't safe. The park was too big, and it was impossible to watch all the animals all the time. Owen Sutcliffe had been on the radio the day before, reporting on the worst poaching wave inside Tsavo in years. He and Maya were making plans for a fresh assault against the trade.

It was never-ending, Hawthorne thought, and yet things had been different since the Enemies of Man. They'd all been changed by it. Sutcliffe had become harder, less of a showman. Before, Owen's involvement with African wildlife had been like an extravagant hobby, but it wasn't that way anymore. He was deadly serious.

Wangai had changed as well. He was a superintendent now and head of Special Operations. Hawthorne had last seen him six months earlier, when they met by chance on the terrace outside the Norfolk Hotel. They shared a couple of beers, and during that time maybe a dozen people approached Wangai, some merely to greet him, others to ask outright for help.

"I have learned to keep my mouth shut," Wangai whispered to Hawthorne. "The other day I mentioned to somebody that my wife wanted to get a barbecue, and you know the very next day there was a barbecue sitting outside my house when my wife got home."

On the other hand, Hawthorne found he wasn't as compulsive about his own work as he used to be. The world he really cared about seemed to have shrunk dramatically, centering on Maya and the child to come. She was also more focused on their relationship. She fought the same battles for the elephants, but she came home at the end of the day.

He pulled up near Longinye and found Maya's vehicle parked in deep undergrowth. She was up on the roof as usual with the video camera pointing towards a clump of thornbushes. Quietly, he climbed out of the Suzuki, crossed the strip of ground between the two vehicles, and was soon sitting beside her, slipping an arm around her thickening waist. She smiled at him, then looked back at the elephants. Just in front of the thornbushes, on a smooth stretch of grass, was the dull-grey shape of a crouching elephant. Solo was about to give birth to the offspring of Rameses, the massive bull she'd mated with twenty-two months earlier.

The rest of her family ignored Solo while filling their stomachs with the juicy grasses that grew along the edge of the swamp. The matriarch's temporal glands were streaming, staining the sides of her head. She changed position, straining with her head up, legs spread apart and her tail raised in the air. A bulge appeared below the tail.

Solo rumbled low, a slow sound full of relief that shuddered into a sigh. On the crest of the sigh, her body shook and she dipped slightly, giving the baby an easy ride onto the ground. It slipped out in a glistening black sack. Solo stepped back, over the sack, touching it with her trunk. The other elephants abruptly ceased feeding, flocked around, surrounding the bundle, and, working together with trunks and feet, they released the baby inside. Some minutes later the tiny infant stood up, completely covered with hair; wet and black with birth fluid.

Trunks surrounded him, touched, caressed, felt and smelt his small wobbling body. He fell often. His knees seemed double-jointed; they flexed awkwardly, buckling underneath, collapsing to the ground. His trunk whipped around, out of control, and this also sent him off balance. He struggled to regain his feet, aided by the gentle lifting of the other elephants.

Solo tried to ease the new infant towards her two large, human-looking breasts, which were swollen with milk and hung from her upper belly. The baby groped around, searching, but abandoned the quest, distracted by the other family members. He wobbled awkwardly away from Solo and found Star, freshly out of adolescence, and tried to suckle from her breasts instead. Star patiently let the infant explore. For a while he seemed to latch on, then broke away again.

The baby was ever curious, whipping his trunk around, shaking his head, making odd little squeals. Solo was there, stretching her trunk around the infant, coaxing him back under her enormous belly. He followed willingly, but then struggled alone in his den, under the great shelter of his mother's body. The breasts hung above. Tipping back his head, his trunk fell across his mouth. He twisted the mouth to the side, but still the trunk was there, blocking the gap between his mouth and the nipple. Finally, he pushed his face fervently into the breast, hooked his trunk to the side, slid his mouth across, and clamped on hard.